D.C. STONE

EVERNIGHT PUBLISHING ®

www.evernightpublishing.com

Copyright© 2017

D.C. Stone

Editor: Jessica Ruth

Cover Artist: Jay Aheer

ISBN: 978-1-77339-201-1

D.C. STONE

DEDICATION

Publishing a book is an intimate process for an author. It involves everything from creating worlds and characters, driving their actions through experiences imagined, and laying bare a hope that others will like the story just as much as the creator. Being an introvert, this process is all a little soul baring for me, but the hero in INTIMATE FEAR, Dwayne, made it so much easier. He demanded his chance, wanted to have others understand him, and wouldn't give up until I had his story on paper and perfected—sorta like the man he is.

There are many, many individuals I want to thank for helping me get this book ready. Ruth S., Nicole D, and Lea B…your support means the world to me, and your encouragement keeps me going. I know I sat on this story for over a year before submitting it, I think I finally got to the point you all said I was in, to make it ready for the world. I appreciate you more than words can explain.

To Evernight Publishing, and my lovely editor, Jessica. Thank you for taking another chance with me, and making this story shine.

And to my father, who will never read one of my romances because they have sex in them. (laughs) I love you, Pops. You walked through hell this past year, and made it through even stronger than before. You have taught and shown me the meaning of strength and willpower, and because of that, I'm pursuing my dreams. You amaze me.

And last, to my husband who holds the fort down, entertains the children, and gives me the peace needed to write. Thank you, honey. This is for you…

D.C. STONE

INTIMATE FEAR

Empire Blue, 2

D.C. Stone

Copyright © 2015

Chapter One

"Wake up, Brooke."

The sultry voice of John Mayer penetrated her subconscious. Brooke Mason latched on to the sound and envisioned the dark-haired man with hooded eyes, the slight tilt of his lips for her alone.

"Hurry, girl, time is running out. Wake up."

Brooke lingered on the edge of consciousness. She stood in a dark room, no one else but her and this sex god. Held in his stimulating trance, she swayed along to his music. His voice called to her. She wanted to go, to be wrapped in his promise of pleasure.

"Hailey's waiting. You have to stop it."

With a shift, her face brushed against something soft, a comfortable feeling associated with plush bedding. Long nights…this man spread out across her bed. His body a wonderland, just as he crooned.

Her bed…

"Wake up, girl!"

Her eyes snapped open as the local DJ for Z-100 interrupted John's voice with a brief on traffic. Sunlight shone brightly through the blinds, glaring against her vision and the reality she'd been thrust in. Her gaze snapped to the clock. Eight fifteen.

"Shit!"

She jumped out of bed and shoved her legs into a ratty gray pair of house pants lying on her desk chair. She'd slept through the alarm again! Stumbling past her desk chair, she stubbed her toe and pain ran a line up her leg with the force of a punch. "Ow! Shit, shit, shit!"

It was the third time this week. She cursed her late-night hours and rushed from the room.

Brooke darted down the hallway, passing rows of pictures: a giggling baby reaching for her first flower, the bottom of a toddler's feet taken from behind as she sat on her knees, a toothless grin staring up at the camera as the girl stood still for the frozen memory. Their lives—her and her daughter's—splayed across the wall with hardly any white showing beneath. The display was a constant reminder of their happiness, a treasure, more, a declaration of the forbidden four-letter word she no longer believed in.

Love.

She skidded to a stop and slapped a hand on a door, the sign "Enter at your own RISK" shaking with the impact. Pushing the door open, her gaze darted to the empty bed before landing on her daughter, who sat at a vanity table applying pink gloss to her already pink lips.

"Hailey, I overslept again. I'm so sorry. Give me five minutes and I'll have breakfast ready."

Her seventeen-year-old's deep brown eyes met hers in the reflection of the mirror and paused. One brow lifted and Brooke fought a smile. Hailey looked too damn cute with that look on her face.

"Again? Mom! You know this isn't healthy. How late did you stay up this time?"

Brooke, still trying to brush off the remnants of her weird dream, shook her head and lifted a hand.

"Never mind that. Are you almost ready?"

She nodded and pursed her lips. "Just about."

"Okay." Brooke paused, taking in Hailey. She was growing up so damn fast. It seemed as if it were just yesterday she learned how to walk, to talk, to throw a ball.

"Mom?" Hailey lifted a brow. The impatience—and yes, aggravation at being stared at, because the girl couldn't stand it—was written clearly across her face. Brooke struggled with the sigh that wanted to escape. Her beautiful daughter was in that stage all young women went through, the one where they were so self-conscious about their bodies, their looks. It was a wonder they didn't have men of all ages knocking on the door to get their shot with her teen.

"I'm going, I'm going." Brooke drew back and rushed down the hall and into their bright kitchen. An island sat in the middle of the room, decorated in blue-and-white broken tiles. She and Hailey had built that countertop piece by piece. Between Brooke's father and her daughter, the two had more fun taking a sledgehammer to the tiles before starting the process of getting them together in grout. It had been painstakingly slow, four weeks to complete, to get everything to fit like a puzzle. The laughter, though, the conversations and bonding experience they went through made it well worth the time.

Especially now—her lips thinned with sadness—when her parents couldn't remember those memories. They'd both been diagnosed with Alzheimer's six years ago, and each sad verdict of this disease had been within three months of each other. Now when she visited her father, which she needed to do soon, she was lucky if he remembered his name. And her mother had unfortunately succumbed to the illness.

She shook out of her depressing thoughts and skidded across the floor. A large, dark stainless steel refrigerator stood behind the island, and to the left was a door leading to a small yard behind the house. To the right were the sink and a window that overlooked the backyard. Countertop wrapped around the corner of the room before stopping at the stainless steel stove.

She yanked open the refrigerator, grabbed orange juice and coffee creamer, butter and jelly. She pulled two pieces of bread from a loaf and tossed them into the toaster.

Her hand slipped behind the *Keurig* machine and turned it on. Whoever had invented a machine that brewed cups of coffee on demand, and in single rations, should be deemed a god. The familiar, soothing sound of water heating inside filled the air.

Several minutes later, she was in the process of setting butter on toast when Hailey breezed in. Brooke took in her outfit and bit her tongue.

Jeans sat low enough on Hailey's hips to cause a traffic accident, and her white t-shirt didn't hide the very visible pink bra she wore beneath.

"Hailey..." Brooke began, wincing at the telling tone, but really, this outfit couldn't be fit for public consumption.

Hailey grabbed a piece of toast and bit off a chunk. "Mom, don't start," she said around a mouthful of food.

Brooke narrowed her eyes and leaned forward on the center island. "I'm your mother. I'm supposed to start—and end it. How do you even know what I'm going to say?"

Eyes matching the color of dark chocolate and framed with long lashes met hers. A trait Hailey shared with her deadbeat father, and yet another daily reminder of Brooke's failures in love. Hailey tossed a long, thick braid over her shoulder and let out an exaggerated breath. The color of her hair matched the clay of Arizona's desert, deep, rich shades of red and gold, intermingled with blonde. Besides her stubbornness, the color was another trait she shared with Brooke. And it had always been one that thousands of other women paid hundreds of dollars to replicate in the salon.

"I know what you're going to say because it's written all over your face. And from the way your eyes practically bugged out of your head, I'm sure I can guess what it's going to be. This is the style now, Mom."

Brooke bristled. Her hand curled around the coffee mug, the brim almost as big as her face. In most instances, she needed at least two cups to start her day, and today she figured she'd need a lot more. But for now she used the warmth coming through the ceramic to comfort her frayed nerves. The day had started out wrong, her dream interrupted, her daughter's outfit... She could only guess what else was going to come her way.

"It may be the style, but really?" she asked.

Hailey huffed. "I'm not a little girl anymore."

She wanted to give Hailey a chance to grow on her own, but she needed to keep the boundaries tight, as well. It wasn't too long ago that she had been a teenager herself. And even if Hailey didn't know it, they were alike in many ways. She saw herself in her daughter and fought an impulse to point it out. That argument, the repeating of her past mistakes, had never been one to get through to Hailey, and it wouldn't help matters now.

Before she demanded Hailey go and change, she took a deep breath. Her smart daughter retained knowledge faster than anyone she knew. Brooke hoped her daughter would get over this need to act out soon, and get back on track. She had tried to stand back and not harp on Hailey too much, give her space, and encourage communication. Lately, though, it seemed as if the girl deliberately tried to push her buttons in what she wore, in who she'd hang out with, in the late hours she would come home. Her grades even started to slip, and while Brooke really wanted to get that under control, to set her daughter straight, she didn't know how to get through to the teenager standing across from her. The slip was minimal, mind you, nothing rash compared to the four-point-oh Hailey held, but it was there.

"Hailey," she started again, "you're beautiful without having to draw attention to your…assets." She raised her brows, emphasizing her point, and tried another tactic. "Honey, I get that you want to grow up, feel like you can take on the world, think you understand what it's like being an adult. But really, don't rush it."

Hailey rubbed the back of her hand across her forehead. "God, Mom." She bit her lip and looked around, her words fading.

Brooke's hackles rose again. "What, Hailey? Just spit it out."

Hailey's expression grew harder, reminding Brooke of when her daughter had been two and thrown a tantrum in Walmart. That fit was over the fact that she'd said no to getting the new holiday Barbie. Brooke braced for the explosion.

"I'm not going to end up like you. You want me to be myself, well then, stop trying to make me into someone you want me to be." Her face softened with an undeniable amount of pity. "I understand your fears, but I'm also smart and know what I'm doing. All I do is go to school, play softball, and come home. I need to break out of the box."

Oh. Well, shit. "Hailey, listen."

"No, Mom, *you* listen."

Hailey came around the island. Her daughter brushed the hair from Brooke's shoulders, and she sighed. Such a small touch, but damn it, she didn't even get hugs anymore.

"I get you're scared. I do. And I love you for it, but you need to trust me here."

"I want to, Hails."

Hailey wrapped her arms around Brooke's shoulders and smiled. "Prove it."

She raised a brow. "What do you mean?"

Hailey shrugged and looked away. "If you trust me, then hear me out and really think about it before you answer."

Ding, ding, ding! That was the sound of an alarm. She shouldn't ask, but she couldn't resist. The brow she raised came down tight and she frowned. "What do you want?"

As if she were bracing for impact, Hailey let out a slow breath. "Jaxon asked me to go out on a date and I want to say yes."

Brooke sucked in a sharp breath. "Jaxon." She didn't ask it as a question, but it was stated. *Oh shit, shit, shit.* This couldn't be happening already.

"Yes," Hailey answered with a smile, slow and sweet as honey.

"You're only seventeen," she said and winced at the whine in her voice. "A date? Jaxon is older," she rushed on. "I don't know if it's such a good idea. Plus with everything going on at the school, with the investigation, I don't know if I want to have to worry about you dating while things are...tense in the community."

Hailey huffed and stepped back. Brooke fought with the loss of the little girl who used to give hugs out as if a necessity to life. It seemed she only got any kind of affection when her daughter wanted something.

"See? This is what I'm talking about. He's only two years older," Hailey said, with what Brooke noticed was a complete disregard for anything involving the drug investigation going on at her school. "And he's nice. Has a good job and his own place. He's smart and funny, and totally cool. You've known him for two years. Come on, give me a chance to go out on my first date with someone I really like."

Brooke saw the hope in her eyes. It was there like bait to a fish, straining to do its job, and it worked. Hailey was a teenager who could manipulate with the best of them. Caught on the hook, Brooke closed her lids before opening them again. "Okay, under one condition."

Surprise flashed across her face before happiness. She jumped up and down, laughed, and wrapped Brooke in a tight embrace. The sweet innocence of her daughter filled her lungs—baby powder. Such a simple smell but one that reminded her of a hundred memories. Her heart clenched as Hailey hugged her tightly. Brooke did not know if she was ready to take this step, but holding on forever wasn't an option. She needed to teach Hailey about taking responsibility, about making the right decisions, and the first step to that would be *cutting the cord*, so to speak.

"Anything, Mom." Hailey pulled back, her smile as big as the GW Bridge was wide.

Brooke nodded. "Number one, go change your bra. Put on a white one."

She nodded with rapid movements.

"And two, promise me you'll concentrate on your grades. They're slipping, Hails."

Hailey bit her lip, looking sheepish before she nodded again, the movement slower than before. "Of course, I promise. Anything else?" She ducked her head and looked up beneath heavy, long lashes. Brooke bit back a sigh at how beautiful she was. What if this was too soon?

"You won't come home too late. And you're not allowed to be alone in his house. And you will keep in constant contact with me. Understand?"

Hailey beamed before she jumped forward and kissed her cheek with a giggle. At that sound, the sigh she tried to hold broke free. Love swelled unconditionally. Hailey was the one person Brooke felt comfortable giving any affection to.

"Understood." Her daughter's gaze darted over Brooke's shoulder before widening. "Crap, I'm going to be late."

With a whirlwind of movement, she dashed off down the hallway, thanking Brooke over her shoulder.

Brooke looked over at the small wooden kitchen table and sighed at the bags left behind. She picked up Hailey's softball bag and made sure everything was inside before moving it next to the rest of her daughter's things. With another small wince—this one for herself— she tried to ignore just another reminder of her ex-husband. Leo Mason had been the star pitcher for their high school's baseball team. He was good, phenomenal actually, and had dreams to back up his star playing abilities. He was also pretty damn dreamy when it came to how a young woman might view him.

She'd been more of an academic teenager and sat on the other side of the cafeteria from where the jocks did. He was a year ahead and bounds more popular. She never thought he'd ever give her any kind of attention, much less look in her direction twice. So, when he approached her one afternoon, she'd been shocked and wary. It took him months to build their friendship, her always thinking he couldn't possibly want her. He could have had anyone, but he'd chosen her and that was unbelievable. She questioned every step they took before finally giving in to him.

Time was relative in everything one did. It took months to build the friendship, moments to break through the affection, years to grow a relationship and a child, and mere seconds to have it all shatter.

An exuberant Hailey rushed back into the room and grabbed her bags, tossed them on her shoulder, and shoved the remaining piece of toast in her mouth.

"Is Dwayne picking you up again this morning?"

Hailey turned and pressed a sweet kiss on Brooke's cheek. "Yup," she said, then dashed out of the kitchen with an, "I love you, Mom," over her shoulder.

Brooke followed on her heels and held the door as her daughter sped outside. Sandy hair reflected off the teenager's head as the sun rebounded from the strands.

A dark police cruiser pulled up to the curb as Hailey reached the street. Brooke smiled at the familiar sight.

Detective Dwayne Gonzalez.

This was common as Dwayne normally drove by her place at about the same time each morning to pick Hailey up for school. While this should be a parent's job, making sure their child got to their destination safely, Dwayne had been a fixture in Hailey's life for so long it wasn't something any of them thought twice about. Since he had a major drug investigation going on at the school, the pick-ups were coming every day now.

The passenger's tinted window drew down and a deep voice rumbled out of the vehicle.

She closed her eyes against the involuntary shiver. Dwayne's voice oozed sensuality and sin. Combined with his looks, he was a lethal combination to a woman's senses.

They'd known each other since elementary school, and while that was close to twenty-five years ago, it seemed just yesterday that he was running behind her, snapping her bra against her back. Despite the teasing, and regardless of her irritation, he'd remained at her side, a loyal friend ever since. He had been a rock when she needed him most, and now, a friend to help when she required a crutch.

Hailey laughed at something he said before nodding and opening the side door. She slid inside and flashed Brooke a smile, leaning out the window, blowing loud kisses, and waving as the cruiser pulled away. Lifting a hand, Brooke caught a flash of white teeth and a masculine hand wave before she turned and went inside.

Chapter Two

Dwayne pulled away from the curb and checked his side view mirror as he eased back on the road. His vision still burned with the perfect picture of Brooke standing in the doorway. Long, thick sandy blondish-red hair fell around her shoulders. Eyes a blue so pale they reminded him of Alaska's melting glaciers shone across the expanse of space. The encounter lasted for all of ten seconds but refused to leave his mind.

He glanced over at Hailey, a younger clone, no less beautiful than her mother. Amazing how time sped the older you got. It seemed to be just yesterday when he had been hit with the gut-wrenching news Brooke was pregnant. From afar, he watched as she grew round with child, happiness radiating from her rosy cheeks, which were flushed with the making of life. It seemed like only last night when he coached Hailey's peewee softball team. At eight, the girl had been a mass of uncoordinated limbs but had more drive than any other on her team. She worked to get where she was today, the star pitcher of her high school squad. It wasn't the regular practices that pushed her skill level. It was her dedication and patience in learning and practicing a skill until it was perfect. There had been more than one late evening he'd worked with her in the backyard, building strength and endurance. Those memories were often followed by Brooke chewing him out for keeping her up so late, pushing her too hard, and even at times being just a general pain in the ass.

He chuckled under his breath at that very vivid memory.

And was it only an hour ago that Hailey transformed into a young woman? He'd watched her grow—faster than he liked, if he had to admit.

Learning what had been going on in her school, a protective instinct raised its head. There were too many things he wanted to shelter her from, too many uglies of the world she'd yet to see, and with what was happening in her school, he had a feeling things would be introduced to her far too soon.

Hailey changing the radio station brought his attention back. He glanced over to find deep chocolate eyes studying him. Dwayne arched a brow and pointedly turned his gaze to her hand.

"You having fun, Hails?"

She flashed a quick grin and sat back as the sound of some boy band filled the car. He shuddered. Give him ACDC, Metallica, hell, even Dave Matthews Band, but this techno beat with boys who hadn't hit puberty yet wasn't his style. Music was *not* made in the same way anymore.

"I love this group."

He made a face but didn't respond. Instead, he turned their focus to his investigation at her school. "Listen, I need to talk to you about something."

She groaned and shifted on the seat. "Not you, too."

He shook his head, confused. "Not me, too? What does that mean?"

Out of the corner of his eye, he watched as she ran a hand through her hair, grabbed the bottom of her braid, and proceeded to play with the end.

"Mom got on my case this morning. She doesn't want to accept I'm growing up. And I love her, I do, but lately I'm feeling smothered. Honestly, I need her off my back. It's like I can't breathe. I don't know if I can handle being around her when she gets like that. I know she means well, D, and I understand what my father did to her. But I'm not going to let it happen to me. I just wish she understood I'm smarter than that. I wish she trusted me."

He sat an elbow on the door rest and scrubbed a hand over his short hair. Hell, he was the last person Hailey should be talking to about this stuff. It was one thing to offer her advice on softball and even in school, but on anything dealing with decisions or discussions with her mother, he didn't want to touch it. Getting involved in any rift between them, especially involving her jerk of a father, wasn't an avenue he wanted to think, much less talk, about. Being the man he was, and denying himself what he truly wanted, didn't make him anywhere near close enough to dish out relationship advice.

"Your mom," he began, carefully choosing his words, "is just looking out for your well-being. She knows how smart you are. Hell, we all do. I don't think it's you she doesn't trust, but instead the male gender." He pulled up outside the school, tossed the cruiser in park against the curb, and turned to Hailey. "And trust me when I say men, or boys in this case, only want one thing. And that's not to make cookies. Plus," he added, "your father running out on you all like he did does have something to do with why she protects you the way she does, but she does it because she cares for you. We all do. I don't believe any of us are ready to see you grow up."

Her expression softened and she reached over to brush her fingers down the side of his face. "I care for you, too." She drew back and nodded with a smile. "I understand all that, but really, I can't handle being suffocated. You can get that, right?" She cocked her head and his mouth quirked as the movement brought a rush of memories back from his high school days when Brooke used to do the same.

"I can. This isn't what I wanted to discuss,

though." He arched his eyebrows, pinning her with his no-nonsense stare, and again chose his words with care. "But I do want you to know you can always come to talk to me, no matter what. I'll listen and try to do what I can to help, understood?"

Hailey deliberated his face for a few moments, then nodded. "Got it. What's this thing you wanted to chat about?"

Dwayne cut his gaze out the window behind her, studied the students milling around the walkway. The red brick building rose from pale concrete like an imposing monster. Dark windows gleamed under the morning light and the green grass sitting outside was starting to brown with the impending winter. "I'm looking into something here at the school. I want you to tell me if you've heard anything, okay? And if you have, no matter what it is, you can tell me."

He shifted his attention back to her and waited. She bit her lip but nodded. He focused on her body language, the pulse on her neck, her breathing. He didn't think Hailey would lie to him, but the reports they'd been getting at the Nyack Police Department were unsettling. Being thirty minutes northwest of New York City kept the village plenty busy, but this latest influx of drug activity was something that hit a little too close to home. Especially with his past.

"There have been some reports of drugs here, Hailey. Do you know anything about that?"

Her eyes widened and her gaze darted away. He clenched his teeth. *Fucking great. Come on, the truth, baby girl.*

"What, like people smoking weed?" Her gaze returned to his, but she fought to keep contact. He ducked his head and held her hesitant stare.

"No, not marijuana. More like ecstasy,

prescription pills of Vicodin and Adderall, even cocaine." With each drug he listed, Hailey grew more and more still. He stifled the urge to shake her and demand answers. Her body language more than told him she knew something.

She twisted away and he silently urged her to turn back to him. His right hand clenched and released on the seat behind her head before he reached over and pulled her face back to his with a gentle tug on her chin. "Hailey…"

She interrupted. "Of course I've heard things around school. How could I not? But I'm not using those things if that's what you're asking."

Like a geyser, he released the breath he hadn't realized he'd been holding. Tension eased from his shoulders, his body slowly relaxing from the stress of thinking she may be doing drugs. With the initial question of her possibly using out of the way, he pushed forward. "That's good, that's good." He dropped his hand and glanced back out the window. A young brunette, a teacher here if he remembered correctly, sashayed up to his cruiser. He focused on her for a moment before remembering. She taught freshmen literature, wild in the sack, open to different things, stuff he was more than willing to indulge in. What the hell was her name, though…?

"Do you know who is selling, Hails?" He kept his focus outside, still trying to remember the teacher's name, but listened for Hailey.

"I-I don't think so," she stuttered

That snapped him out of his trance. He swung his gaze back to her. She stared ahead, worrying her lower lip. He bit back a sigh at how uncomfortable this must make her. "Get out, but wait for me."

He pushed open the door and stood to his full

height, towering over many of the young students walking around, bustling for the front entrance. Latching the middle button of his blue suit jacket, he walked around the front of his car and met Hailey outside the passenger side.

"Listen, just mull it over. If you think you may be able to help me or identify something that you believe I need to know, you know how to get ahold of me, okay?"

She didn't meet his gaze. She was hiding something, he knew it. He just had to get through to her.

"Hailey, this is important. We have a kid in the hospital right now from an overdose. Drugs he bought from this location put him there and he may not make it out. So if you know something, I will listen."

"Okay, D. If I see or hear anything, I'll come to you."

She shifted her feet until he reached out again and caught her chin with his forefinger. With a slight tug, she turned toward him. He flashed her a smile and was rewarded with one in return. "Have a good day, Hailey, and knock 'em dead at tonight's game."

Her smile grew and she winked. "You've got company." Her chin lifted to point behind him. The young teacher waited by the hood of his cruiser. When he turned back, Hailey was strolling away. She walked up to an older kid and tossed her long arms around his neck. The dark-haired kid dipped down and brushed his lips over hers. Dwayne narrowed his eyes and watched as the kid's hands landed on Hailey's hips, then slid lower before curving over the bottom of her jeans. With a growl, Dwayne stepped forward.

"I wouldn't if I were you, Detective," a raspy voice said, drawing him to a stop.

His vision turned red as the kid groped and prodded Hailey's ass. She didn't fight against his hold, though, just turned her head back and laughed. "Fuck." He turned toward the woman who'd spoken. Her hooded gaze ran along his body. She bit her bottom lip and he read the blatant invitation.

"You never called," she accused.

He shrugged, still trying to figure out her name. "I lost my phone." An outright lie, but small ones didn't hurt.

Her red lips parted and a vivid memory struck him, a reminder of how nice her mouth had felt wrapped around his dick. The beast in his pants gave a painful jerk as if it remembered her, too. *What the hell was her name?*

"Do you have one now?" she asked.

He nodded and reached into his suit pocket, pulled out the device, and held it in the air between two fingers. "Are you going to fix my problem?"

Those red lips curved into a slow smile. "I'm going to fix your problem and then some, Detective." A slender hand grabbed the cell from his hand. The movement brought her body closer and he took in a deep breath. Apples. He suddenly craved pie. He glanced down as she worked something into his phone and handed it back.

"Lucy." Now he remembered. He remembered well.

Lifting an eyebrow, she tittered. Fingers playing with her red V-neck top drew his attention to the swells of her breasts. "I expect you to make it up to me, Detective Gonzalez."

One brow rose as his gaze returned to her face. "Make what up to you?"

Lips curved more, a hint of white teeth flashing from behind. She stepped closer, her mouth a hairsbreadth from his cheek. "Forgetting my name, of course. Talk to you soon, Dwayne."

She brushed her breast across his arm before strolling off and he sucked in a sharp breath. He twisted and watched her long legs strut away until she vanished. The tempting minx out of view, he turned to where Hailey had been standing and found she had disappeared, too. He searched around, but kids were piling inside the school and the warning bell rang.

Remembering the older kid with Hailey earlier, Dwayne started up the walkway, needing to speak with the principal before he looked around. The way the kid put his hands on her raised protective instincts again, ones that drove all reasonable thought from his head. That wasn't the real thing bothering him, though. It was the expression the male had when he glanced down at her that drove Dwayne insane. That one look spoke of possession and a hint of danger. A look he had seen too many times from the men his birth mother brought home...before she was murdered.

Chapter Three

Ugh. Brooke sat back and stared at the screen of her laptop as if it were the bane of her existence. The words which normally came out like water from a faucet now felt forced, the same water dripping with an annoying sound. *Dlub, lub, lub.* The writing looked all wrong.

This was her chance at last, the point where after years of putting everyone else first, she had her moment of opportunity to break through. After spending so much time dedicating her entire life to her marriage and raising her daughter, she'd never been able to go after what she wanted. Now, with Hailey older and more independent, Brooke was able to pursue her dream.

After her ex, Leo, left, she'd jumped into the raging waters of her life and fought to make sure Hailey had not wanted for anything. When he stepped out of their life, Hailey, at seven years old, took it hard, worse than Brooke. The crying jags at night, the back talking. Everything Brooke had guided her to do—*everything*—Hailey did the opposite. And while her sweet little girl had tried to hide the hurt, a mother would've had to have been deaf not to hear the sobs coming from Hailey's room at night.

Luckily, her daughter had outgrown that stage, and the constant drama that had been their lives. So now, since Hailey didn't require her full focus, Brooke was able to move from a freelance reporter to an associate writer. She'd done small pieces up until now for a decent food magazine out of the city. Just last month, though, she'd been picked to write for *Time Magazine*. Her first article was due in less than a month to the editor who had so bravely taken a chance on her. With another four thousand words needed, she hoped she would make the deadline and get the deal.

"No, no, no!" Brooke clenched her fists next to the keyboard and stared at the screen with nothing less than extreme hatred. This! This had been her problem for weeks. The story kept making its own path. Her focus was supposed to be on home decorating and personal beauty, but everything sounded lame and droll—something even she wouldn't read.

While the hiring manager initially tried to talk her into a dating column, Brooke had promptly steered the conversation in another direction. She didn't write romance and had no desire to do so. That wasn't her interest. She didn't do lovey-dovey crap. Hearts, flowers, and all that wasn't something she could give. With her past, she would be cheating her readers. The words of love were foreign to her. A fake story of her life. Her history was filled with nothing but heartache and betrayal and lies that led to the death of her marriage.

Wanting to toss her laptop out the window, she pushed away from the desk, folded her arms across her chest to keep from doing the aforementioned, and turned to the small office window. Outside, the sun shone bright and bathed the lawn and aster bushes in vitamin D. Pink blooms framed the orange disks of the flowers and butterflies danced around the colors, drawn to the sweet smell of the garden. The image stood out in stark abundance, the white fence popping in the background.

She frowned. The beauty of the world around her glimmered while she sat inside, in a darkened room, typing away at what was supposed to be an interesting column. Outside, life was robust, teasing her with the cheerful circle of living. It didn't seem fair.

No more.

She surged out of the chair, mind made up, and

grabbed her running shoes.

After slipping them on, she dashed outside. Her feet pounded against the asphalt, and Pitbull sang to her alone about how he knew she wanted him. The warmth from the bright orb heated her neck, and Brooke did what she had intended the run to do, she gave in to her thoughts and allowed her mind to wander. This was where she could think, where her thoughts calmed, and the words of her article flowed.

Air, humid and with the threat of turning any day into the cold winds of winter, flowed in and out of her lungs. Flowers were still in bloom, and colorful leaves hung on trees. The cloudless sky didn't show any threat of fall. No one not from the northeast would have been any wiser.

Strength in her legs bounded each kick. Her arms pumped as she turned down street after street, sticking to the back roads and away from traffic. Even with a dark voice singing in her ears, now about hotel room service, she basked in the quietness of the village and was thankful that the recent crime spree no longer existed.

How her village had come to house a madman who terrorized women and took away the peace of the community was a nightmare she didn't want to relive.

She turned down Piermont Avenue and stretched her stride, passing the park. Keeping a conscious mind on the time left before Hailey's softball game, she glanced down at her watch. School had ended an hour ago and the team was meeting for a quick practice before this evening. This game would decide if they were going to the county championship. After the county, should—scratch that—*when* they made it through, they would go to state. It was an exciting time in Nyack, the girls being reigning champions from the year prior. They had a name to live up to. Another trophy to bring home.

Brooke rounded a corner, lifted her gaze, and jumped to the side as a large shadow filled her vision. "Shit!" Her ankle collapsed as she hit the bumpy lawn. After breaking it one too many times in soccer, it was still weak and without warning, simply twisted. With injuries she sustained as a kid, she really should get it looked at, should probably get physical therapy, but damn if she was willing to give up any more time living in the past.

Strong arms gripped her shoulders as she started to go down. Belatedly, she heard a little voice in her head, one that reminded her of the same strong arms waiting for Juliette in the novel next to her bed back home. She wanted to scream in frustration. *Get your head in the game, you're friggen falling, and you're thinking of romance!*

"Easy there."

Brooke snapped her head up at the familiar voice and found herself staring into eyes dancing with humor, a deep green gaze that gave the lush lawns in the village a run for their money.

"I'm sorry, Dwayne, I need to pay better attention to where I'm going, I guess."

He flashed a grin and her attention shifted to the dimples outlining his smile. Those two indents should take away from his ruggedly good looks, but instead they did the opposite. It gave him a boyish charm she found all too enticing, adding to his handsome appearance.

"Not a problem. It's not every day I have women falling into my arms."

She snorted. "Yeah, right." Was it her imagination or did his arms tighten around her for a moment? She didn't have too long to wonder about it before he set her away from him. Gingerly, she tested her ankle and winced as pain shot through her leg. She rolled it in circles, gave weight to it in increments. "Crap, I really do need to stop putting this off." She hoped she could get home and that no additional damage happened to the already weakened ligament.

"Are you okay?" Before she could utter a response, Dwayne's dark head ducked into her view. He knelt to take her ankle in his warm hands. A zip of electricity having nothing to do with pain sizzled where he touched. She tried to push away the fleeting pleasure his large palms against her skin gave. He wouldn't have it, though, and held her ankle firmly. She blew out a breath and turned her face away to try to hide her reaction. If her cheeks were as red as they felt, then surely he'd see.

This reaction confounded her. Dwayne was her friend, had always been around and while he was extremely easy on the eyes, she'd never felt anything other than friendship for him. Then again, he'd never touched her, had he? It must be her. Years of going without physical contact from the opposite sex had left her body starving, craving for any touch.

That's all it was.

Or at least that was her story and she was sticking to it.

Bright eyes looked up at her. His warm fingers danced along her ankle, pushing on the now-throbbing limb.

"It's fine, I wouldn't worry. Really." Was that her voice, all breathless? *For Pete's sake, Brooke, get a damn grip!* She gently tugged her leg away and stepped back.

Dark brows drew down with his frown and he rose to his full height. As he uncoiled, she gingerly took another step back. He moved with the grace of someone half his size, almost like a dancer unfurling from a ballet pose. Smooth. Fluid. Gorgeous. "Too many breaks as a kid. I'll just walk it off, take it easy on the way home."

"Dwayne?" a sultry voice called from behind.

Brooke turned to recognize a teacher from the high school. The woman lounged in a doorway. Long, brown curls fell in silken waves around her shoulders. A black skirt dangled around her hips and was partially covered by an untucked starched white dress shirt. Several buttons were undone and the look on the young woman's face painted a story.

She'd interrupted something here, and if patience was anything to study, the woman's face said it was anything *but* a virtue.

The earlier blush Brooke had felt now flamed to life again. Just as suddenly, regret lifted its head. She took a step to the side, and embarrassment prevented her from meeting Dwayne's eyes, although she felt his gaze taking her in. It was like a caress against her skin. "Shit, I'm sorry. I'll just, I'll go now."

She winced at her stuttering voice and turned away.

"Brooke, wait."

Every muscle locked, but she kept her back to him. It should be illegal to sound so delicious, and despite being outside, his scent seemed to wrap around her—fresh mown lawn combined with the raw and undeniable trace of sex. Her heart pounded a hardy pulse in her ears, rivaling the beat Pitbull established before. The road ahead looked so damn long, and with her ankle screaming, the walk home would be anything but fun. Yet she wanted to be anywhere but right here, right now.

He sighed and stepped up next to her. "Do you need a ride home?"

She bit the inside of her cheek, feeling like ten times the fool. For one, she enjoyed his touch on her skin more than a friend should. And two, she'd interrupted something that he was obviously heading to. Damn it, this wasn't her. She didn't do this kind of thing, get caught in anything resembling connection to a man. Dwayne was Dwayne, and she did not want to put a damper on his plans any more than she already had. "I'm fine, don't worry about me. I'll see you at the game later, right?"

He nodded, then mumbled something under his breath, but it was so soft she couldn't catch it. She really wanted to get the heck outta there and not cause any more of a scene, so she offered a weak smile. "Great."

She limped away and got about twenty steps down the block before she glanced over her shoulder, unable to deny the urge to look at him one more time. That small mumble he had made jumped around in her mind like beans from Mexico, and with each bounce, the words grew in clarity.

Dwayne sauntered across the green lawn, his back to her, his stride toward an eager-looking young woman. The words, though, they had to have been her touch-deprived body playing tricks. She swore she heard him say, "But I do."

Chapter Four

A low, pulsing throb wrapped tentacles around her ankle, but rather than staying home and nursing it, Brooke sat in the bleachers at Nyack High School, waiting on the game to start.

With the sun low in the sky, it painted the horizon in shades of orange and red. A lush line of green on the trees dotted the horizon, and leaves trying to keep up with the changing colors of the sky—another hint that fall was coming—combined to make a scene that could be the perfect shot for a postcard.

The girls, decked out in their black uniforms, came running out on the field, and the crowd stood and cheered. The sound was deafening. The community supported the girls and between the size of the crowd and the support of family members, it showed with packed bleachers. Shrill whistles pierced the air. Enthusiastic remarks about what some wanted to do to the other team rang with abundance. And clapping raised the already heightened anticipation for a good game.

Brooke sat after the cheers quieted. She watched as Hailey took her spot at the pitcher's mound. Her eyes stung, but she took it all in and got lost in the emotional tug the scene brought. She blinked rapidly and tried to dismiss her tears on the fact that the sun shone directly on her face.

But deep down she knew it wasn't that at all. Her daughter was no longer her little girl, and watching as Hailey stood tall and proud on the pitcher's mound brought memories back in a rush.

It seemed like just yesterday that Dwayne stood in their backyard and taught Hailey the basics of a sport that had become her life. They spent hours working well into the night on throwing and catching. At one point she'd even become concerned that softball was taking over her daughter's life, and she'd kicked Dwayne off her property, told him not to come back for days.

Hailey had been such a sweet little girl, her eyes bright with a thirst for knowledge on something she wanted to master. Looking at her now, there was only a hint of the little girl she used to be. Her curves gave her athletic form more of a feminine look. And her legs went on for what seemed to be miles. A few weeks shy of eighteen, the contours of Hailey's face slimmed, taking youthful expressions and turning them sexier, more mature.

Brooke did not know what she thought about that. She didn't want her daughter to grow up, didn't think she was ready for this. With her little girl changing into a young woman, she grasped at the last of Hailey's childhood innocence as if it were air to breathe.

Then again, remembering what she'd promised herself about letting Hailey be free echoed in her mind. She took in a lungful of air and pushed the panic, the threat of losing her child to womanhood, away.

A deep voice filled the speakers, welcoming everyone to the county championship game, then introduced the singer for the Star Spangled Banner. A girl no older than ten squared her shoulders and sang her itty-bitty heart out, not missing or confusing a word through the whole song—unlike some adult celebrities—which said something. The game kicked off with more cheers, each team moving to give the other a run for the title. As the innings progressed, the sun sank lower, and Brooke's fingernails grew shorter as she bit on each with her nerves jumbling.

The game tied four to four at the bottom of the ninth.

Hailey stood on the plate, had two runners on base and a strike against her. Her long ponytail trailed down her back as she bent over. After concentrating on pitching for so long, her daughter was not the best with her batting average, but with two outs, the game centered on Hailey at least getting one of those runners in.

The pitcher wound her arm and sent the ball flying. Hailey did something she had never done before and uncorked her best swing, sailing the bat through the air and—*crack!*—the connection vibrated through the stands as everyone stood.

Brooke followed the path of the ball and out of the corner of her gaze, Hailey sprinted to first base. The ball sailed over the back fence. Brooke jumped, ignoring the pain in her ankle, and shouted.

With the setting sun, Hailey's hair looked bright orange against the sky. She rounded first. Missing the tag, she turned and went to the base again and froze. It was a split second, but noticeable, and the crowd's murmur brought more attention to it. In that moment, something happened, because Hailey collapsed. Brooke moved before realizing and headed down the stairs, still watching her daughter. The coach stood to the side of the base, talking to Hailey. Her daughter gave a shake of her head and crawled back to the base. *What the heck was going on?* The coach turned to the umpire and the conversation between the two turned heated as the older plump man turned red and the coach tossed his hands in the air.

Brooke walked around the field and stepped inside the fence, her intent to get to her daughter. To find out what was wrong and figure out why the coach looked as if he wanted to wring her neck. But before she could take another step, strong arms captured her shoulders and drew her to a halt. Startled, she glanced back and found

Dwayne's grave hazel eyes watching not her, but Hailey on the field.

"Easy now, you can't help her."

She bristled. "What do you mean I can't help her? She's my daughter, who is obviously hurt. And I have no idea what the coach is saying to her, but I don't like it."

He looked down at her and set his lips in a grim, flat line. "You go out there and help her, or if her teammates try to do something, she will be called out. They're discussing bringing in a pinch runner now, but if you look at Hailey, she seems determined to get through this herself."

Brooke drew her attention back to the game, and her daughter stood, one leg bent, weight distributed to the other. She tried to talk to the two men arguing, but between their heated conversations, she seemed at a loss.

Before anyone could do anything, the two runners who had the chance to cross home base because of Hailey's hit walked over to first base. They ignored the ump and coach. Each took an arm, wrapped them over their shoulders, and began to walk—to her daughter's limp—around each of the bases.

With the ball gone, Hailey had hit her home run and obviously wanted to get around *each* of the bases.

The act was so touching, independent, and such a true measure of teamwork, that tears stung the back of Brooke's eyes. Dwayne, who still had a grip on her arms, tightened his hands against her until the girls crossed the last plate.

Cheers once again filled the air, and the ump called the home run—Hailey's first of her entire life.

* * * *

Brooke turned and pressed her face to his chest, her arms around his waist. Dwayne fought against reacting in the way he wanted with this woman in his embrace. Rather than tossing her against the fence and taking her hard and fast here, he gave a gentle squeeze and smiled when she drew back, laughing.

The affection was short lived, though, as she pulled away and bounded over to her daughter, who sat on the bench in the dugout. A local physician examined Hailey's leg. He could still feel Brooke against his body, lush curves, long limbs, and the sweet smell of lavender. Damn, he wanted her back in his arms, wanted to feast on her lush mouth for days, not hours. But Hailey had been hurt and both he and her mother needed to focus on her.

He caught the gaze of the young woman he had spent more hours with than any female in his life and winked as she grinned. His fondness for Hailey had grown stronger over the years, and no matter that she wasn't his blood, he considered her family. It was not lost on him that this had, in fact, been her first home run. Being the bottom of the inning, the game was called, Nyack won the title, and congratulations jumped back and forth.

He pushed away from the fence and bounded into the dugout, dropping to a crouch next to the doctor.

"How's it looking, Mike?"

"Nothing's broken, but I suspect she may have stepped on something wrong out there and strained a ligament in her knee. It'll need some rest."

"It hurt like hell."

He snapped his head up just as Brooke warned, "Hailey, watch your mouth."

The teen looked contrite and muttered an apology.

"I'll go home and get the car, Hails, then come back. I don't want you walking on that tonight."

"It's no bother," Dwayne filled in. "I can take you both home. I have my cruiser out front."

Brooke opened her mouth, but Hailey's voice beat

her to it. "Actually, I was supposed to hang out with Jaxon tonight, remember, Mom?"

Dwayne stood and stepped back, not wanting to be in between these two when they worked out whatever was going on.

"I do, Hails, but don't you think you should reconsider since you got hurt?"

"No, I think I should still go. Even Doctor Smith said I'd be fine as long as I took it easy."

Said doctor stood and backed away, looking uncomfortable as well. He rubbed the back of his neck, and dark brown hair fell and covered one side of his face. "That is true, but maybe you should take it easy tonight, Hailey."

In a classic teenager move, Hailey crossed her arms over her chest and glared at the doctor.

"Mom, please?"

Brooke bit down on her lower lip and, drawn to the sight, he stared. The plump pink bud was shiny when she finally released it, and instead of taking his attention away, it pulled him in further.

Christ!

He shouldn't feel this damn horny after the afternoon he had spent with Lucy, learning more than one way to make the teacher scream. And more so, his thoughts should be staying PG-13 in a high school softball field.

Brooke nodded and said something to Hailey. The girl jumped off the bench and limped her way over to her mother, tossing long arms around the star of his fantasies for so long.

Hailey left shortly after. Brooke pivoted to him and shrugged. "I have no clue how she gets away with it, playing that cute little face on me when she wants something. Am I foolish?"

He flashed a grin and followed her out of the dugout. "Not at all. Hailey has a good head on her shoulders. She knows to take it easy and understands she'll only hurt herself more if she doesn't."

Her sigh reached his ears. She turned to him again and stopped walking. "I know, but still, a mother will always worry." She glanced around, but instead of following her gaze, he kept his on her. Hair matching the color of her daughter's, the soft light behind her seemed to give it a glow, brightening the golden highlights sparkling over the tendrils. Azure eyes gave a startling contrast against the afternoon sunset. The color and uniqueness grabbed him by the balls and refused to let go.

"What are you doing tonight?" He didn't realize the words came from his mouth until she turned to him, arching a brow. Why had he asked her that? He knew better than most that Brooke was not someone to mess with. Asking her out would only have her drawing back, especially after her past.

"Probably falling into the tub with John, a bottle of wine, and a good book. Why?"

His brows furrowed. "John?" Who the fuck was John? Moreover, when the hell did this happen? And why did the surge of jealousy in his gut feel more like rage?

Her expression danced with humor. "Yeah, John. As in John Mayer?"

He resisted the urge to roll his eyes. "Ah, got me there."

She grinned and poked his stomach. "Was that jealousy I heard in your voice, Dwayne?"

"No." *Fuck yes.*

"What, you want to be the only man for this town?" She laughed.

"No," he grumbled. *Actually, not for the town,*

just you. Always you.

He shrugged. "I'm meeting up with Charlie and Trent for a drink down on Main. You should come with us."

Charlie was, without using the high school saying for BFFs, his closest friend and confidant, as well as a fellow NPD detective. Last summer some crazed lunatic had been set free on the streets of Nyack and managed for over three months to put the community in turmoil, his crimes escalating from breaking and enterings, on up to rape and murder. The chief, normally so protective of Charlie and never assigning her a violent case, had given her what he thought to be a simple Peeping Tom investigation. As the attacks and B&Es increased, the activity had garnered the attention of the FBI and brought two agents to assist, one of them being Trent Rossi. Besides working together to get the suspect caught and locked away, the two had fallen head over heels for one another and were inseparable.

Dwayne had never been one to envy anyone for anything. He believed you made your life what you wanted it to be and you were responsible for what accomplishments—and happiness—you could get alone. In recent days, though, each time he visited or hung out with the couple, he found his life lacking something, his vision turning green.

She grimaced. "Sounds a lot like a date. You know, with two couples there."

He laughed, the sound awkward. "Who cares what it looks or sounds like. Besides, could it really be all that bad? You know, being on a date with me?" Who the hell was this fool who couldn't seem to get an intelligent sentence out? What the hell was wrong with him?

Brooke wrinkled her nose and glanced away. He resisted letting out a sigh, already knowing she was going to turn him down. "You don't want to go out on a date with me, nor be seen with me in public, Dwayne. I'm a mom, have so much baggage it's not even funny, and just don't have time for getting all dolled up and playing that scene. You don't want to waste your time with me."

He had to hold back so many words he wanted to say. They would scare the shit out of her and probably send her screaming for the hills. "I think you look fine how you are now." He openly scanned her from the tips of her brown Sketcher boots, on up the length of those legs that seemed to go on for miles and were encased in jeans, over the thin white camisole and gray cardigan, past the sapphire-colored eyes sitting inside a heart-shaped face. "More than fine."

Were her cheeks turning red? He smirked, enchanted by the sight.

"Ah, well, thanks. However, I think I'll have to pass on this one. I have some writing to do. Maybe another time."

He tried not to let disappointment show on his face but it flashed anyhow, because she said, "I promise, Dwayne. I'll let you know."

Yeah, when hell freezes over you will. "Sure, give me a call if you change your mind."

She nodded, unable to hold his stare. *Damn it.* "I will. See you later."

"Yeah."

She lifted a hand and pivoted, then walked away. He kept his gaze on her, watched the sway of her hips, studied the glow the setting sun seemed to give her, and cursed being a chicken shit back in high school, as well as now.

Chapter Five

Hailey stepped out of the shower and grabbed a towel. Her mom would have a shit-fit if she knew that she did this at Jaxon's, and that's why she had no intention on telling her. It wasn't like he was in the bathroom with her anyway. The door was locked—another quick glance confirmed that—and besides, Jax was engaged with his friends out in the living room. She heard the low beat of bass as it shook the walls, with the occasional laugh leaving her very secure, and very alone while she cleaned up.

She grabbed her clothes from her bag and donned a white thermal and a pair of pink velvet track pants with the word "Juicy" written across her ass. She chuckled, turning to look in the mirror. They were a present from Jaxon, ones she wouldn't normally wear, but having never received a present from a boy before—the only man ever to give her something was Dwayne, and he didn't count—she could not refuse the gift. It was sweet.

Thoughtful.

And made her swoon.

Like she told her mom this morning.

After running a brush through her hair, she braided it behind her head and tossed everything back in her bag, then limped out of the bathroom. Jax's room needed a bit of sprucing up, with a king-size bed and a few sheets in disarray across the width, some IKEA nightstand off to the side, and a poster of Bob Marley where the headboard to the bed should be, it looked more like a bachelor's pad than anything in her house.

She tossed the bag on the bed and followed the sounds of what she guessed was a small party in full swing. Hobbling down the hall, regret settled in her stomach like a two-ton piece of concrete. She had wanted to spend a quiet night with Jaxon, just the two of them. There hadn't been any days like that in the past few weeks. After he moved out of his parents' house and into a place with his friend, it seemed as if people were always here, either smoking, or drinking, or shooting up.

She had yet to try any of it, both a little apprehensive about her first time with drugs, and the fact that she knew her mom would flip if she came home high. There would be no hiding it from her, either; she was too perceptive. And there wasn't a night she went to bed that her mom hadn't come in to say goodnight. Yeah, there'd be no way to hide any of it from her.

As she reached the living room—as bare as the bedroom—Jaxon bounded up from the ratty brown couch that had seen better days. He arrived at her side within seconds. She smiled at him and took his offered hand. She was so lucky to have such an understanding and thoughtful boyfriend. More so, while things got a bit hot and heavy the last few times they had been alone, he hadn't pressured for more. Sure, he was horny and let her know just how much, even guided her hand to his package, but when it came to "the deed," he didn't seem to be in a rush to push her.

They reached the couch and Jaxon knocked some guy in the head. The guy lifted his head and glared, his brown eyes narrowed, then his gaze shot over to her and he promptly moved away.

Hailey sat next to Jaxon and took in what they were doing. Little foil packs were scattered across the wooden table, some sort of brown powder held inside of the bowl-like pieces. Bags of weed were tossed haphazardly across the table, and a lit bong was in the center as if a flower arrangement at a wedding.

A girl with short purple hair—whom Hailey

deemed Mrs. Barney, seeing as no one introduced themselves—picked up a spoon and took some of the residue from the foil tins. She grabbed a lighter and ran the flame beneath the utensil for a few minutes. The ash turned to a liquid and bubbled before the black-haired male—*who in the hell were all these people?*—took a syringe and pulled the dark liquid inside. Mrs. Barney set the implement down and turned toward him. Jaxon wrapped a piece of latex around her arm, like the ones they used to tie off your arm when you gave blood at the hospital.

Adrenaline and a tiny bit of excitement shot through her as the pointer pierced Barney's arm and the liquid disappeared. The girl looked up and sat back in her chair, contentment relaxing her features. Her eyes went hooded and she focused on Hailey across the table.

"Your turn."

Something very like a snort popped out of her mouth before she could stop it. "I don't think so."

The guy—since he still had not been introduced to her, she would call him Emo—started preparing another spoon of what she suspected was heroine and spoke. "Princess too good?"

Stung with the remark, she flinched and waited for Jax to say something. He avoided her stare and reached for the bong, started to pack it with weed. She turned back to Emo.

"Of course not, but if I go home high, my mom will kick my ass."

"Eh." A flash of a lighter from Emo, but this time Jaxon spoke up. "The high only lasts for about four hours, tops. It won't even be midnight, which is your curfew." Popping bubbles filled the air as he inhaled from the bong and blew out a breath.

Hailey bit her lip, wary of the situation. She didn't

want her boyfriend to look at her with pity, nor did she want to embarrass him. All she wanted was to spend time with him, since they never got the chance to do it. She doubted her mom would let this happen too often, so she craved the time with him now.

A low pain still wrapped around her knee and she reached down to rub at it. Emo nodded his head toward her action. "Take a small shot. It'll help with the knee. Take the edge off."

Jaxon turned to her and studied her limb before agreeing. "A small shot won't hurt. Hell, you probably won't be high as long."

She furrowed her brows, still worried about what she should do. As if sensing her indecision, Jaxon leaned over and brushed his lips across hers. Her breath caught, as it always did. He pulled back and she met deep violet, intense eyes. "Trust me, baby? You know I wouldn't let anything happen to you."

She considered his words and, remembering it would be a small shot, she nodded with hesitation. It only took a small movement of her head for Jax to flash a wide grin. "You won't regret it, babe. I promise."

He reached for the latex string and grabbed her arm, tying it off, then took the needle Emo prepared and brought it to her vein. Her heart pounded in her throat as the needle pierced her skin. Her pulse kicked up a notch as the liquid disappeared inside.

A snap, and the band was removed. Relief hit her arm and she blinked, wondering if she was immune to the drug. She didn't feel any different.

Just as the thought popped into her mind, waves of euphoric warmth spread through her veins. It seemed as if a thousand little flames, the cuddly kind you see in Christmas movies, danced along her bloodstream, spreading and growing until her back bowed off the couch, the pain in her knee forgotten.

Hell, she couldn't think of anything but the hot, pulsing pleasure throbbing between her thighs and across her body. Her breath hitched and she cried out as an intense orgasm swept over her. Beneath the pound of her heart, she heard Jaxon groan and his lips brushed against her ear.

"God, babe, that was so fucking hot. You feel good?"

The tingly sensation wasn't going away and she turned to meet his gaze, took his hand, and set it between her thighs. She reached for the back of his head to draw him down.

"Make this ache go away, Jax."

He growled and took her mouth in a ravishing kiss, his teeth clashing against hers.

Music, something akin to beautiful bells, filled her mind. The bass from the speakers heightened the hazy sensations running through her. But his hand held her attention the most. He rubbed along the outside of her pants, and she wanted more.

Inhibitions gone, she came over the top of him, setting her thighs on either side of his as she kissed him again.

He stood, warning her to wrap her legs around him before moving, and carried her away. She didn't pay mind to anyone else, her focus on him and the way her body brushed against the hardness in his jeans.

A door slammed and a second later, she landed hard against the mattress. She had no time to react as his large body covered hers. Roughly he pushed her legs apart so he could settle between them. She tugged at his back as he lapped at her neck. He murmured incoherent words, pulled at her clothing, and ripped her shirt over her head.

She lay back as his head moved to her breasts and he worked the bra with jerky and frantic pulls. Staring up at the brown-stained ceiling, her mind struggled to keep up. The room spun and her stomach turned. She whimpered.

Jaxon took it for something else and cooed, "It's okay, Hails. I'll take care of it."

His hand snuck under the waist of her pants, spearing beneath her panties and touching her core. She grabbed at his wrist with both hands and shouted a startled cry. "Wait."

"No," he growled and pushed a thick finger inside her. Cool air invaded her skin down there and gave her a clue of how wet she was, but his touch wasn't gentle at all. It cut through the haze. Hurt.

She bit her lip and tried to tug his hand again. Her spinning head made nausea rise up the back of her throat. "Jaxon, please, stop."

He lifted his head and gave her an incredulous look. "No, you asked for this." He shifted his hips, rolled a hard ridge against her hip. "Stop teasing and give it to me. I'll make you feel good, better than you do already."

He dropped his head again and tore down her bra with his teeth, baring her breasts to the cooler air. His mouth clamped over her peak, sucked too hard, and she bit her lip, tears stinging her eyes.

What had she done?

He lifted from her and before she could react, he ripped her pants off. Moments later, warm, bare skin lay on top of her. His knees forced her legs open. She tensed when his erection prodded at the part of her no one had touched before.

"Jax, wait, please." Tears trailed down her temples and dipped into her ears. She pushed at his shoulders. He grunted, then slammed his hips forward.

Oh, God, what have I done?

Chapter Six

Brooke stirred the creamer in the coffee, watching as it blended with the darker color until becoming a light shade, the same matching Dwayne's skin. The fact that she compared her java to the man who'd haunted her dreams last night said far too much.

She wasn't some willy-nilly teenager who swooned at the words of young men. Nor was she some woman who hadn't lived and learned from her mistakes. Dwayne equaled everything she promised to stay away from, a man who could be her ex-husband's clone. Leo, voted most popular in high school, had been the man on campus, so to speak. She remembered seeing too many females' eyes get all starry when he walked by. But she ignored it all, simply happy to be beneath his arm. His girl. She'd been too naïve at the time and believed they would be together for life. After all, didn't true love last forever?

Getting pregnant, while it had been alarming, was a blessing. They married weeks later, months after graduating. Blind to what occurred behind her back, Brooke considered herself lucky.

Finding him between Hailey's kindergarten teacher's legs had not been the first time she caught him engaged in illicit activities with other women, but it sure had been the last.

Dwayne, while she could not say he ever cheated on a girlfriend, and never married, may as well have been cut from the same crop as Leo. The man did not settle down. Instead he seemed to jump beds like it was some kind of sport. He was easy on the eyes; hell, the man was a sugar-coated treat to look at, and damn sweet with her kid, but outside that, no future existed for them.

No way she'd jump into his bed and become one of the countless females he had sex with. There was no doubt he would be a treasure between the sheets, but she wasn't one to get involved in a casual sex relationship. Her mind was not built that way. Nor her heart. It had been years since she gave in to the touch of a man, and Leo being her only conquest, that wasn't saying much.

So no, getting involved with Dwayne would be a bad idea despite his sexy smile, his bedroom eyes, and his dark, good looks.

What a shame.

Hailey walked into the kitchen, pulling her from remembering her too-hot dreams last night, starring her very own Eliot Stabler. She frowned, taking in Hailey's appearance. Her normally smiling face had a look of sadness to it, purple shadows beneath her eyes, and strain darkening the lines on her forehead. Brooke jumped from the chair and her only thought was finding out what was wrong.

"What's the matter? Are you sick?" She reached out, but Hailey drew back, avoided her touch, and refused to meet her eyes.

"No, I'm just a little under the weather is all. Think I'm getting my period."

Brooke didn't believe the lie for one second. They were on the same schedules and TOM—time of month— was weeks away from visiting. The avoidance spoke volumes, but she tamped down on the urge to push. If Hailey wanted to talk, she would. While Brooke didn't like secrets and still worried, she knew it would only get worse and her daughter would pull away.

Therefore, instead of taking Hailey in her arms and holding her tight, promising to help with whatever, she stepped back and fixed a smile on her face.

"Do you want something to eat?"

Hailey grabbed her bag and shook her head, gaze still evasive. "No, I'm going to school."

"Are you sure?"

She nodded. "Yeah, sorry, we'll catch up later, Mom." She turned away and walked from the room. The sound of the door closing moments later clicked something in gear and Brooke rushed out of the house.

"Hailey! Hold on."

Hailey froze on the lawn but didn't turn. Her daughter's shoulders shook. An alarm went skittering in Brooke. "Hailey, what's wrong? Talk to me." She grabbed her shoulder and turned her.

Hailey took a step back again, out of her reach. "Stop it." Tears tracked in lonely rivulets down her precious face. Her nose was red and her cheeks blotchy. Something was seriously amiss, but damn it, what could she do?

"I don't have to tell you everything, you know? Why don't you get a life and stay out of mine?"

Brooke bit her cheek and forced a breath in and out before she responded. "Now you listen here, Hailey Marie Mason, you may be going on eighteen, but you are still my daughter. You will watch your tone. I'm not trying to push myself into anything, but I want to know why you are upset. You're not acting like yourself this morning, and the tears are proof that there's something the matter. If I can help, I will."

Hailey rolled her eyes but refused to meet her gaze. She could handle the attitude, all a part of being a mom to a teenager, but the distrust, the secrets, cut deeper than anything else. The thing was, Hailey knew that, too. Especially after everything with her father.

"No, Brooke, you do push. You dig your way into each part of my life, and I'm sick of it. No wonder Dad ran off, you can't seem to stop clawing at the blackboard.

I'm sure if you would have been a bit more into him, he would have stayed."

Brooke drew back, her jaw popped open, and damn it all to hell, her eyes filled. She took a step back.

Regret crossed Hailey's face and she moved toward her. "Mom, wait, that didn't—"

"No," she interrupted, "it came out perfectly clear. No need to say any more, Hailey."

Brooke turned away and heard her call out again. She couldn't turn around, though. The pain in her chest scratched with an impending breakdown. The sob building physically hurt, but she held it until she stepped inside. Then, letting everything loose, she slid to the floor, back to the door, and cried.

* * * *

Dwayne leaned against the front of his cruiser, his eyes hidden behind dark glasses as he studied the schoolkids, watching for anything, something being passed, or maybe whispers of impending deals.

Another kid had been admitted to the ER last night, this one found by his mother, dumped in a tub full of ice. The drug on the street, the dealers selling this shit, needed to stop. Someone was going to die and he had no doubt *if* it would happen, but more so *when*.

Teenagers bustled around the lawn, heavy backpacks slung over their bodies, short skirts over black leggings bringing back more than one memory of high school, while at the same time making him feel like the biggest pervert for noticing. He folded his arms and cut a glance down the street. Hailey was walking toward the school, shoulders slumped, head down. He frowned, recognizing something wrong.

A deep male voice called out for her and she snapped her head up. Dwayne's gaze tracked to the kid, the same one he recognized from the day before. He refocused on Hailey. She tore her attention away from the young man and met Dwayne's gaze. Her expression changed, going from dissolute panic to almost a cry for help. He pushed off the vehicle and headed in her direction, unease and alarm skittering down his spine.

"Hailey!" That damn kid again. She glanced toward Dwayne one more time, with that same damn look on her features, but then went to intercept Mr. Grab Ass.

"Hold up a second, Hails." He reached her. She continued to stare at his shoes, so he tipped her chin up with a finger. "What's going on? You okay?"

She jerked away, her eyes rimmed red and puffy from crying. Dark shadows said she'd barely slept. "I'm fine. Please, I'm just having a bad day."

He arched an eyebrow. "Having a bad day is running late, not having a pair of socks that match, and being out of milk. You, little lady, look like shit. No offense. Is everything okay with your mom?"

Fresh tears pooled in her eyes and he drew up, shoulders back at the alarm clanging in his head. "Is Brooke okay, Hails?"

She shrugged, then looked away again. "I'm sure she will be." The bell rang and she shifted again. "I gotta go, D."

He rubbed the top of his cranium as she walked past. Following her progress, he frowned when Grab Ass literally grabbed her. Hailey's face turned to stone and she looked up at the young man. Dwayne cocked his head at the exchange which, for his taste, grew a little too rough.

Grab Ass got within inches of her face and said something. Hailey shook her head, lips pressed in a tight line. The male jerked her arm to pull her closer, and Dwayne had enough of the little exchange. He proceeded across the lawn, intending on intercepting and teaching shit-for-brains a little lesson on how to treat a woman. Hailey's gaze snapped up and cut over to him. She was forced to turn away when the kid dragged her around the corner of the school. Dwayne picked up his step but got cut off. Lucy stepped in front of him and purred, "Detective."

He glanced down at her and back up, trying to find Hailey in the crowd. "Hey, morning."

"Is that all you wanna give me after what happened yesterday? A 'hey?'"

Shit. He looked at her and smiled. "I had a blast, really did. You're okay with this, though, right?"

Her brows drew together. "This?"

Christ, this was why he needed to watch whom he tumbled in bed with. He saw the stars and hearts in her eyes, could practically hear the wedding bells ringing in her ears. He dropped his voice, lowered his head. "Yes, this. You remember I don't do commitment, right? I'll tangle in the sheets any day, Lucy, but I can't give more. I'm not *that* guy."

Her face, which still held interest and a blatant invitation, fell a little. "I remember, Dwayne. I just thought…" She shrugged.

He leaned forward and brushed his lips across her cheek. "Let me take care of something and then we'll talk about this, okay?"

She nodded, and he flashed a smile before jogging over to the corner. When he rounded it, though, the parking lot held cars but was devoid of people.

"Shit."

Chapter Seven

"Come on, Hails, let me make it up to you."

She studied Jaxon's face. His dark eyes pleaded with her, contrite features masked to reveal sullen emotions. He looked upset enough, but she was unsure if the display was true.

Turning away, Hailey watched the horizon pass, colorful displays of houses breezing by in a kaleidoscope of images. Blinded by her thoughts, she wrapped her arms tighter around her midsection, trying her best to keep the fear and humiliation of last night from showing. She'd slipped out of his bed early this morning and snuck back into her house. The hot water that she tried to douse the memories with did nothing to the dirty distrust surrounding her when it came to Jaxon. She'd stayed in the shower so long that her skin felt as if it would peel off. Then she had switched the water to cold, sending icy shards of glass raining upon her. The distinction between two temperatures cleared her head. The red trail cascading from between her legs evidence of the degradation she'd went through and cemented the final goodbye to her childhood innocence.

The car jarring to a stop brought her from that nightmare and into the present. Jaxon shut his door and skirted the hood before helping her out. In the early morning light, she took in his handsome features, but instead of her legs growing shaky with a hazy lust, trepidation boiled in the pit of her stomach. He took her arm and led her forward, drawing her inside the place she'd wished to escape yesterday.

This time, the living room was empty and the quietness of the house spoke of their solitude. He tugged her along, bypassing the living room table still containing reminders of last night. He pulled her down the hall and into the one place she had experienced not only enhanced pleasures but also her biggest fears—his bedroom.

After he shut the door, he coaxed her to sit on his bed and joined her, finally releasing her hand and leaning forward, forearms resting on his thighs, gaze drawn to something on the ground between his feet. He rubbed his hands together. Sweat beaded along his neck and at his temples. With fall rolling in, the heat had begun to wash away and cooler air pushed in, but she supposed he was just as nervous from what had transpired last night.

"Hailey, I can't begin to tell you how sorry I am."

She remained silent. There was nothing left to say.

He tilted his head and looked at her, his body still bent over his legs. "It's no secret I've wanted you for so long, right?"

She shook her head. Each time they had moments to themselves, she recognized how much he wanted her as he ground against her body. She wanted him, too, but not in the way that had happened last night and not until she was ready.

His chocolate gaze darted around her face, glanced to the door, and back to her again. Unease skittered through her veins, but she shook it off to the action being so fresh in her mind.

"Well after waking this morning, everything from last night came barreling back. At the time, I was so high I didn't realize you told me to stop. Then, when I woke and you were gone, I got scared. Not that you'd try to get me in trouble, but because I'd hate to lose anything we have going on, Hails. I want to turn over a new leaf, and I promise you that we'll be better. I'll be better." He took a deep breath and blew it out between puffed cheeks. "I'm going to get rid of the drugs. After today, they will be out of my life forever. And you, I want you to stay. I want to work on us."

She wrinkled her nose, his words both confusing and piercing a piece of her heart. "What do you mean after today? Why not now?"

He shrugged his big shoulders, ones that had held her head while she cried her frustrations out. "The stuff is expensive. I'm just going to use the last of it today."

Hailey drew off the bed, paced to the door. "That stuff almost ruined us. If you're serious about kicking it to the side, wouldn't you want to be done with it now?"

The bed creaked and she pivoted. He drew closer and took her into his arms. A large palm ran along her back, the act so familiar, she fell into the embrace. She gave in to the moment to close her eyes and pretend as if last night had not happened. "I wanted our first time together to be so fucking special, Hails." His harsh voice and ragged breath sounded heartbreaking in her ear. He tightened his hold around her and trembled. "I don't know if I'll ever be able to forgive myself for what I did, but with how I feel today, I cannot say no. The pain is too fresh. Just one more day."

He drew back until their noses brushed. So close together, she saw golden flecks dancing within his eyes, like honey. She felt entranced. His lips pressed against hers and she gave in, parted her mouth, and let him swoop in for a tender kiss. Like all other times, the fusing of their bodies ignited a low moan from her chest. She wrapped her arms around his shoulders and he moved in to press the length of his body to hers. Her back hit the wall, and she gasped as she hadn't realized they moved. His fingers dug into her hips. One hand dipped to cup her ass and draw her closer.

The same rigid need she always recognized in him pressed against her core. Between his body's response and the words he spoke, the soft way he tendered care at her mouth, she relaxed, allowing the heat to take over and follow the buildup of lust.

He whipped both their bodies around and walked her backward to the bed. When her legs hit the mattress, she fell, him coming down on top of her.

Jaxon trailed kisses, laving paths down her neck. His touch, his roaming hands, reminded her of their true history, not of last night. This was her boyfriend, not the drugged fiend who stole her virginity like a modern day Robin Hood.

He took her hands in his and moved them above her head, held her there as one of his palms wrapped around her wrists. His hips rotated between her legs, and the feeling was so nice, she bowed toward him. This she could do, the lazy, loving way he made her feel. The switch to keep things on a PG-13-rated level. He did not work to remove her pants. But when he pushed up her shirt, she looked down as he pressed kisses over the swells of her breasts, between the valley of her cleavage.

"Hailey." His voice shook and she understood. She trembled.

"Yeah?"

"Let me make last night go away."

He looked up, set his chin on her stomach, and waited.

"What are you saying?"

"I want to make love to you. That's what I'm saying. The right way."

She swallowed, forcing the lump of fear down her throat. "I don't know, Jax. I'm really sore down there."

His head tilted and he licked a languorous path beneath her bra. "I can make you forget," he said against her skin.

Indecision weighed. As if he sensed it, he spoke. "Let me fix this, baby. I want to replace those memories with better ones."

He rested his forehead against the curve of her breast, eyebrows scrunched up, and her heart shattered. He looked so regretful and utterly devastated.

"Okay."

His head snapped up and he studied her. "You sure?"

The tears stinging her eyes released and her vision grew watery. "Yes," she whispered.

His smile blinded her. He came up and kissed her hard and fast, then rose again. "Do you trust me?"

Not wanting to hurt his feelings, willing to make things right, she nodded. "Of course."

He moved and reached to the table, brought a syringe into her vision. "Jaxon, wait."

"No, let me explain. This is the last of it, Hailey. Let's share this, take the edge off your pain, and give a little more to this experience. You'll only have half of this, which is a little more of what you did yesterday. I'll do the rest."

She really didn't want to. God, she hated this. She only wanted him. Why did he have to bring the dirty liquid into this, a chemical that made her feel unclean?

Taking her silence for an answer, he reached for her arm and tapped her veins at the crease of her elbow. "This will be good for us both, baby. I promise you."

She couldn't speak—*why in the hell wasn't anything coming out?*—and watched as he pierced a fat purple line in her arm. When the entire contents of the needle released inside her, she glanced up to him in surprise. Her mouth opened, but a rush ten times the scale as yesterday flooded into her. She groaned, arched her hips, and all else fell away.

Jaxon pushed her back to the bed. He pumped the hard ridge of his erection against her and hissed in her ear. He pulled back, began to work at his belt. Behind him, the door opened and in walked several men, one being Emo from yesterday. She didn't pay attention to any of it, though; she was feeling way too good as spikes of pleasure roamed through her.

Chapter Eight

Brooke pulled back the curtain again and peeked outside. Children sped by on their bicycles, cars passed through the neighborhood in a lazy way, and the sun sank lower, sending contrasting rays of pink, orange, and yellow scattering through the sky. The view would have been beautiful, had she not been so worried about Hailey coming home.

A quick glance at the clock confirmed the time, four hours after school had been let out, and eleven since their fight.

Ugh!

Fed up with standing by watching, she flung the cloth aside, opening the curtains as wide as they would go. She would not miss her daughter coming home.

What if she doesn't? The little voice nagged, had been doing so all afternoon. She ignored it or, at least, tried.

Pacing across the carpet, she didn't pay attention to the wear she gave the rug, nor did she see the couples and kids stopping outside, watching her walk back and forth. She scrambled for purchase, tried to reassure her heart all would be okay. She didn't know how long she had been walking back and forth because when she brought herself out of her morbid thoughts, ones that had no place in a mother's mind, the window reflected darkness. The area around her pitched in shadows. Several hours had gone by in a flash and yet her daughter hadn't returned.

A quick trip down the hall confirmed Hailey's room was still untouched, as it had been earlier. Now, with it closing on midnight, the panic she'd tried to keep at bay all afternoon rose to the surface. She whipped out her phone and tried Hailey's cell for the umpteenth time, squeezing her eyes shut as the call went unanswered. A young, sweet voice announced the missed call and prompted to leave a message. Brooke's skin grew clammy, and a chill swept down her spine.

With only so many friends Hailey hung with, she made a handful of calls. Each one woke a groggy teenager, but all of them gave her the same answer.

They did not know where Hailey was, nor had they seen her the entire day. The last bit was new information, seeing as she should have been in school today. Brooke's hands started to tremble, making the call to Jaxon much more difficult.

After three separate times of inputting the wrong numbers, finally ringing on the other end of the phone connected the call. She paced, waiting for the young man to answer. Seconds turned into minutes, slowed to an almost unbearable pace until the sound cut off. No voicemail, no pick up, no anything. Just absolute silence and an operator relaying the caller was busy and to try again later.

Her gut pitched, swirled as if caught up in a tornado. Bile boiled and surged. She sprinted for the hall bathroom, flung herself to the floor, and tossed the contents of her stomach into the porcelain bowl. She heaved, the pains in her belly constricting as if someone squeezed her body into a tiny fist. Tears leaked from her eyes, snot ran from her nose, and she gasped for breath as she purged.

Moments later, after washing her hands and face, she clutched her phone and continued to try to get through to Jaxon—her last hope.

Several hours later, still no answer from Jaxon or Hailey, she rubbed the back of her neck and tried to ease out the knot in her muscles. The tension had tightened to the point where the sledgehammer in her head grew worse with each minute. At the window, she gazed outside, her phone still clutched in her hand—silent as it had been all night.

The sun outside crested over the horizon, signaling dawn's arrival. It sent pink-and-yellow rays out in every direction. The serenity of the sky, the beginning of the day, seemed to be the start of her nightmare. There was no beauty in the touch of nature, the fresh breath of day. No, everything clouded in a dark shade of gray for her, the worry and fear of last night settling into something so much more—despair.

Hailey hadn't returned and the calls to Jaxon continued to go unanswered. Her daughter wouldn't have stayed out overnight without calling, despite their fight yesterday. Something was seriously wrong, and she was helpless to stop the oncoming train of panic from crashing into the barrier of her life.

She unlocked her phone and without thought to the time, placed a call to the one person she knew would be able to help. Ringing started on the other end, and she waited with barely contained patience. One ring, two, three… Just as she thought he would be yet another one who didn't answer, the gruff voice muttered an oath, then spoke. "Hello?"

"Dwayne? It's Brooke." She glanced at the time and winced. "I realize it's early, I'm sorry."

"No, no, no, I'm up. Everything okay?"

Two words, so simple, tumbled down on her already tight shoulders and sent her slumping to the floor, back against the wall. "No," she choked. Unable to get out another word, she sobbed, a sound so raw it surprised her.

"What? What happened, Brooke? Do you need me there? Where is Hailey?"

Tears fell in rivulets down her hand that still clutched the phone. She struggled to breathe. Fought to gasp air. "She didn't come home last night. She wouldn't j-just disappear."

"Oh hell, I'm getting up. When was the last time you saw her?"

"Yesterday, before school. I don't know what to do," she cried. The words ripped from her mouth. Helplessness tore at her, and she drew her legs up, tried to keep her chest from splitting open.

"Listen, Brooke. I understand you're upset, but try to take a deep breath. We're gonna figure out what's going on."

"Dwayne?" a sultry, feminine voice asked on the other end of the line. Brooke closed her eyes, and a wash of heat flamed her face. Of course, she should have thought it through before calling him. Known as the village's playboy, there was not a single night—she was sure, at least from the rumors—he went cold.

"Oh my God, I'm so sorry, Dwayne."

"No, wait, don't—"

"No," she interrupted. "I shouldn't have called. I'll figure out something." Hope, the little flame that sparked upon hearing his voice, sputtered. Her world, the light at the end of the tunnel so to speak, cast into complete darkness. She didn't know what to do, but she would figure something out. Oh, God, what could she do, though?

"Brooke, hold on."

"It's okay," she said around another sob. "I'm sorry."

She hung up and tossed the phone across the room, despair eating her alive.

Chapter Nine

The sun shined on the back of his neck, doing nothing to warm the chill in his blood, the one present since he'd heard her sob just before she hung up. He rushed up the front steps to Brooke's peach-colored rambler. The echoing sound of her despair rang through his head, causing very real panic to run through his veins, so much so that he pounded his fist a little too hard against the wooden door.

"Brooke! Open up." *Come on, sweetheart. Get the damn door.* Inches from the bright red paint, he waited with screaming impatience for her to answer. Mere seconds passed and his patience snapped. He tried the knob and found it unlocked. He cursed, opening it. While Nyack wasn't like the city, or most villages around the area, the fact she left her house unbolted spoke volumes of her state of mind. His Brooke—and didn't that grate on his nerves, her not being his—never left her door unsecured. She was the most careful person he had ever met.

Sunlight doused the front room in fresh light. A quick scan revealed it devoid of her and he pushed past furniture, glanced in the blue-and-white kitchen, and continued his way down the long hallway leading to the back bedrooms. Dwayne went motionless at Hailey's room and his heart stopped. It did not stutter, didn't skip, but just stopped. In that one moment, no blood pumped through his system, and the life-sustaining beat of his heart ceased. He thought of all the regrets he would have—many involving the sweet, petite woman laying still on top of the cream-colored carpet.

Her face tucked into her elbow, her form did not rise and fall with steady breathing. Maybe it was his already jumbled nerves, but he didn't see any movement coming from her.

"Brooke!"

He dove into the room and tumbled to his knees next to her prone figure. When she—*thank God!*—lifted her head, her red-rimmed, bloodshot eyes stared up at him. They welled with moisture and as the tears fell, he gathered her into his arms and breathed out a sigh of relief. Only then did his heart start to beat again.

"What the hell is going on?"

She clutched at his shirt, and each sob made his stomach curl in on itself, a sickening feeling growing with each sorrowful sound. He tugged her closer, set her on his lap, and straightened his legs as he leaned against Hailey's bed. Dwayne scrambled for purchase as his fears raced to the surface. He studied the room, looking for a clue, anything to tell him what the hell was going on.

"Sweetheart, Brooke, where is Hailey? Is she hurt?"

A sound reminiscent of a wounded animal tore from her. He closed his eyes and brushed his lips on the top of her head. "Come on, I need to know what's going on. Let me help."

"She's—she's gone. She never came home last night."

He frowned. That wasn't like Hailey. Hell, he had practically raised her himself, and her not coming home was out of character.

"When was the last time you saw her?"

Brooke sat up, pushed damp tendrils away from her face, and wiped her nose with the back of a hand. "Yesterday morning. When she left for school. We had a huge fight. Nothing physical," she tacked on. "But an argument. She promised we would talk about it when she got home, but she never came home last night. Something is wrong, I know it."

He ran a palm up and down her back and drew his thoughts back to yesterday. "Before school yesterday?"

She nodded and swiped at the tears trailing silvery tracks down her cheeks. "Yeah. I don't know what to do. She wouldn't stay out all night. You know she wouldn't."

He nodded, his mind playing over the events on the lawn. "That kid she's been hanging out with was there yesterday. At the school. I remember not liking the way he handled her, but when I went after them, they had already disappeared."

Brooke frowned, tiny arched eyebrows scrunching together. "What do you mean how he handled her?"

He shook his head. "I don't know, nothing violent. But the grip on her arm stood out to me, but then Lucy intercepted, and in those few moments, I lost them."

"Lucy?"

Yeah, he didn't miss how her spine stiffened. Taking a deep breath, he turned to her and spoke in the same tone he would use to talk someone away from the ledge…or into putting down a gun.

"You met her two days ago. She teaches at the high school."

Recognition dawned across her features. "Oh you mean the girl whose house you were at when I ran—literally—into you?"

He nodded. She tilted her head. *Uh-oh.*

"Was she pissed I woke you up this morning?"

Shit, there was no easy way of saying this, but growing up the way he did, and being the man he was, didn't allow him to lie. "I wasn't with her."

"But I thought…" She trailed off. Her lips thinned and she scrambled off his lap. He sighed.

"Brooke—"

"No, no, you don't need to explain. It's nothing

new. Really, I'm glad you came over to help."

Why the hell, then, was she avoiding his gaze? He unfolded from the floor as she practically sprinted for the kitchen. He followed her, and she wrapped her arms around her waist, pacing back and forth, her gaze darting to the clock every few seconds.

"Something is wrong. I tried calling Jaxon, but he doesn't pick up. Not even the voicemail picks up. If something has happened to her, I don't know what I'd do."

Rambling, her voice grew louder, her sentences jumbled together. He itched to take her in his arms but understood it wasn't time.

"She's my world, and yesterday, those hateful words. Good God, what if that was the last thing we said to each other? What if that was it? Oh, God!"

The tears started again and this time he gave in to temptation and rushed across the room, drawing her against him. Tiny fists pounded against his chest, pushed at him, but he didn't let go.

"Hush," he soothed. "We'll figure this out. You're gonna drive yourself nuts."

Heart-wrenching sobs tore from her again and finally—*thank fuck*—she fell into his embrace and clung with desperation against his chest. Despite the situation, he could not help but notice their perfect fit. Their bodies came together like two halves of a puzzle. He stroked the back of her head and held her, unknowing of how long they stood there. When she calmed and the tortured sounds stopped, she drew away.

To him, it happened too soon.

"Here's what we're going to do." The cop in him took over. "You, sweetheart, I'm sorry to say, look like hell. Unsurprising under the circumstances," he tacked on. "When was the last time you got some sleep?"

She shook her head, golden tumbles of orange flying around like a halo. "I won't be able to sleep, not with her missing."

"I understand. How about trying to get something in your stomach?"

She grimaced, features tightening in a pained expression. "I don't think I could."

"Okay." He stepped away. It was either that or pull her against him again. To keep from reaching out, he jammed his hands into his pockets. "How about I make you some toast, maybe a cup of tea?" It was not a question, but her features scrunched up again.

"You make tea?"

That earned a laugh, despite everything. "Yes, I do know how to make tea. Boiling water isn't that hard," he said wryly.

A ghost of a smile flittered across plump lips, and bright blue eyes the color of pure Alaskan waters looked away. "I wasn't making fun."

He leaned into her gaze and smiled. "I know, I'm teasing. How about you go take a shower, I'll make you something to eat, and then we will get a plan. My momma always said best laid plans are made when you have something in your stomach, and a clear head. Okay?"

She glanced at the clock again and worried her lip. He gave in and took her chin between his forefinger and thumb, turned her sweet face back to him. "Trust me. We're gonna work this out."

Her face relaxed and—*thank you, Jesus*—she nodded.

"I'll take a quick one." She stepped away. At the kitchen archway, she turned. "Dwayne?"

Still in the same spot, he lifted a brow. "Yeah?"

Sad eyes met his, but hers held an expression

close to gratitude. "Thank you."

Unable to say anything past the sudden lump in his throat, he nodded.

Several minutes later with two pieces of toast buttered and set on a white porcelain plate, a cup of steaming tea next to it, along with milk and honey, he pulled out his phone and placed a call to Agent Trent Rossi with the FBI. The guy had helped on a large-scale case last year and was now engaged to his best friend, but more, he had access to things Dwayne couldn't get his hands on.

"Six o'clock in the morning, this better be good."

"Nice greeting, Rossi."

"When you call at the butt crack of dawn, it's the best you're gonna get. Especially when you interrupt something a whole lot warmer, and better, than hearing your voice."

That earned a quick smile. "Is my Charlie in bed with you?"

The growl on the other end had his grin widening. "Your Charlie, my ass."

A low, throaty feminine chuckle sounded in the background. "Play nice, D!"

His grin grew. "Good morning to you too, sexy."

"You know," Trent began, "I should kick your ass, but I realize and recognize how very much you like to get under my skin. And as much as I'm enjoying this foreplay, I take it you didn't call to flirt with me at six o'clock in the morning."

Dwayne laughed, surprised at the release of pressure it allowed, then sobered. "No, I need a favor, though."

"Why am I not surprised?"

He pinched the bridge of his nose, the weight of a thousand boulders on his shoulders. "It has to do with

Brooke."

"The cute little redhead?" A muffled sound followed. "Ow, babe, I'm just saying, it's not like I'm dead." The phone was covered while more smothered talking occurred. "Hell, babe, I'm sorry. Come back to bed. I promise I'll make it up."

Dwayne shook his head. *Like that was going to happen.*

"Fuck, Dwayne, now you've gone and done it."

"What? I didn't say *anything*. And I know enough about females to never mention another one while in bed."

"You know, I seem to remember you needing a favor from me."

"I do, sorry. Look, Hailey, Brooke's daughter, didn't make it home last night and I realize we need at least forty-eight hours before a missing person, but this is really out of character for her. Something isn't sitting right."

"If my memory serves correct, and it usually does," Trent started.

Dwayne resisted the urge to roll his eyes. Fucking feds and their egos. Having four brothers working in the same capacity, he had grown used to it.

"Her daughter is seventeen," Trent finished.

"Yeah, so?"

"Well, you sure Mom and kid didn't get into a tuffle and now she's sleeping it off somewhere?"

"No." He shook his head again. Then, remembering Trent couldn't see, he said, "It isn't Hailey. I know this girl, have helped raise her when her dad skipped town ten years ago. Hailey is smart, has a good head on her shoulders, and is one of the most empathic teens I know. She wouldn't let her mom worry like that."

"Okay, what do you need me to do about it?"

"I need you to look into the background on her boyfriend. I've got a bad feeling about this."

"All right, let me get a pen, seeing as my morning doesn't seem to be looking like I'll be staying in bed." The sarcasm wasn't lost on him, and Dwayne flashed another quick grin. "Give me what you got, I'm ready."

He relayed the kid's information and turned at the shuffling steps behind him. Brooke stood in the entranceway, cheeks flushed from the shower. Long, orange hair kissed with color lay in wet tendrils around her face. A pink thermal and black yoga pants framed her curvy body. He swallowed the lump of hard need in his throat and watched her cross the room to take a seat on the stool behind her plate and mug.

His attraction to Brooke had grown year after year, getting steadily worse as time passed. He tried to ignore it, tell himself she was taken by another when they were younger, and again, that they were better off as friends when she left the cheating bastard. Instead of this gripping craving disappearing, it surged like a tsunami, but in this instance, hadn't receded.

"All right." Trent pulled him from the trance Brooke managed to ensnare him in, every damn time. "I'll run a few things and get back to you."

"I appreciate it."

He hung up and slid the phone back into his pocket, gaze trained on Brooke again. She looked better than before, but sadness and worry lurked behind her eyes. He tried not to think about the hot shower she came out of, the way her skin would still be holding the warmth from the spray, how fresh she would smell, how supple she would feel pressed against him.

Christ!

He closed his eyes, urging the traitorous thoughts out of his mind.

"Are you okay?"

He cleared his throat and focused on her again. "Yeah, I'm fine."

"You look like you're in pain."

He pushed off the counter, ignored her question, and crossed to the center island, then pushed her plate closer. "Eat."

Her cheeks puffed and she exhaled in a slow breath of air. "What am I going to do?"

She looked so lost, adrift at sea. Unable to help it, he walked around the counter and drew her into his arms once again. Giving in to the urge, he brushed his lips against her temple. "We'll figure something out."

She did not draw away. At least he would have this.

Chapter Ten

Worried about Hailey, exhausted to the bone, and slightly swaying, Brooke clung to Dwayne, took strength from this solid, very real protector. She would have to be dead not to notice his firm body beneath her fingertips, the hardness of his chest pressed to her breasts, and the wicked, clean scent drifting from his skin. While they were no longer hugging, but more her clinging to him, she didn't want to turn away, couldn't find the power to do so. How easy would it have been to end up with this man? She'd caught the looks he had given her before. But that had all been in the past, a separate life for them both.

She had become a mother, someone who dedicated her entire being to making sure her daughter was well-rounded, cared for, and knowingly loved. Not only that, but she wasn't a young pup any longer, and from the few women she'd seen Dwayne with, his type seemed to have a list of traits all very similar: young, perky breasts, tight asses, single, and free of major responsibilities.

His hand tightened on her back and she held her breath, waiting to see if he would push her away.

Just a few more minutes, please.

She needed him, this close contact with another being. It had been so damn long.

Hailey refused to slow down to cuddle on the couch as she had once done as a young girl. Her daughter had her own life now, one currently held in peril, but Brooke had faith they would find her. They had to. Failure wasn't an option.

Dwayne trailed his hand up her back and pressed a palm to her head, his other arm tightening around her waist. She went with the direction, pressed her face into his warm neck, and breathed. His skin emitted heat rivaling the summer's sun. She grasped the back of his suit jacket, wishing she could be closer. He shifted their bodies, and her aggravation spun to something else. His lips brushed her temple, and moist air fanned across the side of her face. He hovered there. So close, all she had to do was turn her face and take his mouth. She knew he would let her, too.

So near to him, starved for human contact, she wanted to get lost for a while. She trailed her nose along his neck, took another deep breath, and pressed closer.

He grumbled something unintelligible, the sound coming from his chest more than his mouth. His hand at her waist laid flat on the small of her back and urged her closer still.

The situation was moving fast out of control. Tendrils unraveled, but she was helpless to stop it. This strong male held her as if she were a treasure. He had the power and ability to make her forget everything, to make all the stresses and danger go away.

His hand slipped beneath the back of her shirt and made direct contact with her skin. They both hissed and his breath pushed her hair from her face. His cruel yet sensual mouth continued to drift in a teasing caress across her temple. She turned her head, like molasses on a cold day, up and toward him. Her lips tingled in anticipation, waiting for his kiss. She brushed her mouth across the line of his jaw, a hairsbreadth from his skin.

His heart thudded against hers, a matching hammer between their bodies, telling her he was just as affected. The hand at the back of her head tightened. She trailed the caress over his cheek; his lips were right there, centimeters away.

The rest of their surroundings faded. She didn't know if it was because of this man drawing her absolute attention, or because of her exhaustion.

She touched the side of her mouth to his and thought she'd be prepared for the rush of desire.

She was so wrong.

Her stomach clenched and her sex tingled, waiting. So rare a feeling, she realized she had missed this, the buildup before lying with a man.

A shrill ring pierced the air and she jumped back from Dwayne, then lunged for the cell phone on the counter. Out of breath, she answered.

"Hello?"

"Good morning, ma'am, I'm calling from Trade Services International and we'll be in your area on Tuesday conducting free personal reviews of finances." Brooke wanted to scream at not only the interruption, but also at the false hope this call would be from her daughter.

"I'm sorry, not interested."

The telemarketer went on as if he didn't hear her. "So I have you set up to meet with me at ten in the morning. All you need to bring is your latest bank statement and last year's tax return."

At her wits' end, she hung up, not giving an answer, and set the phone back down. Behind her, she could feel Dwayne's questioning and expectant gaze. With the glaring sun shining inside, the moment before now seemed as if it had been a dream.

Her attention flipped to the clock on the hanging microwave, and she drummed her fingers on the counter. Try as she might, she couldn't ignore him. His presence had the hair on the back of her neck standing up.

"Dwayne..." She pivoted to face him but closed her mouth at his expression. His eyes, dark and hungry, did not reflect the normal green she had known more or less all her life. In their place was a deeper color, almost like twilight. She wrapped her palms around the ceramic counter behind her to keep from jumping on him. From the way his pants stuck out between his hips, she figured the earlier encounter had affected him as much as it did her. Still, they couldn't do this. She would never be able to look at sex as just a casual thing.

She wasn't wired that way. And unfortunately, Dwayne was.

He took a step and she lifted a hand.

"Wait. Look, about earlier," she trailed off when he blinked and the darker color left his eyes. He shook his head.

"There's nothing to it, Brooke. Who was on the phone?"

She frowned at the dismissal but skipped over what was sure to be an uncomfortable topic. "Just a telemarketer. No one important. Hey," she said and glanced back to the clock. "I think we should head over to the school and get some questions answered, see if anyone knows anything." She pushed from where she stood and took an unsteady step, reached for her coffee, and tried to gulp as much of the hot liquid as she could.

"How about you stay here and get some sleep? I'll go to the school."

She shook her head. "No. I can't sleep, won't sleep, not until I find out where Hailey is. You go to the school. I'll go to Jaxon's."

He crossed the room so fast she barely had time to react. She sucked in a breath as he loomed over her. "Absolutely not. Let me handle this. I am the detective here. It's my job."

"It's mine, too. She's my daughter."

His gaze softened and he cupped her face. "I know, but something doesn't feel right. And I'm not about to let you get in the middle of something that could get you hurt."

"What about Hails? She could be hurt."

His head tilted. "That's true, but I'll be able to concentrate and move faster if I didn't have to worry about what kind of situation we were walking into. Please, I will need you on your toes later, and you really should get some sleep."

"I won't be able to sleep," she whispered. The despair she thought she had battled returned full force. She felt useless.

She went to take another drink of coffee, wanting to wash the taste of fear from her mouth, but he removed it from her hands. "Not drinking that you won't. Come on."

He tugged on her hand, pulling her from the room and down the hall to the back of the house. Once in her space, he guided her to the bed and despite earlier, and against all claims that she would not be able to sleep, she looked at the covers with longing, exhaustion settling on her head.

He drew the covers back, sat her on the mattress, bent to take off her shoes, and directed her to lie down.

"I'm going to go check a few things out. I'll call as soon as I hear anything, okay?" Dwayne didn't sit on the bed, but he leaned over her prone form until she had no choice but to take in his features. She understood why women tossed themselves at him, felt the temptation drawing at her with his dark, raw looks. He was a man built for danger and seduction. An irresistible combination.

"Okay. Please, just keep me in the loop."

He brushed hair back from her face and studied her. Their faces were only a few inches apart, but she couldn't hold his gaze so close. Not after earlier. Being so tired, she didn't think she'd have enough strength to *not* pull him down on top of her.

"I will." He pressed his lips to her forehead. Then he was gone.

* * * *

About a half hour later, Dwayne pulled his cruiser to a stop against the curb. He studied the rancher across the street, frowning at the brown grass, the weeds climbing up the side of the house, and the trash littering the yard. Nyack was a sensible town, a noble village that took pride in their appearance. Folks traveled far and wide to settle here during the summer months. Hell, even a few from Hollywood owned mansions up on the hill overlooking the compact space and the Hudson River.

But the house he looked at now stood out like a white dress at a funeral. What used to be white shutters lay on the ground and the windows were cloudy, as if parchment paper lined the panes. You couldn't see a thing inside. At least from this distance.

He set his jaw. Typically, the papers on the windows led to one of two things: drug use or heat insulation.

He doubted the latter and unfolded from the car, unzipped his jacket. The comforting weight of his Glock sat on his hip. He crossed the yard, tried to ignore the crunch of dead grass, and bounded up the three cement steps to the front door.

Silence met his knock, and while patience had always been a strong suit for him, something didn't sit right. It was too quiet, so much that he knew, before he looked inside, the house would be empty. He leaned close to the door and was able to get a look inside through the small, rectangular window at the top, or at least make out the bare rooms. Slapping a fist against the glass, his thoughts took a nosedive into worst-case scenarios, which this was it. Nothing, not even a scrap of furniture.

"Shit."

Dwayne pivoted and scanned the neighborhood, his mind screaming on code three, lights and sirens full ahead. He tapped an old high school drumbeat against his legs, something he did when he was deep in thought or in anticipation for a big response on scene.

Brooke had looked so damn defeated, and this news would kill the small measure of hope in her eyes. He wanted to keep it there, build it up until she smiled again. He'd always been a fan of her smile, adored the way her face lit up. All he saw this morning was pain and sadness, helplessness he had no way of saving her from.

Where could these kids be? What the hell was going on? How was Hailey wrapped in all of this? He dug his phone from his pocket and hit the contact for her phone again. It continued to ring as he crossed the yard. The fact that he'd seen Hailey yesterday morning with a boy whose house was now empty sat in his gut like sour milk.

Mrs. Wilshire stepped out from her house across the street, and he lifted a hand in greeting.

The complete opposite of the piece of shit shack sitting behind him, the eighty-two-year-old woman's house was doused in a plethora of colorful roses that played peek-a-boo between full hydrangeas. Her grass was lush and green, and the tall oak that stood in the center of her lawn buzzed with windmills and birdhouses.

As if her house wasn't loud enough, Mrs. Wilshire's outfit made up for it in spades. She wore a bright pink muumuu with prints of every different type of bird imaginable. Never one to be outdone with the likes of the ladies down at City Hall who played bingo, today she sported a pastel wig atop her head and sunglasses larger than his palm. He held back the inward laughter as hot crimson lips pursed and blew a kiss his way.

"As I live and breathe, if it isn't little Dwayne Gonzalez."

He bounded up the step to her yard, flashed a grin, bent low, and kissed her wrinkled cheek. Baby powder and lavender assaulted him in a thick wave. "Mrs. Wilshire, have you made up your mind about running away with me?"

Her high chuckle sent a team of birds scattering into the sky. "Always such a flirt. I've told you once, and I'll tell you again, you couldn't handle this old woman." She pressed her forearms beneath ample breasts and pushed them higher. A smile hovered on his lips.

"Of that I have no doubt, but a man has to try." He removed his dark shades and stood to the side, pointed across the street. "I'm actually trying to find the owners of that house. Do you have any idea where they are?"

"Florida."

He gaped at her and she patted his cheek. The action brought back memories of when he had been in middle school, darting along hallways, and finding Mrs. Wilshire, who had been the principal at the time, waiting at the back door they were trying to skip out of.

"I see I can still shock you." She giggled and her entire body shook with effort. "The Ramseys own that place, but they moved to Florida two years ago. A few months back some rough-looking hoodlums came in. They had people coming and going at all hours, I tell you." She leaned closer and he dipped his head to listen. She whispered like a conspirator. "And some of the young women they had coming in looked a little loose, if you catch my drift."

He nodded. "Ah, yes, I think I do. Have you seen them recently?"

She shook her head and he tried to ignore the double chin jiggling for a few more seconds after she stopped. "No, yesterday evening they packed up everything in a white truck and took off."

His unease grew, but there had to be something, some way to track them down. "Did you notice any markings on this truck?"

"Nope. Plain white. I saw a bunch of them young ladies get in the back, too. Yes, I did. Think it's the oddest thing and against the law to boot." She gave him a pointed glare as she said the last. "Would have thought they needed the truck for furniture, but all they put back there were mattresses and a couch. Everything else got set on the curb and the trash people picked it up this morning."

Dwayne cursed, and the word tinged the air blue.

"Dwayne David Gonzales, just because you're grown doesn't mean you can color the air with your filth."

His face warmed and he reached for her hand, then brought it to his lips. "I'm very sorry, ma'am, I just really need to find the previous tenants."

Her cheeks, already stained with pink circles, reddened. "Well, I'm sure you can apologize and come by for tea next week. An old lady does get lonely every now and again."

He grinned, knowing he was forgiven. "Are you asking me out on a date?"

She drew her hand away and set it to her ample bosom. "Well, no, just tea."

"Ah," he laughed. "So you just want to get me alone."

Her musical, high-pitched squeal rang out and she slapped him on the chest. "You're such a flirt. I'll see you on Tuesday." With that, she walked away, up along the sidewalk, heading toward City Hall.

He grinned after her and fished his phone out of

his pocket as it started ringing. A glance told him it was Charlie.

"What's up?" he answered.

"We've got a real issue here at the high school, D. You might want to get here as quick as you can."

In the background, several women shouted, but one voice stood out. He turned and rushed for his car, jumped inside.

"Shit, she's supposed to be in bed."

"Yeah, well she's not," Charlie answered wryly. "She is accusing the principal of some pretty foul things, and she's refusing to leave until someone brings her Hailey. I gotta say, D, so far Mr. Rodgers hasn't pressed charges, but I think if she throws one more book at him, we're going to have to intervene."

"Christ! She threw a book at him?"

"Books," Charlie answered, emphasizing the s.

He flipped on the lights and squealed away from the curb. "You tell the principal I'm on my way. And you tell Brooke I'm gonna paddle her ass if she doesn't calm the fuck down."

Charlie laughed, the sound deep and hearty. "Yeah," she said in a sarcastic tone, "I'll get right on that."

Chapter Eleven

"I can't possibly understand why my daughter isn't here!" Brooke slapped her palms on the dark wooden counter and glared at the principal.

"Mrs. Mason—" the tall, balding man began.

"It's Ms.," she hissed. She rose on her tiptoes, leaned over the platform, and spoke through clenched teeth. "You will damn well find an answer about how my daughter disappeared off school property. Someone here knows something. You," she said and thrust a finger at him, "have some explaining to do and my patience is running thin, Mr. Rodgers." Out of sorts, she realized she was acting crazy, placing blame where it wasn't due, but thoughts of Hailey's safety were at the forefront of her mind, and she couldn't seem to stop the runaway train that was her mouth.

Mr. Rodgers glanced over at Charlie, who stood at the wall behind her. She followed his expectant stare. The female detective had long, dark hair tied in a ponytail atop her head, blue jeans, a white polo, and a smirk. In the past, Brooke always thought women cops had no femininity, that it somehow got lost underneath the uniform or the persona of who they had to be. This woman, though, broke those misconceptions. She was tall and curvy. Her confidence radiated through her body with the power she needed to do her job. Petite shoulders shrugged as she returned the principal's contact.

"She's got a point, Tom."

Brooke clapped her hands together, then whipped around to him again. "So help me, if something happened to my daughter…"

"Now just you wait a second, Ms. Mason, I am only responsible for the children once they are inside the school. Since she never showed for her first class yesterday, there is no way of knowing if she truly did come in the building."

"She was here," she interrupted, but he continued on, talking over her.

"However, I do understand the concern for Hailey, and the school will do everything in its power to help. Perhaps if you kept a tighter rein on your daughter, then we wouldn't be in this predicament."

"If I what?" she shrieked. "Listen here, you son-of-a—"

The door behind her crashed open and Brooke spun around. Dwayne stood in the doorway, dark eyes menacing and focused entirely on her. "You're supposed to be in bed."

Her breath caught, and she turned back to the man and small plump woman who hovered nearby. "Find her."

"Ms. Mason…"

"Find her!" she screamed. Tears stung her eyes and her vision wavered. "Find her!" With her fists clenched by her sides, chest splitting wide open, she screamed over and over again, chanting the two words until strong arms surrounded her. "Do something! Don't just stand there." She pleaded with them to listen, but all the man and his secretary did was pass her a look of pity.

It was too much.

She wrenched out of Dwayne's arms and reached for the closest thing. Charlie's shout of warning was the only thing she heard before the glass vase flew out of her hand, crossed the high counter, and missed the principal's head by an inch.

The sound of glass breaking shattered through the air.

"Goddammit, stop it!"

Iron bands grabbed her at the waist and hauled her

out of the office. Incoherent words babbled out of her mouth. She didn't understand anything she said. And as if she were watching from above, looking down on the out-of-control scene, she could see her own erratic behavior.

She was so damn tired and worried for her daughter, her focus had been to get answers. Coming to the school seemed like a good idea at the time, but now dozens of students looked at her like she belonged in a mental institution. She was carried out of the building by the Nyack Police Department, and now she realized how wrong she had been.

"Put me down."

"Nope." His short answer spoke a thousand words with the tone alone. He stepped outside and the thick, humid air wrapped around her like a heavy cloak. They bounded down the stairs, him carrying her as if she didn't weigh any more than ten pounds. He crossed the front yard and headed for his cruiser.

"My car is in the parking lot."

Dwayne ignored her and made a beeline for his vehicle.

"Detective Gonzales!" she squealed.

He stepped up to the backseat, tossed open the door, and unceremoniously threw her inside. She landed on the cloth-covered seat in a tangle of limbs and scrambled to get back out of the vehicle.

A large finger appeared in front of her and she glanced up to meet storm turbulent green eyes.

"Don't." That one word, uttered in a voice she had never heard before, with such dominance, as if he expected her to listen, had her frozen.

The car door shut and he pivoted. He crossed back over the lawn to meet Charlie and Mr. Rodgers. The sad, pitiful eyes of the principal met hers, so she sat back with a huff.

"Damn it, I just want to find my daughter."

* * * *

Every muscle in Dwayne coiled tight like a serpent ready to strike. Pissed beyond reason, he fought to keep his face impassive as the balding dictator of the high school droned on and on about responsibility. Dwayne knew his responsibility, damn it. It was sitting in the back of his car.

He had never seen her—in the twenty-plus years they had known each other—act with such reckless abandon. Her wild eyes spoke to him, uttered a desperate plea he wanted nothing more but to answer. Shit, he wished to find Hailey, too. Every one of his instincts screamed something was wrong, that she was in danger. He couldn't concentrate on what to do, though, without making sure Brooke was cared for. That drive, the urge to provide protection for the damn woman who had driven him crazy forever, seemed ingrained into his DNA.

He cared for her. Had a soft spot for the sweet woman. He had pushed his feelings to the side for years, and while they were still there, he thought he had them under control. At least until she'd embraced him in her kitchen earlier.

He'd been wrong to think he could push her from his system, slake his lust on other, more willing partners. And every skirt he laid with was willing, almost eager for what he provided. He wasn't cocky about it, but it was a fact. He recognized lust and gave in to it, taking what they both wanted in a mutual agreement of pleasure.

"She really should have been keeping an eye on that boyfriend of Hailey's."

Mr. Rodgers' statement cut Dwayne from his musings. "Excuse me?"

The tall, lanky man puffed his chest and tried to stand straighter but fought to keep eye contact. "All I'm saying, Detective, is that kid has been bad news since day one. I suspect he was the one behind the drug dealings around the area, too. However, where he chose to make horrible decisions in what to do with his life, and to others, he was smart in how he hid it. I never saw any dealings on campus, and each time I asked him to leave, he did."

Dwayne bit his tongue to rein his temper. Getting into a schoolyard fistfight would do no good.

"Do us a favor and keep an eye and ear out. If anyone hears anything, give us a call." Charlie passed the principal a card and they all turned away. Dwayne crossed the yard and cursed when his best friend called for him.

"Not right now, Lopez." He faced her, softened at the concern in her expression.

"Look, D, maybe you need to take a step back and let someone else handle this."

He crossed his arms and glared down the length of his nose. "No."

She tossed her hands. "Why? What good are you going to do for them in the mood you're in?"

"I'll handle it. Don't push me on this."

She cocked her head and studied him. Silence stretched, the sound of cars passing on the highway behind the village filling the air. "This isn't the way to get close to her, Dwayne. Tread carefully. This is her daughter."

That did it. The coiled string in his stomach snapped, the last of his patience whipping out. He dipped his head and got in her face. "I'm going to pretend I didn't just hear you say that. I, of all people, know exactly who is missing and what she is to Brooke. I've spent countless years trying to give her that male figure in her life, taught the girl how to play softball, gave her instructions on the proper way to toss a right hook, and goddammit, Charlie, it has nothing and everything to do with that stubborn woman in the backseat of my cruiser. This is every bit of my fault as it is the school's. I was here yesterday. I could have stopped her from leaving."

She held his stare, didn't even flinch. "When did you see her last?"

He sighed and straightened, pinched the bridge of his nose and tried to hold in impatience. "Yesterday morning, right before school. She was hanging with Jaxon Williams and he got a little rough with her. I tried to intercept, got interrupted, and when I finally managed to break free, they were gone."

She glanced around the neighborhood. "You've been talking with Trent." It wasn't a question.

"Of course. He's looking into it. Did he tell you?"

"Yeah, a little. I'll go see what he's found out." She glanced to his backseat. "Take her home and try to get her to see reason."

"I plan on it." Without another word, he got in his cruiser, started it, and pulled away from the curb.

Once at Brooke's house, he opened the back door, and she got out. She stayed silent and pushed past without looking at him. They entered her residence in quiet. He followed Brooke to her bedroom, watching as she grabbed a duffel bag. He clenched his jaw when she began to stuff clothing inside.

"Where do you think you're going?"

She didn't answer him. *Of course!* Why would she? Instead she disappeared into the attached bathroom and came out minutes later with a brush, a small bag, and her toothbrush. She tossed the items inside with the clothing.

"Stop."

She didn't. He growled under his breath and

grabbed her arm. She wheeled around and slapped him across the cheek. The sound vibrated around the room and stunned the hell out of him. Electricity filled the air as if it were a living thing. Without realizing, he reacted. He held her body to the wall, his large frame pushing into her, holding her wrists behind her back with his hands.

"Damn it, Brooke. I'm trying to help you!"

"Help? Help! Bullshit, you treated me like a child and threw me in the back of your cruiser like some hooligan."

"You were acting like a spoiled brat who wasn't getting her way. Shouting orders, throwing things, and demanding answers isn't going to get us to find Hailey any faster. Let me do my job here."

Her expression grew cold and she lifted her chin. "Fine. You do yours."

He narrowed his eyes. It couldn't be that easy. "You're going to listen to me?"

"I didn't say that."

He switched his grip on her hands, held them with one of his own, and brushed a tendril of red hair from her cheek. "Listen, I need you to trust me. You need to understand that I would never neglect my duties when it comes to Hailey. I will find her. You have to believe that."

She studied him for several tense moments. Her gaze jumped back and forth between his eyes, as if she searched for an answer. He swallowed, trying like hell to show his intent, to let her know he wouldn't stop for anything until her daughter was home. It would have to be enough. It was all she would take from him. At least, for now.

Seconds turned into minutes and finally she nodded.

"Promise me."

Her blue eyes swam with tears, reminding him of drops of rain falling into the ocean. Catching a tumbling tear with his thumb, he released her hands and cupped her jaw. "I promise you, Brooke. With everything I am, all I could ever hope to be. I will bring her home."

A sob tore from her mouth, and he crushed her to his chest, his heart breaking as sounds of her despair filled the air. She clung to him with a fierce grip and he closed his lids. He hoped like hell he'd be able to keep this promise.

Chapter Twelve

The continual rocking of the truck, the constant swaying back and forth, soothed Hailey. The drugs in her system, the ones making her mind scatter in every direction, unable to latch on to one specific thought, kept her in and out of consciousness. Memories of getting in the vehicle were fuzzy at best, and she'd only woken for brief periods to see other girls being loaded in with her. They shivered against each other. The tank top she wore wasn't much of a barrier against the cool air.

She tried to sit up, to pull her face away from a foul stench that reminded her of spoiled milk, but she couldn't move. Her arms were heavy and failed to answer to the call her brain tried to send.

Someone groaned, another gagged, and Hailey's stomach lurched. The truck took a sharp turn. The group shifted and pressed together with each motion. Everything spun around her and she groaned. Rocks hit under the truck next, the *ping, ping, ping* sounds slamming through her head. They must have turned off to an unpaved road as the vehicle shook and bounced until she thought her head would explode.

She pushed against the body lying on her face, desperate to take in fresh air. Her arms wouldn't move. They felt laden, out of sorts, and itchy. She yearned to shower, wanted a meal, but more than anything craved something darker.

No!

The heroin injections took over her body and mind. She couldn't respond to the things done to her and was powerless to stop the doses. Tears burned behind her lids as she wished for her mom, pleaded to go home. She hadn't realized she'd spoken aloud until a loud thump rattled the metal above her head and a harsh voice demanded for her to shut up.

The truck braked suddenly. Bodies tumbled one over the other, and someone's hand smacked her in the face. Pain exploded, blossoming out from her nose. She gagged at the distinct taste of copper trailing down the back of her throat.

Bright sunlight pierced the interior, the first she remembered seeing in several days, as the back end opened.

"Get the fuck up, and get out. Your new life is about to begin, whores."

* * * *

Brooke stretched, her fingertips touching the beige velvet headboard above. Her room was doused in fading orange light that dropped indiscriminate shadows behind picture frames and the large six-drawer dresser in front of her. She stared at the ceiling, watched the play of blades as the fan rotated in a slow and constant speed. The motion almost hypnotized her, the scene and day coming to a false relaxing tranquility.

Memories rushed in, crashed into her mind like a jolt of electricity, and her heart slammed against her ribs before pounding away at a breathtaking speed. The insistent demand told her what she already knew. Hailey had disappeared, was taken from her, and could very well be dead.

"Oh, God," she choked, the building beat of her heart scrambling up her throat. She gave in and set it free with a sob.

She scrambled out of bed, rushed to her phone sitting on the dresser, and jumbled the device until it turned on. The red light blinked, alerting a need for charging, while the lack of icons displayed across the top revealed no missed calls.

No contact. No hope. No Hailey.

The digital second hand ticked away precious time. She groaned, realizing she had been asleep for six hours. Her mind spun with implications, her biggest fears, and a dead quiet that bellowed how alone she was, how helpless, and how utterly useless she was in ensuring her daughter's safety.

Tears trailed down her cheeks unchecked, and she let the remorse free. It pressed on her chest and weighed her shoulders. She dropped her phone on the side table, plugged it in for juice, and grabbed her calf-length sea-blue silk housecoat. After settling it on her body, she headed down the hall, bypassing memories she couldn't face. Stepping into the kitchen, she drew to a halt. *Dwayne.* He'd stayed. She hadn't expected him to, but that he had brought something akin to gratitude through her chest.

He stood by the back sliding glass door, facing at an angle, arms folded across his chest. A black long-sleeved shirt looked as if it had been painted on, the muscles in his arms straining against the material. The cloth tapered at his waist and covered the distinct bulge of his belt buckle holding up dark washed jeans that encased his ass in perfect display. A dark blue baseball cap sat on his head, pulled low, shielding her from the piercing green eyes he turned her way.

With unhindered focus of him, she sucked in a sharp breath. Dwayne hardly ever seemed so casual to wear something this normal. Usually impeccably dressed, he wore suits for his job, and for the past few years that's all she'd seen him in. This man—and he was *all* male— seemed a stranger. The hat on his head defined a strong jaw and plump, full, tanned lips. His mouth didn't curve as she was used to seeing, though, and instead tightened. A muscle ticked in his cheek.

"You're up."

She didn't acknowledge his statement. There was no need for idle chitchat. "Have you heard anything?"

He sighed, lifted the cap, and scrubbed the top of his head. He averted his gaze, looking anywhere but at her, and settled the hat low. "No, not really. I've been trying to call Jaxon for hours now, but each time the phone goes to voicemail. No one else has reported anything and the truck companies in the area haven't rented anything resembling what was reported this morning."

She blanched, sure she heard wrong. "What do you mean a truck?"

He grimaced. "Shit, Brooke. I meant to tell you. This morning at Jaxon's house, Mrs. Wilshire mentioned seeing a truck leave his residence early yesterday. Some sort of moving truck. And while I was there, I checked the place out. It was empty."

She cried out. "No!" Her lips trembled and she fisted her hands. Behind her breastbone, her heart pounded against her chest like a wave crashing ashore. "A truck?" she asked in dismay. "Tell me that's not true. Where's my little girl?"

A look of helplessness crossed his features. "I don't know, but I'm going to find her."

He crossed the room, cupped her shoulders, and refused to let her look away. "You need to trust me to do my job here. I want to find Hailey as much as you. I need you to hold it together."

Her eyes stung, but she forced the tears back. Shedding them wouldn't help anything. She had to be strong for her daughter, keep her head together, and show Dwayne she could help. Sitting around and letting others do all the work was not the woman she wanted to be. She was more than that, had grown in confidence when Leo left.

She swallowed, forced the lump of guilt down, and nodded. "I do. I will. I'm just really scared. I don't know what else I can do to help here. I don't know how to get her back."

"I know. We are doing everything we can. I won't rest until she's back in your arms." He searched her face, and his lips thinned. It almost looked as if he held something back. Hiding things, keeping secrets, and refusing to tell the truth had led to the demise of her marriage. She wouldn't let it have a part in the finding of her daughter. Impatience wove its way through her fear.

"What is it, Dwayne? What aren't you saying?"

He leaned forward, a passing moment, but then stepped back and released her. A battle raged over his face like a movie playing out his indecision. His body rocked back and forth as if he was having a difficult time staying in place. He cursed, a foul word so low she didn't quite hear. Then he turned away, paced to the door, spun around, and came back. Just when she thought he wouldn't answer, he did. His voice was devoid of emotion, calm, flat, and lethal. She shivered.

"Trent," he started, "that's Agent Rossi with the FBI, has been looking into a few things while you were asleep." Pivot, pace back. "He's doing it as a favor, you see. So, the information I'm about to tell you can't leave this room. A lot is riding on this and it's our best shot at tracking Hailey down."

She bristled, opened her mouth, but he held up a hand and continued, still pacing back and forth.

"We've tracked Jaxon's phone. The little fucker may not be answering it, but with the GPS inside, Big Brother has made it easy to keep track. And really, I could have done that without Trent's help, but it's still appreciated. I mean all you have to do is *Google* 'how to track a cell phone' and you get a bunch of hits. Pay a few dollars, log on to a site, input the number, and there you go."

Why was he rambling? She struggled to keep up.

"It tracks to a hundred yards, but hell, that's close enough, right? Well, the FBI can get closer. I mean real close, like satellite lock and all. I wouldn't be surprised if they could actually see the phone from space, but Trent wouldn't answer that question. The fucker."

"Dwayne!"

He stopped pacing and snapped his head up, eyes wide.

"Please," she pleaded.

He gave a distinct nod. "Sorry. Anyhow, we've traced Jaxon's phone up north. To Rhode Island, just outside Providence." He drew up straighter, lifting his head high. "And his credit card charges in the past few hours have led us in the same direction, so there's no doubt it's him."

She stared at him, speechless. What was he saying? She would not, could not, let hope surge…yet.

As if he heard her unspoken question, he heaved a deep breath. "I'm going after them."

* * * *

"Okay, when do we leave?"

Brooke looked so damn small standing in front of him. He had never paid much attention to her size, but with the blue housecoat that clung to her shoulders—her very small and petite shoulders—she seemed fragile. Her eyes filled with hope and trust. It physically hurt his heart. He couldn't make her any promises, but damn he was going to try.

"I'm leaving as soon as I hear back from Trent."

"Okay." She turned and took a step. "I'll go pack a bag."

Her words caught up with his sluggish mind. "Wait." She stopped, then spun to face him. "You're not going anywhere. You're staying here, Brooke."

Her spine snapped and he saw the fury—and braced—before it released. "She's my daughter."

"Stop it." He held up a hand, palm out, and took a step closer. "This is dangerous. I will not put you in jeopardy. It's safe here, and this is where you will stay. What if she comes home?" It was a long shot going there. They both knew—he knew—Hailey was with Jaxon, up fucking north, and there'd be no returning anytime soon.

Her mouth opened, closed, and repeated until she resembled a fish out of water. Sea spun blue eyes swam with moisture and it was like a kick to the gut.

Fuck.

"You will not keep me out of this." She tried so damn hard to keep those tears from spilling. The fight for control rode over every taut muscle in her body. "You won't." A sob broke free on the last word.

His resolve wavered. Hell, he didn't want to think about her coming with him, putting herself in danger. As it was, the fact that Hailey was wrapped in something dangerous was enough to rub like salt across a wound. All day he had been unable to get her out of his head, the memories hitting him one after another: Hailey learning to ride a bike without training wheels, her first day of middle school, trying out for the varsity softball team, going on her first date. He had been present for each one, held her hair back when she blew out the candles for her thirteenth birthday, and damn it, she may not be his daughter by blood, but the affection he felt put her on a pedestal in his life.

"Brooke," he began. She chose that moment to jump into his arms. He had no other choice but to grab hold to keep her from falling to the floor. And fuck him if he didn't feel *every* curve of her sweet body pressed to him.

"Please." Liquid bubbled up and spilled over the rims of her eyes. She clutched his shirt, pulled and tugged in an attempt to stay upright. "Please, Dwayne. Let me help. Don't keep me out of this. I'll go crazy not knowing what's going on. She's all I have."

He fought for control. In the past two days Brooke had never been so close to him, never touched him as much. While he would give anything to have Hailey home, he also wished the woman he held was there for other reasons and of her own choosing.

"I'll call you every hour." His decision was already cracking.

"Please." She pressed closer. He closed his eyes. She was too damn close. Her cheek laid against his and her breath shook. "Please, Dwayne. Not just for the sake of Hailey, not even for the point in making sure someone is there to help, but please, for me. I couldn't live with myself if anything happened to either of you."

His chest caved and what air he had in his lungs came whooshing out. The clock behind them ticked, marking the passing time. She trembled in his arms and he shook with the hope that he wasn't about to make a mistake.

He turned his head, kissed her temple, and held her close. "Okay, go pack a bag."

Chapter Thirteen

The vehicle surged on I-287 east, heading out of the Village of Nyack limits and therefore away from Dwayne's rightful jurisdiction. The chance he took with his career had a ball of unease coiling in his gut. He glanced at Brooke, who stared out the car window at the blur of colorful trees they passed. The risk of his job was nothing when compared to the risk he took with her life. That coiled ball clenched and burned through his stomach. He mused over everything that could go wrong or what they could find up north.

When he told Charlie and the chief he needed a few days off to take care of some personal business, he knew he hadn't gotten anything over their heads. Charlie, acting as the great detective she was—and his best friend—looked at him as if she knew what he'd arranged. He hadn't liked leaving her out of his plan, but damn if he wanted to bring anyone else in on what he was doing—which, depending on how much he got involved in up north, could be against the law. Charlie had thinned her lips but otherwise kept her mouth shut. The concern sitting in her eyes, though, said more than the silence she maintained.

Leaving Hailey to the local LEOs wasn't an option, and after the phone call this morning to Rhode Island State Troopers, his decision to take matters into his own hands just reinforced his need to do something. He recognized bullshit, and the gruff man he had spoken to was spouting it out of his mouth by the second. Seemed RIST had a different thought process on juveniles crossing state lines than he did, despite the fact the asshole who possibly took her was her boyfriend.

They passed through the toll after the Tappan Zee

Bridge, and he rested an elbow on the side panel. *No turning back now.* A glance at Brooke showed her sitting in the same position, legs tucked beneath her petite frame, tendrils of wavy desert-red hair falling around her shoulders, hands clasped in her lap. She wore a gray hoodie sweatshirt and black yoga pants, her black Uggs forgotten on the floor, no makeup, no perfume, but she was still as beautiful as the first day they met. They'd played hopscotch on the playground all those years ago— what seemed like a lifetime ago—and age had only drawn out sensuality in this remarkable woman.

"Whatcha thinking about?"

Her voice broke his gaze away from the steady rhythm of the road. She leaned against the door, watching him through piercing ice-blue eyes.

"When we first met."

That drew a smile, one he hadn't realized he missed.

"Ah, first grade, right outside Ms. Kladarky's classroom. You were new, stood against the wall looking so lonely," she said.

He grinned, then shook his head. "And you couldn't let it go. Had to get the new guy to open up, didn't you? Sometimes I think you should have been the detective with your nosy ways."

She sighed and stared out his side window, trouble fleeting across her face. "You looked so sad. My heart, no matter how young I was, felt yours calling out for companionship."

His mouth tightened and he turned his attention back to the road. "Well, my life prior wasn't peaches and cream, if that's what you're asking."

"You haven't talked about it. Why?"

He cleared his throat, more than a little uncomfortable with this topic. It wasn't that he didn't want to talk about it. More so, it was the memories that came along. He shifted and wiped a hand down his face. "It's not something real pretty. I mostly think that people don't want to hear about the ugliness in life, so I keep to the pretty parts. You know, the family I have now, the life built from then on."

"I didn't mean to pry. I've upset you, sorry."

He shook his head and cut in, "No, you didn't. I just never talk about it, not even with my brothers." He heaved a deep breath, fighting against the urge to remain quiet and squash the question between them. Hell, as much as he wrestled with them, the words hovered on his lips. He wanted to tell someone, maybe even this woman, just so he could have the empathy of a close friend. She would listen and understand.

"You know I'm adopted, right," he began.

"Yeah. You don't have to talk about it, if you don't want to." Her voice was so small and sad he couldn't refuse it now.

"No, no, I think it's time I get this out and besides, we have a few hours on the road." He flashed a smile, one he didn't quite feel.

"Well, the earliest memory I can remember is my birth mom coming and going at all hours, leaving me alone to fend for myself for periods that lasted sometimes days. There were even times I grew so hungry I'd eat the puppy food for the dog we didn't have."

She gasped. "But I met you when you were six."

He turned and met her gaze. "Exactly."

Her lips trembled. "How old were you when this happened?"

He refocused on the road, his mind lost in the past. "I had to of been three, maybe four, I'm not real sure. When she came home, she would bring a *Happy Meal* or something, apologize for being gone, but she'd stink to high heaven. Stale cigarettes clung to her, and the stench of alcohol seemed to seep from her pores. At the time, I didn't know it wasn't normal, so I associated the smell to her, to comfort.

"Sometimes she'd bring these guys home with her, too. And sometimes I'd be forced, seeing as we only had a studio apartment, to watch what the two of them would do in front of me. Being an open loft, there was not a lot of privacy, you see.

"A few of the guys would get rough with her, knock her around a bit." Brooke gasped and he rushed on. "Never anything she didn't just clean up. And there was only one time any of the men laid a hand on me, and it's a lesson I'll never forget." He ignored her sound of outrage, and pushed on. "She'd take cash from them and set them on their ways." Until that one fatal day.

Dwayne blinked hard, kept his gaze in front of the vehicle, but his mind was stuck in the past.

"One day this guy came over, screaming about his money. I remember her telling me to get in the closet and do not come out until she called for me. She gave me a kiss, pushed a sippy cup in my hands, told me she loved me like always, and then closed the door. A loud noise a few seconds later and something heavy had been pushed against the door."

"Oh, Dwayne—"

He continued, unable to stop. "She screamed for hours. I pushed my hands over my ears in an attempt to block out the sound of something hitting flesh. It didn't work." A sound he'd never forget. "Her pleas for me to go get help, the uselessness when I couldn't open the door, and then the sudden quiet have stayed with me as if it happened yesterday. It was deafening, and somehow I knew when something wet entered beneath the crack on the door, that she was dead."

Brooke sniffed beside him and reached across the console to take his hand. Her warm skin did nothing to heat the cold seeping inside his soul. Her gesture of comfort held it at bay, though. His emotions were in turmoil as the scared little boy rose to the surface.

"They found me several days later, and her body already started to rot. I was so dehydrated my heart stopped on the table. Twice. We had no family, no friends that wanted to take me. And my father was some nameless man who wasn't even on my birth certificate, so I was placed with the state."

"That's horrible, oh my God, I'm so sorry."

He squeezed her hand, gave a small smile. "Thank you. Seems my mother sold her body for the drugs she was addicted to. Gave her love and affection to men who only wanted her for a few moments. I realize now anything she gave me wasn't real. The false words, the lies of comfort. She never gave anything real to her son. Her pimp killed her, and some scum on the street later killed him. Sort of like poetic justice, if you ask me."

"How did you—I mean, how have you survived this, to, you know, grow into who you are now?"

He smiled, lifted her hand and pressed his lips to her knuckles. "Aw, sweetheart, I didn't know you cared."

She blushed, and wasn't that just friggen adorable? "My mom and dad, the Gonzalezes, adopted me a year later, brought me here to Nyack. My mom had been on the initial crew that found me, one of the paramedics.

"Pops spent countless hours showing me what having a family was supposed to be. Hell, if it weren't for those two, I don't think me or any of my brothers would have made it this far in life."

She took his arm, scooted closer, and set it between her breasts, then brushed a sweet-as-sin kiss against his knuckles. "I'm so glad they found you."

He glanced down before returning his focus to the road. "Me, too."

"I imagine half of Nyack's female population is glad, as well. Where are you from originally?"

Was that a hint of jealousy in her tone? The two statements were so far away from one another, it took him a second to answer. "I'm from Baltimore, Maryland. And what does the female population have anything to thank for?"

She laughed, the sound strained. "Oh, don't play coy. You are very much a ladies' man, Dwayne."

He shifted again, uncomfortable for an entirely new reason. "I enjoy the company of a woman, yes. I won't deny that."

"Well, I'm glad you're here and that I approached you that day on the schoolyard."

"Me, too." While things had not turned out the way he hoped, he still had her in his life and it was enough. For now... "I thought you were the most beautiful girl I had ever met."

She gasped and covered it with a laugh. "You were six. Were you even old enough to know what such a word meant?"

"Of course," he said immediately. Her eyes widened. "It's something I never had a problem with. Don't you remember the first Valentine I gave you?"

She smiled, hugging his arm closer. He tried not to think about where his skin lay, but it was really fucking hard—which was exactly what he was trying not to become. A comfortable affection, though, nothing sexual, and wasn't that just a damn shame?

"I do," she answered.

"I told you, you were beautiful and I meant every word. You still are, Brooke. You could have asked me to do anything and I would have."

She laughed low, the sound deep, sultry. "Are you saying I was your first crush?" she teased.

He flashed a grin. "Yes." And the longest, still.

His phone broke through the speakers, and she released his arm so he could answer with the click of a button from his steering wheel. "Gonzalez here."

"Dwayne." Trent's voice filled the vehicle and he felt the air freeze around Brooke. She went still.

"Yeah, you're on speaker." Her gaze snapped to him, bore holes in the side of his head, but he ignored it. He didn't want Trent saying something to upset her. She had been through enough.

"That area we were talking about? Where the phone signal ended?"

"What's happened?"

"Nothing." Trent sighed and Dwayne braced. Shit, when the agent was worked up, you knew it wasn't good. "But the area has ties to human trafficking."

Brooke cried out, and he cursed.

"Fuck, I'll call you back, Rossi."

"Sure thing, D. Hey, I'm sorry I had to tell you like this, but I have a damn good feeling, especially after talking to Charlie, that I know where you're going. Let me warn you now, you do not want to be buried under something this big without backup. You understand what I'm saying?"

Dwayne pushed down the irritation, fought to keep his composure cool, his voice calm. "I got it."

"Good, don't forget either. And don't forget your jurisdiction."

He didn't say anything, just hung up and wished like hell he had more he could offer. The sound of her crying reached him.

"Brooke, *preciosa*, don't cry," he said, trying to

calm her.

She curled closer to the door, farther from him, and waved a hand in the air. "Don't," she said. "I don't…just let me be for a bit. God, my poor baby girl!"

He sighed and slumped his shoulders. The road stretched out like a long line before him, an endless distance between where he needed to be, and just how far they had to go until he could figure out what the hell was going on.

Chapter Fourteen

Lured to sleep by the rhythmic *thump*, *thump*, *thump* of the road, Brooke roused from a nap when the car slowed and pulled to the right. She lifted her head, winced at the crick in her neck, and rubbed the aching muscle. Her entire body felt laden, heavy under exhaustion, and out of sorts. The world moved around them as if in slow motion, like they were slowly working their way toward the light at the end of a long tunnel.

Said light in this case was a large sign rising out of the ground reading "Motel 8" and a dreary building that rose two stories and was dotted with various doors of orange and brown.

Still trying to blink away the slumber and the fog from her mind, she turned to Dwayne. He stopped the vehicle in front of a sizable glass-enclosed office.

"What are we doing?" she asked.

Tight lines around his eyes, he scrubbed his face, shook his head as if clearing his mind, and pointed in the general direction of the motel. "Getting us a room. I'm exhausted. We need to rest and think over the next step."

"Wait, where are we? Maybe we're close and can go get her now?"

His lips thinned and he faced her. "Sweetheart, look, we can't get her now. It's close to eight o'clock, we've been on the road all day, and even if we hadn't hit that traffic, I still wouldn't have acted on anything tonight. We don't know what situation we're walking into. And I'm not willing to risk Hailey's life charging in there unprepared. No one knows I'm here. We need to think before we do anything. I need to get a gauge on the situation."

Feeling like a child scolded, she sucked in a harsh

breath. "I didn't mean it like that."

His face softened and he ran the back of his knuckles along her cheek. "I know you didn't. We really need some sleep. In the morning we can work out the details. And to answer your question, we're right outside Providence. Still a good fifty miles away from where we think Hailey might be." He glanced over at the clerk who sat inside behind a desk, watching TV. "I'm going to get us a room and then we'll get something to eat, talk a bit more about what's going to happen next, okay?"

She nodded, her mind still screaming for her to keep moving. The shadows sitting beneath Dwayne's eyes stopped her from making a deal out of it. He did look exhausted.

He got out of the car, stretched his arms and when they dropped, so did his shoulders. This entire time he hadn't stopped to take a breath, much less sleep. Gratitude grew inside her chest. Here was a man who had no blood ties to Hailey, no obligations, and yet he risked his life, his career, everything, trying to help her out. Chastising herself, she waited until he returned. Without a word, he backed out of the parking spot, drove around to the rear of the building and parked at the far end, then turned the car off.

"I didn't realize this place was so hopping, but apparently some rodeo is in town. You're not going to like this, but they only had one room, one bed, and we got it."

Without waiting for a response, he got out of the car and disappeared to the back of the vehicle.

One bed... Sure, it was uncomfortable, but she was more than willing to put up with a night in the same room with him in order to sleep. That thought didn't stop trepidation from spreading at the intimacy they would share tonight. She had never been in such a close setting with Dwayne, or such a vulnerable one.

Her car door opened and she glanced up to see Dwayne, both duffel bags slung over his shoulder. His face had lines of exhaustion, but his eyes were focused on her.

"Do you plan on sleeping out here all night?"

Heat rose in her cheeks, quick like a whip. "Of course not. Sorry, I guess I'm a little out of it still."

She stood and followed him to the door, number 150, then stepped inside.

The room, furnished in your basic hotel setting, had lines running vertical in orange and beige strips along the walls. Two tan side tables sat at the head of and outlined a king-size bed covered in a typical almost blinding, definitely unpleasant floral design only found in these establishments. Next to them, sitting beneath a window unit air-conditioner was a silver table and a pair of chairs. Across from the bed remained a large dresser, six drawers, and a black television on top.

Dwayne brushed by her and dropped their bags to the bed. He rubbed a bulky palm over the top of his head and looked around, avoiding her gaze. "Well, it's not much, but it'll do the trick." He pivoted and opened a drawer on one of the side tables, then withdrew a binder, which held multiple takeout menus. "Anything in particular you want to eat?"

Her stomach chose that moment to grumble. Between the long drive, the exhausting days, and her lack of appetite, she wasn't surprised to realize she hadn't been eating. She crossed to him and looked down at the binder.

A menu for a restaurant named, "Ma and Pa's" listed off basics and claimed to be the best home cooking in the county. She scanned the items, bypassing cheeseburgers, steak sandwiches, and salads.

"How about a plate of spaghetti and some garlic bread?" His resonant voice seemed much more intimate so close to her in this small room.

She nodded, inching back. "That sounds fine."

"Want something for dessert?"

Brooke lifted her eyebrows. "You mean to tell me you eat sweets? With that body?" She blushed, realizing her outburst. But there was no way in hell. The man was built like a machine, and there couldn't be an ounce of body fat on him.

He matched her facial movements. "Sweetheart," he started, his voice dropping low, smooth as melted chocolate. "I can eat a peach for hours."

She stared at him, confounded until it, at last, hit her. "Oh!" Her earlier blush was nothing compared to the fire igniting across her cheeks now.

* * * *

Dwayne tried to ignore the sound of the shower, the thoughts of Brooke standing under the hot spray, rivulets of water running down her slick skin, over the crests of her breasts, dipping down into her navel and sliding between the lush triangle of curls between her thighs. The steam escaping from beneath the bathroom door did nothing to quell his fantasy.

After his comment about peaches, Brooke caught his drift and when her face flushed an enticing shade of pink, she turned, referred to the shower, and disappeared into the bathroom. She returned once to claim her bag and a second time, moments later, to ask for one of his shirts.

That had been his downfall. His mind spun with the vision of what she would look like, how much he would like to see her in his clothing. Her asking was nothing more than her forgetting her own clothes for bed when they'd left in haste this morning. That's at least what he kept trying to tell himself. His body had other ideas in mind. She hadn't asked for a pair of boxers and so that left a very enticing and erotic vision playing. Thoughts of her in panties and his shirt. Would she wear a bra? Maybe she didn't wear underwear…

"You're not fucking helping yourself here, douche. Get your shit together," he muttered.

Deciding to wait for food until they'd both showered, he left the menu on the small table, sat on the bed, flopped to his back and let his mind erect fantasies. Big mistake. He was hard as a rock, despite being exhausted. Yellow stains dotted the popcorn ceiling and he tried to count them, thought of baseball, and switched to arithmetic—nothing seemed to help.

The door opened behind him. He tilted his head and caught her coming out of the bathroom surrounded in steam, wearing nothing but his white t-shirt. The material fell to mid-thigh and he soaked her in.

Muscular legs kissed with the hint of sun and blessed with the right amount of curves walked in silent steps toward him. She tugged on the cloth and set her bag down, then faced him, her eyes averted. Pink flushed her face from the shower and her hair fell in a heavy, thick array around her shoulders. In her hand she held a brush and, still avoiding him, she went around to the other side of the bed, sat, and began to brush her hair.

"Shower's ready."

He couldn't resist. The blush and her hesitancy were too adorable. "You want to get sweaty enough to take another one?"

Her bright blue eyes snapped to him and she stared, mouth agape. "Dwayne Gonzalez, you are such a damn flirt!"

He grinned, sat up, and rested his weight on one arm. His fingers itched to run the brush through her hair himself. He'd never been one to do shit like that with women, but for some reason the urge was so strong he had to fist the sheet to keep from moving.

"I'm only speaking the truth, or better yet a fantasy that's been running through my head since you ran away quicker than the Roadrunner."

She rolled her beautiful eyes heavenward. "I did not run."

"Did too."

She huffed, then yanked the brush through her hair with a little too much force. He cringed at the ripping sound.

"Easy," he said. "Don't take your sexual frustration out on your hair. I happen to like it."

She paused before meeting his gaze. "Please. All men like long hair. What is it about the length, anyway?"

He shrugged and gave in to the urge to reach for a tendril. Her expression grew wary, guarded.

"It's nice to run your fingers through, always smells good, and gives us something to hold on to when we take you from behind."

She didn't speak for several moments, and her voice shook when she did. "Being such the ladies' man, I'm sure you have no shortage of women who allow you to tug and pull all you want."

He took in a deep breath and drew his hand away. He got how he looked in her eyes, had heard her small comments over the years. While he tried to pretend the remarks didn't bother him, they did. Sure, he had been with a few women, but both parties involved were more than willing to play, and more so, almost all understood what he was willing—and not willing—to give.

"Funny you should say that. Because I'm feeling very much like a one-woman type of man right now." He would knock the misconception she had about him right out of her mind. It was long past due.

She snorted, and the sound was so unladylike, he laughed. She never did anything like that.

"Your pretty words and smooth pick-up lines aren't going to work," she said. "You and I both know you don't mean them, and I'm smarter than that. We're too close to allow sex to come between us."

The very fact that she still slammed him, despite her being unaware of it, bruised his ego. Yeah, it might have been petty or even a bit childish, but he put as much space between the two of them as he could. He pushed away from the bed and paced across the floor. He didn't want to say something he would regret later, and it seemed he was fucking this up. Or better yet, had chosen the wrong time.

Smooth, Detective. You're a class act.

He wandered to the door, turned, and faced her. "I don't think I'm saying this properly." He shoved his hands into his pockets and rocked back on his heels. "Look, Brooke, maybe we'll just come back to this another time."

Frowning, she dropped the brush and stared at him. "What do you mean, come back to this?" She looked genuinely confused, which reinforced his decision to hold in what he felt for a bit longer. Surely, she would have figured it out by now. And if not, in the middle of rescuing her daughter wasn't a time to profess his feelings—or affection—for her.

He pressed his lips together, crossed the room, and grabbed his bag. "Nothing. I'm going to take a shower." When he stepped toward the bathroom, he found her in front of him, all five foot six of curvy, sexy-smelling woman.

She placed a hand on his chest and the contact sent a spark between them. He knew she felt it too. Her eyes widened and she looked up at him as she removed her touch.

"What are you saying? Or not saying?" she asked.

He heaved a sigh. "It's nothing, really."

"Tell me."

"Hell, Brooke, you don't want to hear this," he ground out. "You make jokes about it when I bring it up, practically accuse me of being a man-whore, and toss it back in my face. This is not the time to discuss it. We're both exhausted. Just let it be."

Her head tilted in thought, and her eyebrows scrunched together. *Fuck, she's cute.* She blinked, and as if a curtain parted, clarity entered her eyes. She stepped back and stared at him with shock across her features. "You can't be serious."

He dropped his bag at his feet and tossed his hands in the air. "Of course, I'm not." The words came out more sarcastic than intended.

Her frown grew and she shook her head, laughing without humor. "Oh you've got me good. Please, I know you better than that. You cannot shackle yourself to one woman, Dwayne. Good joke, by the way. Because you know, I am not one who takes sex so casually. You and I are so far away from what the other needs, it's not even funny." Her lips curled and she glanced away, dragged the brush through her hair again and walked to the bed, for all intents and purposes dismissing him. "Good one, though."

He clenched his fists by his sides, torn between shaking the utter living shit out of her and throwing a hand through a wall. Never had a woman worked him up so much. He didn't say a word, couldn't. She'd said it all, and it sounded as if she had made her mind up about what kind of individual he was. He was exhausted, stressed, and worried as hell about Hailey. He shouldn't say another damn word, shouldn't push. He kept repeating that advice in his head but ignored the voice of reason, and his restraint snapped.

"You know me so well, right?" He took two steps across the room, yanked the brush from her hand and tossed it aside. A surprised gasp left her, but he didn't give her a chance to say anything. "You think I'm joking with you?" He wanted to shut that pretty little minx up, was so damn pissed he couldn't think straight.

Dwayne gathered her in his arms, snapped her body against his, and slammed his mouth down. The kiss was bruising, and more than a little possessive. He communicated things he couldn't say, poured his attraction through the melding of their lips. He bit, sucked, and nibbled his way across her mouth until she gasped. He took advantage of her parted lips and thrust his tongue inside, wrapped it around hers, and massaged the tentative velvet.

With the contact, her taste of warm mint, her being soft and compliant in his arms, he slowed his assault, expanded his kiss. One hand tangled in her hair and he tilted her head back, impelled his exploration deeper. She began to return the kiss and he moaned. Her arms wrapped around his neck, and she pressed closer.

He squeezed her ass, urged her against his erection, then abruptly pushed her away. Dazed eyes stared up at him. Her lips were red, plump, and moist from his caress.

His chest rose and fell in staccato, but he glared at her. It was either that or kiss her senseless again.

"Next time, sweetheart," he said, his words cold and cruel, even to his own ears, "don't judge a book by its cover. This conversation has been highly enlightening." Unable to stay there a moment longer, he spun around. Grabbing a room key, his leather jacket and wallet from the table, he left.

Chapter Fifteen

Brooke sat on the bed and stared at the door. The very door Dwayne had left through in a rush, but not before she'd seen the hurt and anger. She was long past memorizing the emergency exit procedures outlined behind Plexiglas attached to the wood, and if she had to read the violations for smoking in the room again—waiting for him to come back—she would scream.

Dwayne had been gone for well over an hour, his words and abrupt departure still screaming through her head. He didn't deny what she said, though, right? Or, was the kiss, the sure way he held her, stating something more? It felt akin to lust, a raw kind of craving, and maybe a furious kind of need. How was she to know what was real and what he wanted? No way he wanted her like *that*. They had been friends too long, been through too much, for sex to get in the way.

But good Lord, the kiss shocked her to her core. Lingering effects of heat pummeled in her stomach, the ache between her legs still present. How she wished she could be like the many women he bedded, so free, so willing to give him whatever he wanted—without consequences.

Sex to her was not the physical act of two bodies coming together, though. It was making love, a connection to another being, the ability to open completely to someone else. Trust played a part in letting a man between her sheets, and while she trusted Dwayne with her life and the life of her child, she wasn't sure she could trust him with her heart. Lying with him would give him the one-way ticket to the organ that sped when he touched her, pounded against her breast when he kissed her, and stopped when his gaze came her way.

She glanced at the clock and worried her lip. Ninety minutes. She rose from the bed, pulled on a pair of yoga pants, grabbed for her gray hoodie, the extra key to the room, and headed outside. This wasn't the time for them to fight, nor was this the time for them to explore these options. He was tired, he'd said so himself. So why wasn't he sleeping? And more, where in the heck was he?

The rear of the hotel held no streetlights and the darkness gave an eerie impression, one that had the hairs on the back of her neck standing. She was in a strange, unknown area, and the pitch-dark setting did nothing to soothe her frayed nerves. The past few days had been long and exhausting. She missed her daughter's smile, her laugh, the way her eyes twinkled when she teased. The hollow ache in her chest spread as she stepped inside the front office and glanced around.

She wanted to find her daughter.

A young, prematurely balding man sat behind the tall brown partition, his white shirt stained with only God knew what. His heavy gut strained against the shirt and rolled over the buckle of his jeans.

Memories of the past assaulted her at once.

"Mom, look. He's got dickey-do syndrome." Deep *chocolate eyes danced with amusement.*

Brooke turned to the local pizza shop owner, an older man with thick brown hair. His plump body showed his love for not only baking pizza pies but also eating them. "Dickey-do?"

Sweet laughter, more precious than the finest china, filled the air. "His belly sticks out farther than his dickey-do."

The rush of the memory caused her eyes to sting. *I just want to find my daughter!*

"Can I help you?" Dickey-do asked. Processed meat with the wrapper halfway down the stick, reading

"Slim Jim," hung from his mouth.

She breathed through her nose, ignoring the stench of an unwashed body, bad breath, and old food. "Um, I'm in room one fifty, and the guy I'm with...well, I was wondering if you've seen him?"

He nodded and motioned behind her. She looked over her shoulder, following his pointed finger. "He crossed the street, went to Ma and Pa's Tavern. Didn't look too happy. Whatcha do?"

She pivoted, already walking toward the door. "What makes you think I did anything?"

His answer reached her as she stepped outside. "Because only a woman puts that kind of look on a man's face."

She ignored his comment and crossed the street, not a hard task seeing this town didn't have a lot of traffic. Despite it being early evening, not a single headlight accompanied the road. Dust kicked up under her feet and spread a thin coat of brown specks across her black Uggs. She bounded up four concrete stairs and stepped inside the black wooden building.

Noise assaulted her. From an old red jukebox in the corner to her left, music screamed out. In the center of the room stood a large rectangular bar. Inside the raised bench were two bartenders, an older couple, one woman, one male. They laughed and carried on with customers sitting around the outside, and despite the ghost town, the place seemed full.

Black lacquered tables dotted the room, patrons intermittently at each. One by one, heads turned her way, gazes sliding along the length of her body. It would not have caught her attention so much had not ninety percent of the bar been male. She shifted, scanning the area quicker, looking for any sign of...

Dwayne.

She breathed a sigh of relief and took a step as he turned. His dark green eyes flashed with surprised before the expression smoothed into a blank mask. He leaned against what looked to be a pinball machine, thick arms crossed over a beefy chest, his black shirt straining. She continued to cross to him, drinking in the sight.

Was she recognizing the sensuality he emitted now? What had changed to allow the line to blur between friendship and lust? Those damn charcoal jeans, faded in all the right spots, molded and wrapped around long, muscular thighs.

He sidestepped as she approached and reached out to wrap his warm hand around hers. Tingles spread from their skin-to-skin contact and she gasped. With a quick tug, too fast for her to realize what was happening, he turned their bodies until they faced the pinball machine.

"What are you doing here, Brooke?"

His voice, smooth like melted chocolate, played across her ear. His hard body pressed to hers, hip to hip, chest to back, thigh to thigh, until they molded together. He placed his hands over hers at the controls on the side of the machine, two silver buttons.

She breathed in, out, tried to control her pounding heart. His touch did this.

"I—I was looking for you."

"You shouldn't be wandering around someplace you don't know. Especially in a town you don't know," he growled.

She fought against a shiver as the vibrations from his voice rumbled through his chest and her body. It was like being surrounded by him, encased in his warmth. And they were so close she knew from the tightening of his fingers on hers that he didn't miss her full-body tremble.

"Dwayne, I—"

"Shhhh," he interrupted.

He lowered his head and brushed his lips against the shell of her ear. He didn't move away, though. Instead, he turned his attention forward and inched closer as if they weren't already close enough. "You ever play pinball before?"

* * * *

Christ, she smelled good. Cheap hotel soap simmered from her skin, but deeper lay the undercoat of lilacs, a softer scent of roses, and beneath? A scent he identified as just Brooke.

She inhaled unsteadily. Pressed so close, he was attuned to every movement she made, each sound escaping, and *her* on a whole other level.

"Not really," she answered, her voice shaky.

Dwayne lifted a brow, surprised, and swallowed hard. The slight curve of her ass fit perfectly against his hips, the slender material of those godforsaken tight pants playing havoc with his imagination. Only a thin barrier between them. Heat from her soaked through his jeans and shirt. He wanted to wrap around her, bask in her warmth. Earlier, with a combination of being hungry and exhausted, he'd let his cool go, exploded with things he knew were better left unsaid. His actions had been harsh in response to her words. He cared for Brooke, knew she was stressed. He didn't want to make things harder than they already were. Regret sat like a concrete ball in his stomach and he would give anything to make it up to her.

First, they would play. Then, he would feed her. After that—sleep. He decided he needed to show her he could be her friend, but on the same token, he didn't really want to hold his attraction back. He would show her both sides and allow her to make the decision on where they headed. Keep the ball in her court, so to speak. But she would know exactly where he stood, and exactly what he wanted to pursue.

"Well then, it seems, Ms. Mason, you're in for a lesson." He flexed his fingers over hers, guided her hand to the plunger and held it there. "The goal of the game is to score points, and to keep the ball from going down the drain. This," he said and squeezed his hand around hers, "is what we use to push the ball forward."

"Where's the ball?" Breathless. That's the word he'd use to describe her voice. His lips curved.

"We haven't put in a quarter yet. Patience, Brooke." He shifted, moving his head to the other side of hers, while keeping their bodies in close contact. He readjusted their hands until they lay over the silver buttons again. "These are flippers. When the ball gets too close to the hole, you use them to keep it from falling into that deep, dark hole."

From the way her breath hitched, she caught his double meaning. He fought a grin and lost. He loved this, their play, a time to focus on just living and not stressing over what was to come. Hailey's danger and the threat to her life still hovered in the back of his mind, but he'd do anything to give Brooke a few minutes of peace.

"You want to score as many points as possible, keeping the ball bouncing around, until you hit the jackpot, perhaps even find the Powerball."

"Powerball?"

"Yup, extra points for being so good. If you guide it into certain places, it moves faster, and you'll have to move quicker to keep up. If your ball goes down the drain, then the game is over. You only get three chances. Do you understand?" Nodding, she shifted her ass against his hips, and he sucked in a hiss.

"Good," he grumbled. "Sometimes you will need to bump the machine, not too much, just a bit in order to get the ball unstuck. When that happens, simply nudge…" He shifted his hips into hers until they hit the machine. The contact almost had his eyes rolling in the back of his head. "Just like that." He readjusted until they were back where they began.

"Do you feel up to a game, Brooke?"

She hesitated so long he didn't think she would answer. Tension ran through her body, each muscle locked against him.

"I don't know," she said.

Doubt, suspicion, and vulnerability crept into her tone. *You're an ass, Gonzalez.* He was pushing her, but the time had come and he was done holding back. He wanted her to experience this, something so simple and fun. More, he wanted her to play with him. In more than one way…but for now, this would do.

"Scoring is a mystery to most. The basic goal for some is to keep the ball from going down the drain. Others, however, are after so much more. Do you understand?"

She tilted her head to the side and her cheek brushed against his nose. He closed his eyes, tensed, and waited.

Hours or maybe seconds passed while he waited for her answer.

"You really want to play a game of pinball with me?" she asked.

God, did he ever. He nodded. "Yeah, I really do."

"I'll give it my best shot. Will you help me?"

His chest constricted, tightening until it was almost painful. It was a question he wanted her to ask but for entirely different reasons.

"I'll be right here, sweetheart."

She nodded and he released her long enough to insert a quarter. They both reached for the plunger as the game's lights started blinking. His hand over hers, they pulled the nozzle back and released. He guided her through the game. His attention faltered and instead focused on her, the sounds of her pealing laughter, the fluid way her body moved with his, her sweet scent surrounding him until all he could think of, every bit of his essence and focus, was wrapped in Brooke.

Behind his fly, he grew hard as stone, and he would not be surprised if the rigid member permanently tattooed with the impression of his zipper. By the end of the game, he was so wound up, tight, and hot, he was about to explode. She clapped, giggled and spun in his arms, then froze. She must have read his face, saw the strain there, and he let it out in all of its glory. He wanted to play all right, and he wanted her to know the rules.

He leaned forward, bending her back over the display. His hands, still on the flippers, boxed her into his body. So petite, she fit inside the makeshift shelter as if made for it. Her bright blue eyes watched him with unspeakable trepidation.

Her face was flushed from the excitement of the game and he vaguely wondered if she looked the same way after sex.

"Dwayne?" His name a question broke him from the moment. He wanted to kiss her, had been about to.

In a bar for Christ's sake!

He pivoted, wrapped his palm around her wrist at the same time and grabbed his jacket. Ignoring the lewd calls behind them, he pushed out the door and urged her across the street. He didn't speak until they were back inside the hotel room.

He dropped his jacket, kicked off his boots, and faced her. Like a skittish animal, she backed up until she hit the wall.

He took in air, then forced it out of his lungs with a slow and controlled breath.

"I'm not going to attack you, Brooke, so you can stop looking at me like that."

She studied him as if measuring the weight of his words. He stayed rooted to the spot, allowing her to gather her courage again. He wanted her so fucking bad he was in literal pain, but he wouldn't force himself on her. He needed to wait until she came to him, until she begged. And she would, he was almost certain.

They stared at each other for minutes. The ticking of his watch and an occasional car passing outside filled the silence. Her shoulders relaxed slowly, and her body sagged with relief until she was only blinking at him instead of cowering.

Apparently satisfied with his answer, she pushed her shoes off, drew off her pants, and slid under the covers of the bed.

He sighed and turned away, clicking off the lights and removing his jeans in the darkness. No need to get her even more scared of him than she already was. Soft moonlight filtered through the white sheer curtain and danced shadows across the room. He double-checked the lock on the door before securing the chain and pulling out a chair. He was about to sit when she spoke.

"What are you doing?"

"I'm going to catch a few hours of sleep before we head out again. You should do the same."

The sound of rustling covers followed. "No, I mean, why aren't you coming to bed?"

He groaned. Christ, again! "Fucking hell, I am not a saint. I don't know if I can keep my hands off you right now. I'm sorry, I realize that is the last thing you want to hear, but I have a need for you. Do you understand?"

"I trust you." Her voice shook and her words, while he knew she tried to be strong, sounded weak. He closed his eyes and called for patience.

"I don't think you do."

"Please," she pleaded. "Come to bed. You've been running haggard for several days now. I trust you won't force yourself on me. And I think you know I'm not quite sure I would be ready to do anything other than sleep tonight."

"Brooke, I'm not sure this is a good—"

She cut him off. "Please, don't make me beg. We've been friends too long. I'm not only worried about my daughter, I'm worried about you, too. Please, come to bed and get some sleep. I don't want us walking into something tomorrow and you being tired. I don't want to beg, but I will if you don't get over here and *sleep*."

He opened his eyes. Her words made sense, and while he could catch some z's anywhere, she was right, it wouldn't be that good sitting in a chair all night. With heavy feet, he crossed the room to sit on the cool sheets as she drew back the covers. He lay back, and she pulled the blanket over him, her body brushing against his like a whisper.

He stared at the dark ceiling and wondered how in the hell he would get any sleep with her so close.

Chapter Sixteen

Brooke was having the most delicious dream. Despite her fear of falling into bed with Dwayne, inside her dreams she gave in to her urges and did things she would not dare when awake.

His skin was warm and hard, like heated velvet over steel. She roamed her hands over his body, taking in each minute detail. He placed his palms over the top of her hands and guided her along, unhindered and unrestrained in their pursuit. Somehow, with him following along on the map of discovery, it was more erotic, intimate, and powerful.

Broad shoulders filled out to muscular arms as thick as her thighs. A light dusting of hair played across his chest. Her hand smoothed down the front of his body, fingers jumping over the rigid six-pack of his abdominal muscles. She shouldn't be surprised. He ran rain or shine and ate nothing but protein and steamed veggies. Always had, most likely always would. Now, she traced along the treasure trail that led beneath the waist of his boxer briefs, glorying in her very own Adonis lying in her bed. He should totally become one of those human models in some university anatomy class. He was perfection.

In her dream, the setting was wrong, though, because the covers were not hers, and the room was unfamiliar. Some nagging thought pressed through, but she batted it down. She wanted to taste, had a hankering for chocolate and Dwayne's skin.

Warm musk, a combination of evergreen and masculinity, filled her nostrils as she dipped her head. She brushed her lips over the swell of his chest, lapped against his tan-colored nipples and allowed him to guide her leg across his thighs. His erection was a hot brand through the cloth. He rolled his hips, driving the length on the inside of her thigh.

They both groaned.

Emboldened, she allowed him to pull her atop until her thighs straddled his waist. He crushed a fist in her hair and, blessedly, brought her mouth on top of his. The kiss did not start gentle. It wasn't even a tease. Instead, he ravished and conquered. Tongues tangling, teeth clashing, biting, and soothing licks. His arm wrapped around her and yanked her body to his. The insistent length of him pulsed between her legs and she answered with a roll of her hips, verbalizing her bliss into his mouth.

Pleasure licked at her, warmth moving from her stomach on out to her limbs. Goosebumps spread across her flesh with each touch of his hand. He held her to him, ravished her mouth, and wrecked her senses. This is what she wanted, to be taken, showed how good it could be between two people. Never had she felt such bone-crushing need.

His mouth broke away and a large palm urged her hips into a steady rhythm.

"God, I need to see you," he panted. "Brooke. Sweetheart, take off your shirt."

"Yes." The cloth restrained her movements, preventing precious skin-on-skin contact. She shed the material with pleasure, ripped it over her head until she sat on top of him wearing only her simple white lace panties.

"Christ, you're beautiful," he hissed.

Growing bolder at his response, she smiled and arched her back. He shifted and his bare chest came against her stomach just before one of her nipples was wrenched into moist heat. She cried out as he sucked and nipped at the tightened bud. Nails digging into his shoulders, she rose and fell in an erotic dance against his body.

The ardor disappeared, but he lapped at the sensitive peak. "Look at me," he growled.

She did not want him to stop. Inside, a coiled spring tightened with each swipe of his tongue.

"Look at me," he repeated, this time a command.

She couldn't think. The pressure with each pass of her core against his straining erection was almost too much. She tossed her head back and rode him with wild abandon, the thin cloth of their underwear an annoying barrier. One she wanted to strip away.

"More, God, please, I don't want to wake," she moaned.

Dwayne cursed and she went falling through the air. She landed on her back in one smooth motion. Her eyes jolted open and stared up into a pair of flashing green ones. "I said look at me."

Brooke gasped, and a cold douse of water pushed through her. It wasn't a dream. "What?" she asked, confused. Dread climbed its way over the warmth in her stomach until it froze, locking every one of her muscles. "Wait," she gasped. "This was really happening?"

* * * *

Dwayne recognized the shock in her expression before she went stiff. He groaned, dropped his head into the crook of her neck and willed his overheated body to calm. She lay so still beneath him, her racing heart the only indication she was alive. Her skin against his, her nipples puckered to his chest, was the most extraordinary thing he had ever experienced.

And that was saying a lot.

He had been with women of all shapes and sizes, colors, and ages. None of them had invoked this response in him. He felt as if he were walking along a tightrope, his limbs heavy and uncoordinated, his mind fogged in a haze. Brooke was his finish line, and it was one he tried so hard to get to as she waited for him with open arms.

At least that was what it seemed like in his mind. Instead, reality crashed its course and dimmed the fantasy, leaving him more than aware of the "back-off" vibes she emitted.

He concentrated on their pulses, somehow coordinated and running as if they had just finished a marathon. His cock pulsed in the same beat, straining behind the tight confines of his briefs. Each jump of his erection had her tensing more, a reaction he could not ignore, and he rolled off her body to lay on his back, an arm over his eyes.

"Yes, Brooke, it was really happening." He sighed.

He was on edge, strung so high he couldn't say anything else. When he had woken to her hands roaming over him, it had been his biggest wish granted, his best fantasy come true. He praised the big man above, thanked his lucky stars, and dove into the moment with her. Never once had he considered her in the haze of a dream, unaware of her actions.

Had affairs continued on the path they had been going, how far would things have progressed? "Fuck," he cursed beneath his breath as the realization hit. It would have equated to rape. Maybe not in a legal sense, but yes, in both their minds. Sitting up, he leaned forward on his knees, dropped his head between his shoulders, and held it in his palms. A shaky breath sounded behind him, and the bed shook as a soft, restrained sob broke through the air. He looked over his shoulder, alarmed. His heart seized.

Brooke lay on her side, curled in a fetal position, her hands holding her head, her sweet face breaking under the onslaught of emotions.

"Brooke...hell..." He didn't know what to say, fought to find words. His chest split open as she set her emotions free and poured herself out from her eyes. Deep, sorrow-filled cries pierced the air.

He was such an asshole!

"Sweetheart, please, you're breaking my heart here." Dwayne curled up behind her and spooned her as she let it all out. *You're such a fucking prick, dude.* Yes, Christ, yes he was.

She wiggled in an attempt to escape from his hold, and reluctantly he opened his arms. But rather than moving away, she rotated and pressed up against him, one bare leg thrust between his thighs. He sucked in a breath. Brooke clutched at his back, looking for purchase and he understood. She wanted, *needed*, to be comforted...by him.

The realization shook him, giving back some of the hope that had kindled upon waking under her touch. He palmed the back of her head, wrapped his other arm around her waist and held her. He hated seeing her cry and fought to keep from shaking as the sound of her heart breaking filled the air.

A long time later, she stilled and sucked in deep breaths.

"I don't know what to say," she mumbled against his chest.

He squeezed her but refused to release her. This felt too right, too damn good.

"There's nothing to say. While it's a new experience for me, I don't think it's anything either of us should be embarrassed about. I'm more concerned about how you're doing. What's going through your mind. You okay?"

She traced a finger over his pectoral and he closed

his eyes against the touch. Small, light, like a butterfly's wings, but it went all the way down to his soul. Their bodies were still skin to skin, and the silence intimate, but her mind was a million miles away. He didn't have to see her to know this; he just *knew*. They needed to get on the road. He was well aware of the sun rising in the sky, but he wanted to make sure she was okay, that *they* were okay.

"I'm real sorry, Dwayne. I thought it was a dream. I didn't realize…"

He grinned above her head. "So you were comfortable enough in your dream to touch me, huh? Took advantage of that, did you?"

Her fingers stilled for a beat, and she snickered. "It's no secret that you're very attractive. What woman wouldn't take advantage of that? I'm sure you'd probably find a few men who'd jump at the chance, too," she added wryly.

He made a face, opened his eyes and released her head to tilt her chin back. Studying her, he searched for what was going through her mind. Instead of finding anything, she met his gaze, eyes still watery.

"While I respect different sexualities, I don't think I'd take any of the guys up on an offer. You, however, can feel free to touch me any time you like." Her cheeks grew pink and he smiled, brushing a thumb across the wet skin. "It does make me curious, though," he continued. "Why you felt as if you could do that in your dream, but not now, when we're both conscious of our actions. I think I've made myself more than clear I'd be willing to reciprocate."

She swallowed and sucked in a shaky breath. Each rise of her chest pressed her breasts against him and despite trying to be patient with her, his body twitched beneath his briefs.

"I'm not made like that," she whispered.

He frowned. "Made like what?"

One slender shoulder lifted in a shrug. "I can't just give myself to someone. It isn't about a body. To me, sex is more than physical."

His eyes narrowed, and he contemplated. "What makes you think it wouldn't be anything more than physical for me? We've been friends for a long time. Do you believe I'd be willing to risk losing you?"

"I—I don't know. It's not like you'd purposefully do something to hurt me. But I also don't think you'd be aware of it. I'm not made like the women you're used to. I just…" She started to pull away, and when he refused to let her go, she struggled against his chest. "I'm not made that way. I'm sorry."

He held her fast, pushed the wave of frustration down. "Hold on, give me a moment here to talk."

"This is too intimate," she said, still struggling. "We're naked and lying in each other's arms."

His lips tightened. "Sweetheart, I just had your nipple in my mouth. That's pretty damn intimate. We're not naked. All the most important parts are covered. Relax. Please, give me a few minutes. That's all I ask."

She froze, studied him, and nodded. "Okay," she said, almost reluctant. Another deep breath from her rubbed her nipples across his chest. *Christ!*

He rolled their bodies until she lay on her back, his frame partially atop her. Their legs were still tangled, hips pressed together, but now he could breathe deep. He took a large inhale of air, tried to keep his gaze on her face and not lower. This was a time to be serious, no matter how tempting she was.

"I don't think you're giving me enough credit here." She opened her mouth, but he cut her off. "Let me finish. I've let you speak, now it's my turn."

Her mouth snapped shut.

"Okay, look, I know this may not be the best circumstance you've found yourself in, and I know you may even think this feels wrong. But I don't. To me, and I'm not real pretty with words, but this, the touch of your skin against mine, feels right. The perfect fit of our bodies, the way my body responded with a consuming demand to have you. I care for you, Brooke. I would never, ever hurt you maliciously. I would never take your trust for granted. You mean more to me than that."

"Your words sure are pretty enough."

He grinned. "Look, how about we take this one step at a time. I won't lie to you, I want you beneath me. I want inside you, deep, so much so that you won't know where I end and you begin. I've never wanted someone with the intensity I do you. I will take this as slow as you need, or go as fast as you like, but I want you. And I intend to have you. Do you understand?"

"Cocky," she blurted.

He lifted a brow. "No, confident."

Her lips turned down in a sad smile. "Why me?"

He stared at her, bewildered. "Have you seen yourself? Do you know what you do to me?"

Her eyes watered and she shook her head. He cursed again and rose from the bed to draw her up with him. She had no choice but to follow as he tugged her inside the bathroom, closed the door, and turned her until she stood, her back to his chest, facing a standing mirror.

At once, she went to wrap her arms around her body, but he held her fast, urging her wrists to her sides. "No, let me show you." On full alert again, all the blood must have rushed south because he suddenly had a case of verbal diarrhea, opening up the vulnerability she gave him whenever she was near.

"Look at your body." He set a large palm on her

bare stomach and pressed her hips back to his. The crease of her ass cradled his engorged cock. Willing his body to wait, he continued his attempt to make her see just what he did. "Your breasts are beautiful, just the right size for my hands." He ran his palms up the smooth, rounded expanse of her stomach, inch by inch, with slow, deliberate movements.

"Your nipples, the perfect color. Like sand dollars." He took the heavy globes in his hands and squeezed. She sucked in a harsh breath, but he didn't stop. Instead, he plucked at her nipples until air shot out of her lungs with exaggerated gasps. "And when distended, they call for my mouth. Do you know what I want to do right now?"

She shook her head. "What?" she asked, out of breath.

"I want to take them into my mouth, suck and bite, see if I can make you come from just playing with your breasts."

Her palm squeezed his thigh.

He dropped his head, ran his nose along the length of her neck until his lips brushed the shell of her ear. "Let me do it, Brooke. Let me show you how much I want you. Give yourself over into my care."

He continued to play with her breasts, tugging at the distended peaks until she cried out. "I don't know if I can."

Her hips pressed into his and he hissed. "Sweetheart, that's all I'll ask of you. We're going to do this slowly. You will trust me enough to give yourself completely before I take you. For now, I'm content to do as I've asked. Say yes."

Hooded eyes met his in the mirror and she gave a minute nod. It was all he needed.

Instead of turning her toward him, he rounded her

until he stood before her, the mirror at his back. He wanted her to witness the wild abandon he was about to put on her face, needed her to see him on her body, get used to the sight. He planned to be there for a long time to come, and it was time she got accustomed to it. He dropped to his knees and wrapped his palms around her hips, urging her closer.

"Watch me. Watch us," he commanded.

Without waiting for a response, he took her breast in his mouth...and groaned. She tasted sugary, like honey wrapped in cinnamon, almost reminiscent of waffle cakes. He tugged, nipped, and sucked the tightened bud, using his free hand to play with the other. She gasped above his head, but her hands, dear, sweet Lord, her hands pressed him to her and scraped through his hair. She cried out, the sound like music to his ears, an erotic song just for him.

He took turns working each nipple and massaging her breasts. He also paid attention to what she liked, did it again to hear her cry out, and took note of it for when he'd do it again. Because there was going to be a next time.

He glanced up. Her eyes were hooded, mouth parted. A sensual fairy sprite beckoning.

"Look at us in the mirror," he growled before ravishing her skin again. Like a starving man hell-bent on taking as much as she would give, he couldn't get enough. She glanced up and when he sucked her nipple in deep—and hard—she tossed her head back and shouted in passion.

He fought to keep his hands on her hips as she rode out the orgasm. Keening cries filled the air, his name on her sweet lips. Liquid seeped from his cock and he sucked in a harsh breath, released her from his mouth, and buried his head between the valley of her cleavage.

He was strung so tight he would snap at the slightest touch. He struggled for control and willed her not to speak. She apparently didn't hear his silent request.

"Dwayne?"

His hands tightened to fists at her waist. "Give me a minute, please."

She rubbed a palm down the back of his head, and each damn move reminded him of how close he was, yet how far. "Brooke," he cautioned.

"What is it? Are you hurt?" She took his face in her palms. He stared up at her, letting the lust, frustration, and need show.

"Sweet sprite," he warned, "I'm trying to stick by my word, so I'll give you a fair chance now. In ten seconds, I'm going to get off this floor, turn on the shower, and shed these too damn tight boxers. If you're still in here, I'm dragging you under the water with me and will end up having my way between your sweet thighs. I know you said you're not ready, so I'm giving you a fair amount of warning to escape."

In less than five, she was out the door.

Chapter Seventeen

Back in the car, lush, green scenery rolled by in a haze of blurred shapes. Brooke took in the pretty slopes of hillside landscapes, the changing colors of fall, bright bursts of red, orange, and yellow. It was far out of reach, existing in a separate plane of the world.

A beautiful sight, but her mind was caught in this morning's scene in the hotel bathroom. Never had she experienced such pleasure, and most certainly not from a man touching her. He had done more than that, hadn't he? He'd worshiped her chest as if a drug to an addict, lapped in loving caresses with his tongue and sucked with erotic delight on her nipples. Her toes curled inside her Uggs. She hadn't known an orgasm could be achieved that way, simply from attention on her breasts, and the crest had taken her by surprise when it broke.

It hadn't come on fast and hard, but instead the peak built slow, like hot lava flowing over the crown of its mountain peak. She had been lost in the mind-numbing pleasure, crying out with wild abandon, uncaring of who heard or what she said. Something she never thought possible. More so, her reaction to Dwayne, and how much more she wanted, had shocked her to her core.

If his mouth produced such results when touching one part of her, what would happen if his focus were directed across her entire body?

Yet, wasn't this what Dwayne did? Give pleasure and take it? Albeit, he had not demanded or expected anything in return. No, he had given her a short warning and allowed her to flee.

And, did she ever escape. It wasn't about the promise he held in his eyes, or even the principle erotic threat. But more about the rush of feelings screaming through her, the very ones she had been trying to protect herself from.

She didn't take sex as a casual affair. The blast of affection blindsided her, scared the shit outta her, and snapped her out of the haze he brought her to.

Jesus—she closed her eyes—*can I do this?*

Brooke focused on the slight rocking of the car, the soft music playing, and the *whoosh* of wind outside. Everything seemed magnified, colors brighter, the gentle rocking of the vehicle more pronounced. She was very, very aware of him, drawn to Dwayne like a magnet. She was all too cognizant of the exact spot where he sat, of the small car they were trapped inside, and of the still-viable sexual tension screaming through the air.

His scent, woodsy and raw, filled her lungs. His presence, larger than life, dominant without trying, demanded she acknowledge him.

"A penny for your thoughts?" he asked.

She sighed, turned and focused on his profile. A sprinkle of light stubble lined the square of his jaw. A sight outside of this normally perfected man who wore his impeccable suits like armor. And his lush lips, so full and plush, brought back the memories of this morning and held her rapt attention.

"Nothing. Worried about Hailey," she lied, too wrapped in this man. No need for him to know how much control he had.

He glanced over and smiled. "We're going to do what we can to make sure she is found."

She blinked. "We?"

He nodded, then shifted in his seat and took her hand. An act so new and unfamiliar, it took her a moment to focus on what he said. "Yeah, I talked to Trent last night. He's done some research and if we confirm Hailey is up here, this matter will move into the FBI's jurisdiction. Moving a minor across state lines is a felony, falls under title eighteen of the United States Code. Not only that," he added, "but if Hailey has been mixed up with what we suspect she has, then there is going to be a whole plethora of statutes involved, and it could end up being a huge bust." He gave her palm a squeeze. "We're going to get her, though."

She swallowed and forced down the bile burning in her throat as Dwayne voiced the fears she had been thinking. "So Trent's going to come up?"

He focused on the road. "It's very likely. Again, I need to verify either she's here first, or get enough evidence to suspect she's present. Right now I can only assume she is because that's where Jaxon is, and that's where his phone has pinged. I'm not acting as a law enforcement officer here, sweetheart. There's only so much I'll be able to do. We need to be smart, otherwise, we could lose her forever. I know you're jumping at the chance to get her back, but I'm going to ask you to trust me with this. If I ask you to do something, you need to have faith it's the right decision."

She frowned. "What aren't you telling me? And who else would Trent bring with him? What's going on?"

He pushed back on the seat and shifted again. She glanced down and realized what must have been bothering him. His handgun, black and lethal, sat at the small of his back, digging into muscle. Before she could offer to help, he spoke.

"Sex trafficking of children is something hard to keep track of. They move these children via highly secretive schedules. In addition, when the first sign of a cop starts sniffing around, the entire operation relocates overnight. Under the statute, even if Hailey hadn't been moved over state lines, it still would have been a felony.

The penalties are severe for those caught, which is why the ones who normally operate these kinds of schemes are quick to move if they even suspect they are being watched." He glanced over at her. "The sentence is a minimum of fifteen years. Not only that, but the defendants in these cases are usually required to pay restitution to the families, as well as payment for the medical treatment needed. All combined, makes this type of operation highly suspicious of outsiders."

Riveted by his words, she grasped his hand and didn't realize how hard she'd squeezed until his thumb traced the skin. She relaxed, fighting to keep her emotions bottled.

"Most times," he continued, "the offenders of this crime—the pimps, traffickers, or bosses—will use drugs, hardcore ones, to control and push the minors to either submit or give in to having sex. They do this not only to control the child in the beginning through the use of drug-induced hazes, but then later when it's so painful to go without the drug, the child will do whatever they need just to get the next hit."

She sucked in a sharp breath and it hitched. Her vision grew hazy. "So you're saying if Hailey…"

His lips thinned and he nodded. "You need to be prepared for anything. If she's involved in what we believe, she could very well have drugs in her system and will possibly have developed a dependency to one."

"What," she began and had to clear her throat against the tightness. "What kinds of drugs?" How had this happened? Her sweet, beautiful daughter caught in such an ugly world and changed forever wasn't something she ever thought would be possible.

He winced, then shook his head. "It's not pretty. It's going to be hard. I won't lie. But we're looking at possibly heroine, crack, meth, the list can go on and on, but they are all hardcore.

"Outside of that, you'll see most of these operations either ran out of a house or nightclub. The place where we're heading looks to be a club. It hasn't been in business for too long, only eight months or so, but has been on the RISP's radar for about a month."

Hailey's future and her well-being flashed through Brooke's mind. If she was caught in what they thought she was, her daughter would never be the same. The lost innocence made her want to cry, scream, and punch at the unfairness of it all.

She drew her head back. "Wait, you know all of this just from a phone call?"

He looked over and winked. "Several phone calls, sweetheart. It's good to know people."

How could he wink when her world crumbled around her? "Who else?"

"My brothers. This is what we do, and they are the other part of 'we' I'm talking about."

Her world brightened just a bit at the mention of the rest of the Gonzalez tribe. It'd been years since she'd seen any of them. "Oh my God, it's been forever since I've seen them. How are they?" she asked, memories of each different boy rolling through her head, all different, but held together by a strong bond—family.

His lips curved, something he always did when speaking of his siblings. "Well hell, you're talking a clan here, Brooke. You're going to have to be more specific. Which one?"

She squeezed his hand, taking in his strength even though he probably didn't realize it. "All of them. Please, talk to me about them. Take my mind off this nightmare."

He looked over, seeming to measure her for a few moments before returning his attention to the road. He flexed his fingers in hers. "If I could take this all away, I would. You know that, right?"

She swallowed, forcing down the knot in her throat. "I know."

Dwayne took a deep breath and let the air out in a measured exhale. "All right, let's start at the top, then. Chris is still in Afghanistan on some deep undercover mission. I don't know exactly where, as he couldn't reveal it, but I do know the country. He's been ghost for a few months now, and the only reason we know he's still alive is he sends Ma e-mails. They consist of a few sentences, but he checks in with regular intervals because he knows she worries."

"What does ghost mean?"

He licked his lips. "Deep black ops. Really undercover, so much so the government has blacked out his file."

"Ah, I get it now. Ghost. Huh, cute."

He arched a brow and glanced over again. "I don't know about cute, but it definitely gets attention." He smiled and turned his concentration back to the road. "Mike just got assigned to the Westchester office for the Secret Service. He's settling in and seems to be running some line on the Ukrainian mafia. Don't ask me what it entails, but it sounds all kinds of complicated.

"Then you have Matt, who's still with the DEA. He's been doing bust after bust at JFK Airport, pulling in a rash of cocaine coming in from Latin America. He's recently gotten himself a girlfriend, and the rest of us have a pool to see how long it lasts."

He grinned, a wicked kind of smile, and she laughed despite the circumstances. "You all are awful."

He shrugged, the grin still in place.

"Jake is still in the city, was assigned a new partner. He's working homicides, and seems to be okay. Then again, he doesn't really talk a whole lot, as I'm sure you remember," Dwayne said with a glance at her. She smiled and nodded.

"And then Luke just finished the academy in Texas for the Marshals. He's coming home for a few weeks until he's shipped off to his first office."

"Do you know where they will send him?"

"Yeah. Looks to be the city. He's only a few hours behind us, so you'll see him before the others."

The weight came crashing down on her shoulders. "You all would do this for me? For Hailey and I?"

* * * *

Dwayne fought to find the answer. He didn't want to scare her, and the words hovering on his tongue would do that. How did he tell Brooke his brothers knew exactly how he had felt about her for so long? How could he explain she was his family and by that link, a pseudo sister to his siblings? He cleared his thoughts and pushed the warnings in his mind away.

"Why wouldn't we help? I'd like to hear your answer before I get to yours."

She hesitated. "I—I don't know. I've never had someone go so far to help us."

"Hell, sweetheart, you're going to have to get used to it. I told you I'm intent to have you, and this is a package deal."

She stiffened. A subtle movement, but then again, he was a trained detective. He tried not to let it bother him, but it was difficult.

"I know what you said, and sex is just sex. There isn't any commitment involved. You've shown that to be the case time and time again. It isn't a big secret," she said.

Frustration surged. So, they were back to this again. "And like I told you, you're different. What makes you think it's just sex?"

She shrugged, then turned in her seat and glanced out the window, her attempt on shutting him out.

Bull. Shit.

"Brooke, answer me," he urged.

She huffed, a heavy sigh. "Because that's all it can be."

She wouldn't look at him and despite him driving the car, he wanted to reach over and shake some sense into her. Why didn't she see it?

"Look," she pressed, "I get you like to have fun. And hell, being a good-looking guy who knows how to please a woman, or one that women *want* to please them…no one is holding that against you."

"You are," he jumped in. "You are very much holding that fact against me." He tried not to let the anger through his words, but from her wince, he failed.

"I'm not," she continued. "But for me, it's different. I've already told you it's hard for me to give in to a physical relationship without my heart feeling the effects. I'm not like that, and while I wish I could be, it's just not in the cards. Moreover, you aren't a one-woman kind of guy, Dwayne. You have never been one. So, while I'll try to give this one side of our relationship a shot, I can't promise anything more. Especially now, especially with everything going on with Hailey. I can't let my heart get too wrapped up in whatever is going on, and I refuse to let you stomp on it."

He released her hand as if he had been smacked. Her words were like a physical blow across his face. He understood she was stressed, got the worry she had for her daughter. Lines had etched into her face in the past few days, indicators this was hard on her. However, how she saw him, how she explained who she thought he was, burned. They had been friends for so long, his affection for her almost as long. Yet, still, seeing himself as she did made him feel cheap…dirty.

He didn't want to press things too far with her, not now when everything was riding on the next few hours. She wouldn't be able to handle the pressure of it all. And while he wanted nothing more than to sink inside her body, he wondered if now, after her speech and low-lying opinion of him, if he was taking the right path.

Damn it! No way in hell he would be any use to anyone if his mind stayed tangled up in the situation he and Brooke had gotten into. It was his fault, but still…

A scenic stop came into view and he jerked off the road, drew the car to a halt, and slammed it in park. She stared at him with wide eyes and opened her mouth, but he cut her off.

"Get out."

She frowned, glancing around. "Dwayne, what?"

"Get out of the fucking car, Brooke. We're going to settle something right now."

She shrank back, and he cursed. He didn't mean to scare her, but damn if his ego wasn't bruised. He started to apologize, but she got out of the car and slammed the door while his mouth gaped.

He laid his head back against the rest for a moment before he followed.

He skirted the hood. Brooke stood against the wooden beams marking the cliff's drop off. This high up, the valley of trees and a blue river spread out beneath them. He had been too involved in his conversation before, but the scene was majestic and glorified Mother Nature's true gift—creating visions that made you stop and enjoy life.

He stopped next to her, looking out across the land. Dots of deep red danced around colors of burnt orange and deeper shades of green. The river, a crisp blue that reminded him of Brooke's eyes, turned the scene into something fresh, clean. Everything unlike what he felt in the moment.

He turned to face her, then tugged her into his arms. She came on her own accord—*thank God!*—and rested her head against his chest. He wanted her here forever. Picturing the two of them growing old, raising children, and sitting in rocking chairs watching their grandbabies was easy. With her in his embrace, this was everything he sought, yet still, the wish seemed so far away. He grasped for the right words, overthought them, and decided in the end, he needed to lay it all on the line.

"I'm not the guy you think I am," he started.

She stiffened and went to draw away. He tightened his grip and held her still.

"No, wait. Let me speak." He waited until she relaxed. "I don't want to push you on this. I don't want it to seem as if I'm pressuring you into doing something you don't want. If you can't reciprocate my feelings I have for you, then let me know now. I won't say that I will not be disappointed. Hell, I would. And I'm not saying this just to get in your pants. This is more. Something that doesn't come around that often. Maybe once in a lifetime. What I feel for you, Brooke, goes much deeper than a friendship. And my past shouldn't have any bearings. I know it does, but I won't apologize for who I am or for the decisions I have made.

"Those women, the relationships or time I spent with each, have made me into the man I am today. I don't regret a single moment of it. I went in to each one's arms where both sides knew what I could and couldn't give. Each one knew I wouldn't be able to offer them more.

"Does that say something about who I've become? Does it make me question who I want to be? Yes, of course it does. But what I feel for you has nothing on that."

He drew back, held her waist to him with one arm and tipped her chin up to meet his gaze with the other. Wind brushed past, sending tendrils of her hair spreading around them.

"Don't assume I'm that guy. I would hate to tell you you're wrong, but I'd be glad to prove it to you."

She searched his eyes, pain and confusion clear for anyone to see. Damn. Fighting for something you wanted so bad shouldn't be so hard. He wanted her to say something—anything!

"Close your eyes," she whispered.

He almost missed it, but the sound pierced his ears. He frowned. "What?"

"Close your eyes," she said louder.

His heart sank. She couldn't even meet his gaze when she talked. This couldn't be good. He gave in to her request and shut his lids, dropped his head and rested against hers. He wouldn't make this hard on her, no matter how fucking much her dismissal would crush him.

She shifted and something brushed against his mouth. Light, comparable to a moth's touch. Her breath played over his. She pressed her mouth to his and he sucked in a sharp gasp. He let her guide the way, allowed her to control the embrace, still too shocked to do anything else.

Her warm tongue traced the seam of his lips, circling until he parted. Their breaths mingled. She palmed the back of his head and kissed him. Air rushed from his lungs. Her tongue pushed inside his mouth to tangle against his. The kiss was sweet, soft, slow, and sensual. It spoke the words he was unable to find earlier and said more than he thought possible.

She was giving him a chance, communicating in the way she knew how. It hit him like a sledgehammer to his chest, driving away all thoughts but the feel of her in his arms. Her mouth fused to his, her grip steady and sure around him.

With a sigh, he gave in and crushed her closer, pushing the kiss deeper.

If this was all he could get for now, it would have to be more than enough.

Chapter Eighteen

Hours later, Dwayne sat back in the leather tub chair, arms crossed over his chest, and stared at the laptop screen. Trent, coming through like the true special agent he was, had sent mounds of information on this local club and the suspected ring inside. With an opening of, *Don't do anything until we get there, and for fuck's sake, keep your head down,* he knew the e-mail couldn't be good.

What followed that joyful greeting churned his stomach, caused bile to creep up the back of his throat, and had his pulse pounding behind his eyes. *Fuck!*

According to the FBI, the club had been under surveillance for eight months, suspected of moving trafficked teens in and out as if they were cattle, changeovers happening faster than one could blink. So close to the shore of the Atlantic, the crew running this operation stayed under the radar and was, to quote from the report, "A highly successful operating scheme."

So why in the fuck hadn't they busted the joint up yet?

Getting behind scenes from the main club proved difficult. If the guards sniffed so much as a cop anywhere in your family's bloodline, they turned you away. Agent upon agent, cop upon detective had tried to get back there and so far, no luck. Moreover, with the club bringing in much of the town's revenue on taxes, the low-key residential placement, and the lack of complaints—no judge deemed it worthwhile to issue a warrant.

Goddamn bureaucratic assholes.

He ran his fingers through his hair, his body itching to run in and pull Hailey out now. He didn't want to picture what must have been happening there, but after reading the report, spending the better part of an hour glued to the screen, images slammed into his mind.

Hailey forced to have sex.

Hailey drugged and left to fend for herself.

Hailey so doped up she did not understand what was going on.

Oh, how he hated to admit it, but he willed for the last to be true. He did not want her to be aware of what was going on. And if his luck changed, from everything Trent had pulled on Jaxon—she would be stoned out of her mind.

In the time the club had been under surveillance, an approximate one hundred thousand children were suspected to have been pushed through. More so, eyewitness accounts and johns arrested put the youngest victim at thirteen. Many of these adolescents were runaways, promised love and companionship, hell, even given a few precious months in an established relationship before they were turned over. It all made sense now, the fast track of a bond with Jaxon, the aggressive and overbearing way the kid had been with Hailey, the alarm screaming in the back of Dwayne's head anytime he saw them together.

Why hadn't he paid more attention?

What kind of fucked up cop was he?

As he read the report further, his gut churned with nausea. Another problem here was what happened after one of those victims escaped. The last one had been killed after apparently being under police custody for only thirty-six hours. It made the hairs on the back of his neck stand—to think that one of his own, a brother in blue, had allowed this to happen. The writing that this cop had allowed this was as clear as the sky in the summer. And that cop was still under investigation.

The victim, before she had been able to give a sworn statement, described to the detectives how she had been wrapped up in the scheme. Only sixteen, threatened with harm to her and her family if she didn't comply, Jessica Garcia would sneak out of her house at night after getting a call demanding her service. With no time to change, a car would pick her up down the street and take her to a client's home.

Once there, she was forced to get undressed, lie on the bed and remain quiet. If a client asked her name, she had to keep silent. She was never left alone with the men, and many times her pimps stayed by her side, watching, sometimes joining in the sexual acts.

"My legs were tied down," the deposition read, "and the guy raped me over and over. I screamed for them to stop, tried to fight them off, but they were so strong, and I was weak. I passed out a few times and each awaking, found a new man on top of me."

Christ! Dwayne stood, glared at the laptop, and paced the room. He couldn't show this to Brooke. She would freak and after the past few days, he doubted she could take much more. Arriving a little over two hours ago, they'd checked into a hotel—this time one with two queen-size beds—and she'd disappeared into the bathroom moments later.

On one hand, he knew she was afraid to be alone with him, but on the other, he understood her need to work things through in her own way. He hadn't held back on the drive up, refused to let her hopes get too high. The letdown, should something go wrong, would kill her. She needed to be aware of what they were dealing with. But this, the report pretty much confirmed what was happening inside the club. There was very little left to give hope to.

A door clicked open behind him and he reached the laptop a step later and shut the lid, then turned to her.

Her cheeks were flushed from the heat of a bath,

skin dewy from the steam. Her hair fell, a sunset over the horizon, trailing in a long braid as thick as his wrist, over one shoulder. Her bright blue eyes dazzled, shone like a piece of heaven. In addition—*fuck me now*—all she wore was the complimentary white bathrobe with the hotel's name over the right breast.

Blood surged to his groin, and despite what he had read, the nightmare entrapping Hailey, he wanted Brooke.

You are a piece of fucking work, Gonzalez.

She glanced at his closed computer and back to him. "Have you heard anything?"

He shook his head. "Not yet," he lied. "Everyone should be up here by tomorrow, though, and then we can put in some more concrete plans about what we're going to do."

Despair etched between her brows, drawing them together. "Tomorrow? We can't wait. She's there now. We're here, so close. We have to go get her."

Her gaze, wild and frightened, similar to a hunted doe, speared him across the room. He crossed to her with long strides and quick steps, took ahold of her shoulders. "I know what you're feeling, but you need to stop it. We can't go charging in there. I've explained this." Dwayne took in a deep breath and pushed it out slow, trying like hell to fight against the urge to act. He wanted to go get Hailey now, too.

"I want to get her home as well," he said. "But, we need to be smart, take a look at what we're dealing with here, and size up what's going on inside that club. From what I've read, it's hard as hell to get in the back, so there's no promise we'll be able to do so. One way or the other, though, we're going to get her," he promised— and hoped like hell he could carry through.

She drew back and pulled away from his touch.

He tightened his jaw.

"I thought you said you hadn't heard anything," she accused.

Shit.

He backpedaled, choosing each word with care. "I did get a report from Trent, yes. However, as far as a plan, no. The report is just FBI bullshit, nothing you should concern yourself with at this point."

Her spine stiffened. "Nothing I should concern myself with? This is my daughter." She spoke through clenched teeth.

His chest ached at the helplessness written across her features. He knew just how she felt. His own hands were tied and bound behind his back. Seeing things from the other side of the law, as a victim, threw a punch to his gut at how people must feel when the police couldn't help, or even worse, refused to. He kept reminding himself things could get much worse. At least now, they had a chance, a direction to move in. Should she disappear from the club...or should she already be gone...

Any chance in bringing her home would be lost.

A chime echoed in the room, Brooke's cellphone coming to life. She tore her gaze from his and gave him her back. He dropped his head and rubbed the bridge of his nose, exhaustion and frustration pulsing, changing into a throbbing mess between his eyes. He had planned to go to the club tonight, just to scope things out, but Trent's words of caution held him back. At least for right now.

The ringing stopped and Brooke's voice cut through his thoughts.

"Hello?"

* * * *

"Mom?"

Brooke gasped and her heart jumped into her throat. Hailey. She sounded tired, her speech slurred, muffled, as if she held a sheet over the phone. But it was her, and she was alive. Relief, so profound and strong, surged.

"Hails? Oh my God, baby, where are you? Are you okay? Tell me where you are, I'll come get you."

Dwayne was at her side in an instant, but she didn't look at him, couldn't. She stared straight ahead at the white wall, trying to hear anything, something that would help her get to her daughter.

"They left us here." Her words rumbled out as if she was inside some tunnel. "They never leave us."

"Who, Hailey? Who left you? Where?"

"I don't—I don't know." Her breath hitched and it tore through Brooke's heart. "Mommy, I want to go home. Please, come take me home."

Her sight grew hazy as tears stung. "Oh, baby, Mommy will come get you. Tell me where you are," she choked.

"I don't know!"

"Hey!" A distinct male voice popped in the background on the other side. Alarm spread, settling like a concrete weight in Brooke's stomach.

"Mom!"

"Put the fucking phone down, bitch. You want to call out, I'll give you something to call for."

"Hailey!" Brooke screamed.

"Mom!"

The cell left her hand and Dwayne brought it up to his ear, a murderous look darkening his features. "Hailey?"

He glanced down at her, brows drawn together, sadness in his eyes. The device clicked shut a moment later and he sighed. "Fuck! They hung up."

"No!" She fisted her hands and pounded against his chest, tears leaking down her face, dropping from her chin. "No, get her back. Get her back, now!" Pressure built in her throat, then broke free and sailed out as a sob. The sweet sound of her daughter still filled her head but combined with it was fear. The terrified voice was so far off from Hailey, was one she almost didn't recognize.

Dwayne stilled her hands, brought her up against his chest and pressed a large palm to the back of her head.

"Please, go get her," she pleaded.

"I will, sweetheart. I promise you, I will."

She sobbed. Pain pierced through her chest, the helplessness of being unable to protect her daughter scraping her throat raw. She didn't know how long she stood like that, held in his strong, warm arms. But after some time she recognized the steady beat of his pulse beneath her ear. He took her face in his hands and wiped at the wetness on her cheeks with his thumbs. His stare pierced straight through her.

"I'm going to take a quick shower and see about heading over to the club. I don't know what will happen, but if anything, at least I'll have a heads-up on the layout. I need you to stay here, and stay in this room. Do you understand me?"

She shook her head. "No, take me with you. I can help."

He dropped his head to hers. His face crumpled in agony. "I won't take that chance." He gave her shoulders a quick squeeze and pulled away, walked over to his bag and began to go through it, then pulled out a dark shirt and black jeans.

"If I take you with me we run into several problems. One, you look so much like Hailey, or rather she like you, that anyone will grow suspicious as soon as you walk in. If they are suspicious, we won't get anywhere and the entire plan any of us come up with will more than likely go down the drain."

He stood and faced her, clothes held in hand. His words made sense, she understood that, but her heart cried out for Hailey.

"Two, if I take you in there, I will be more worried about watching out for you than anything else. I won't be able to concentrate." He shook his head, his next words spoken with more authority. "No, I need you to stay here. Please, Brooke. This is one of those times I need you to trust me."

She didn't like the idea of staying back and fought the urge to demand he take her. To tell him she would go whether he brought her along or not. Instead, she held her tongue. "What will you do?"

He shrugged, dropped his gaze from hers, and moved for the bathroom. "Look around, see how far back I can get."

"What do you mean, how far back?"

He stopped at the door, the muscles in his body rigid. "I've explained a few things to you already, right?"

She nodded.

"So you know what happens in this club, right?"

She nodded again, and her eyes stung with tears. The look on his face shredded her heart.

"I need to get behind the scenes," he stated.

She frowned, his words not making sense. He wasn't telling her something…

"Behind the scenes? Dwayne, you're talking in circles. Stop shutting me out. Talk to me."

"Christ!" he barked and whirled around. She took a step back at the expression on his face. No longer was he the charming man women of Nyack couldn't stay away from, nor was he the childhood friend who had laughed and played with her for hours. Instead, disgust, fury, and a bit of anger etched his features as if it pained him to contemplate, much less speak what he said next.

"What do you think?" he asked through clenched teeth. "I'm going to have to pretend that I'm there to get in bed with little girls. I have no clue what I'm going to have to do, how *far* I'm going to have to go. I'm out on my own here, and I'm putting together ideas as I go along. I'll have to play the part of the scumbags whose faces I want to beat in, the very ones who are probably trying to get to—"

He snapped his jaw shut but she couldn't mistake what he had been about to say.

"To Hailey, is that what you were going to say?" she asked.

His features softened and he dropped his shoulders. "I'm sorry, but I'm not too keen on doing this, pretending to be this type of guy."

She swallowed, forcing the lump in her throat down. To consider what Hailey was going through...

"I know, and I'm sorry to ask you to do this. If I could go to anyone else, I would."

His lips thinned. He took a step toward her and dropped his head until it was inches from hers.

"You're going to stop that line of thinking, right now. Hailey is important to me, too, dammit. I would do this even if you didn't ask me."

She sighed and he spoke again.

"Do you ever consider that maybe these men have more in common with me than anyone else?" he asked, drawing up to his full height and rubbing at his eyes. He looked exhausted, defeated, and worn down.

Her frown grew. "They are nothing like you," she stated, meaning it.

He cut her off with a quick hand through the air.

"My mother brought men identical to these assholes home. All the time. Men who wanted to tie her up and do *things*," he spat the word, "with her, *to* her. I was forced to watch all the cruel disgusting acts. And when they would start beating on her, I tried to force myself between them. Only after my arm was broken by her pimp, did I learn my lesson and stay far away, helpless and too fucking small to do anything but pay witness."

She stared, understanding dawning. "Dwayne…"

Pain crossed his features before he pivoted away but didn't move far. "Forget it. I'm sorry I brought it up."

They stood, silent and caught in their own thoughts for several moments.

"If this is too much to ask…"

He sighed. Loud. But still he kept his back to her.

"Like I said, I'd do it anyways. This won't be a proud moment, this pretending to want things from these women. These *girls*," he corrected. "Damn it," he muttered, his voice smaller than she'd ever heard before. Her heart went out to him. This proud, brave man.

"So you'll get close to them? You said it would be hard to get behind the scenes. Do you think these girls will be in the main part of the club?" she asked.

"No, these will be regular females, strippers, hookers, escorts. They'll feel me out before taking it to the next step."

"How do you know that?" she asked.

He shook his head and didn't answer.

"What's the next step?" She shifted, stepped to his side, and looked up. Disgust, whether at himself or what he had to do, displayed across his face like camo paint.

"Sex."

That made her brows rise. "You'll have sex with them? Tonight?" She fought the uneasy feeling, pushed down on the swirling sensation in her stomach.

He snapped his gaze to hers. "No," he said with a harsh voice. "But I will have to lead them on to believe that I want to. You understand this is a role, right? That I want no part of these women?"

She shrugged and turned away. Feelings she didn't realize she had, more questions than she wanted answered pounded into her mind, comparable to a sledgehammer on the streets of New York City.

"You can do whatever you like. We've discussed this. I have no claim on you. I just don't want you to do something you don't want to."

You are such a liar, girl.

He snorted behind her, the sound unpleasant. "Look at me, Brooke."

She faced him, slowly lifting her gaze to his. Features strained, his body shaking with unspent emotion of some sort, he held her stare.

"You keep telling yourself that. The no claim comment. Here's what I'm going to say to you, and this will be the last goddamn time I say it.

"I care for you. I feel things I've never felt for another. I have now for a very long time. If you want to keep tossing my words, my actions, on the ground, please do me the favor and just stop. I can take rejection, Brooke. Believe it or not, it has happened before. However, what I will not do is not be given one ounce of a thought toward any chance and then have it thrown in my face.

"You may not feel you have a claim on me, but I think that's bullshit. I more than recognize your claim and choose to honor it. If I could stay here and simply hold you, I'd be a happier man than taking any or all of those women in the club to bed. It's *you* I want to be with, not them. But right now, with how you keep shitting on me, I imagine I'd find more warmth in the arms of a hooker."

She gasped, his words like a slap.

He winced, shook his head, and turned, muttering, "Forget it." The bathroom door slammed behind him.

Brooke stared at the wood panel in shock. His words struck a chord inside. Had she treated him the way he said? She tried to remember everything, to piece together the actions with the man she knew, the one who switched beds faster than anyone else. None of it made sense. If he cared for her for so long, why now? Why hadn't he said anything before?

Dwayne had always been there for her. He came when she called, didn't ask questions and at times, dropped everything…for her. Did she take advantage of his friendship? Had she recognized his feelings before now and used it against him?

More so, how did she feel? She cared for him, yes. Her attraction was no surprise or even under question. Just looking at him, being near him and smelling his unique scent had her heating with sexual awareness. And when he watched at her, the fire in his eyes more than spoke of what they could generate.

She dropped to the bed and stared ahead, her mind torn between her daughter, what she wanted from Dwayne, and what she could give.

If she had no claim on him, then why did the thought of any woman other than her touching him bring such a tight pain to her chest?

Chapter Nineteen

Music pulsed through the speakers at a rate double his heartbeat. Bass vibrated through Dwayne's chest, giving him the feeling of free falling off a cliff. He scanned the room, looked past the crowds who danced in the center, beyond the workers, the girls, and the mean-looking guards standing in the back.

The room's black walls had LED decals twirling in unusual shapes and different drawn faces that changed colors from orange, to a vivid blue, starched violet, lemony yellow. In the back corners, women danced on raised platforms, wearing no more than floss and small stickers to cover their assets. Two more erotic dancers caged the bar in at the sides, seeming to catch the eye of any one that passed, and then moved for just him alone, as if they were the last man on earth.

He made his way to the blood-red satin lined bar, leather stools spread at intervals alongside. The bodies packed into the club brought the temperature to the triple digits. But despite that, the bar was devoid of people. He caught the glow of a necklace as a bikini clad brunette passed him carrying a tray full of tube shots. Another crossed his path, her load consisting of plastic cups of amber beer.

At the bar, he slid into a seat at the end, keeping his back to the stripper. There were many threats around him, men walking around with bulges sticking out from beneath their shirt, a shape no one could mistake for anything other than a weapon. A few beefy-looking women were walking around with the same. Then you had the cameras installed in the ceiling, watching everyone and anything that moved. Considering the stripper behind him didn't wear enough clothing to conceal anything, she was the least of his worries. In a club like this, selling goods as they did, he would not have to wait long to be approached.

And he wasn't wrong.

After a few minutes, a dark-skinned man greeted him from behind the bar. The bartender had deep, chocolate-brown eyes, a wide nose, trim goatee, and thick arms, perhaps wider than his thigh. A black t-shirt screamed for mercy across a chest he figured he'd need a climbing harness—or an ATV—to hike over.

"What can I get you?" the mountain of a guy asked.

Dwayne skimmed over the line of taps and each label. "I'll take your best on tap."

Mr. Mountain nodded, retrieved the drink and set it in front of him. He took a red bar cloth from the back of his jeans and wiped his hands, but his attention remained on Dwayne.

He recognized what the guy was doing: measuring him up, determining the threat, gathering information for no doubt who watched from behind the camera. He didn't blame him, would do it himself if the situation were reversed. However, the thing was, it would never be that way, because he fought for the right side of the law. Coming in here to play, pretend and schmooze with scum was not something he looked forward to, but it was necessary.

He met the man's stare. "Can I help you with something?" He had to speak slightly louder than normal, but for some reason the sound level around the bar seemed muted.

Again, with those brows. They popped up in surprise, and it looked as if the guy wore caterpillars above his eyes. He really should talk to the dude about some manscaping.

"Shouldn't that be my line?" Mountain asked.

Dwayne shrugged, took a gulp of his drink.

"Haven't seen you around here before. From out of town?"

He held his gaze. Mountain's eyes were intense and full of questions, but Dwayne refused to back down or give him specific answers. "You could say that."

"I could…but how about I ask where you're from instead?"

Hell…damn nosy bartender. "New York," Dwayne answered.

"Long way from home. What brought you up this way?"

He took another drink, then made a quick look at the mirror behind the bar. He didn't doubt it was a two-way glass. Only question was, what—or who—was on the other side?

"Was in the mood to switch things up a bit. Get a taste for something fresh," he lied.

You're a goddamn piece of work, Gonzalez. Feeling good about yourself now?

No, no he wasn't.

"Fresh, huh?" The bartender leaned forward and set heavy arms on top of the wood, scanning the crowd, but Dwayne wasn't fooled. This guy's attention centered on him and only him.

Dwayne took the opportunity and turned to the side for a better view. Having people at his back made his neck itch, his shoulders twitch, and his cop instincts scream.

"We've got a whole batch of fresh meat for you here. All different flavors. Perhaps you might want to take a look around?"

He made a point to look at each of the dancer platforms. Let his gaze pause on each woman, brought his reactions of disapproval, minimal interest to his face as he passed each one. "Eh, I'm looking for something a bit more tender. Something new, not all that experienced."

"I could put in a good word, for the right amount, that is, and get you some time with a few that would treat you real nice."

He lifted his brows, allowing the interest to show. Eyeing Mountain over the rim of his mug, he gave a distinct, minute nod. He brought the glass down, reached into his side pocket and drew out a wallet. Lesson number one: When going into a strange or crowded place, never carry your shit in your back pocket. All it takes is a female to move close and half your life, along with your cash, would disappear.

He tossed a Benjamin on the counter. "Make sure she's impressionable, if you catch my drift."

You are full of it tonight, dude. Look at you!

The guy nodded, stepped away and picked up a black phone, eyeing Dwayne over his shoulder. The camera above moved and focused on him.

Oh hell, this was going to happen. He needed to keep his head together, his senses up, and an eye out for Hailey. Trying to act on anything tonight would get him a lot of lead and empty air.

Keep your cool, stay calm. Play the part. Forget you're a detective.

A tall and skinny white male, bald-headed, same goatee as the bartender stepped up to his side. "I hear you're in the market for a good time."

Dwayne skimmed the guy's attire. Another black shirt, this one long-sleeved, matching jeans, and dark black boots screamed security. He couldn't hesitate but had to give the impression he was willing to be meticulous and wait. "I like my meals crisp, fresh."

The man stared, unflinching, doing the same as the bartender did earlier. "Going to run you three c-notes tonight. Another four tomorrow if you make it past this first part and want to dive a little…deeper."

Three hundred dollars? Christ. No wonder these people had resources at their disposal. He nodded and passed over the money like he didn't have a care in the world.

"Pleasure doing business with you. This way."

Dwayne tossed back the rest of his beer and stood to follow. It wasn't hard to keep an eye on the guy. He towered over the crowd, the giant mounted like a sore thumb with his bald head.

Surprise skittered through him at just how easy this was, getting back behind the scenes. If it could be so simple, the hope that they'd find Hailey soon could flame. As it was, he pushed down on that thought and added some patience. They'd know soon enough.

He shoved his way through the crowd, receiving more than one suggestion from both genders, seductive glances from almost everyone, and by the time he reached the back wall, he felt more than a little violated.

Suck it up, chump. This is for Hailey.

Instead of going through the heavily guarded area he'd spotted when he first walked in, they veered off to the left and pushed through a curtain of midnight softness. The music from the club muted, and lenient lights skimmed over individual corners of the room, velvet l-shaped couches spread throughout. In the back corner, a woman danced for a man, her bare breasts swaying with seduction. The man had a head full of gray hair, his back to Dwayne.

Giant motioned to a separate blue couch. He slid onto the velvet, facing where he had entered, and waited in silence. A few minutes after the guy disappeared, a soft touch brushed his shoulder.

Shit! A door must have been at the back of the room for he didn't see the dark, exotic girl approach. And girl she was. Most likely still legal age, but with small, elfin features, she resembled a young child with pert breasts, a miniature waist, and even tinier hips. She wore black boy-shorts and a matching bikini top. Glitter was painted across her revealed skin, giving the impression of her shimmering under the black lights.

"Hi, papi. Are you looking for some company."

The guy had given him a test. He recognized it at once. This was the first phase, one to see his reaction, how far he'd let her push. If he were a cop, he would have to stop things before they went that extra step. At least that's what they thought. More than familiar with the law, Dwayne knew there were certain measures they could take while undercover.

He refused to have sex with this woman, but perhaps a bit of PG-13 action would keep the bosses happy and satisfied. Besides, from her glazed look, he doubted she'd even notice.

Her touch left his shoulder and her form appeared in front of him. She leaned over, set her hands on the back of the couch, and set her face within inches of his. Stale smoke, the distinct scent of alcoholic drinks, and cheap perfume invaded his senses. Underneath, the smell of an unwashed body made him want to pull away.

Fucking-a.

"You look good enough to lick," she purred.

Her nose brushed along his cheek and he refused to relax. Waited and watched.

"Do I need to go over the rules for you, sexy?" she asked.

He cleared his throat, fighting the revulsion her touch created. While he saw the age in her eyes, her figure was all wrong.

"Sure."

"First, you can get as aggressive as you like, but leave a mark, and Tom over there will tear you to shreds."

Dwayne glanced in the direction of her nod and saw Giant waiting, gaze glued to a monitor sticking out from the wall. He spoke low on a phone, not sparing them a glance.

"Second, I'll provide the protection if you don't have it."

As if it would go that far. He didn't see how to get out of this, but he would figure it out sooner or later. With any luck, sooner. Like before, he was flying by the seat of his pants here and coming up with things on the fly. Maybe not smart, but it was all he had, and he had to try.

"And last, no kissing on the mouth," she said.

He grunted in acknowledgment and she slipped onto his lap, legs spread over his hips, her slight tits pressed into his face.

The entire situation felt wrong. With this young woman in his arms, no doubt more than ten years younger than his thirty-two, thoughts of a dirty old man speared his mind. He placed trifling kisses over the small rounded parts of her cleavage, pretending like hell he was into her, excited. But he didn't want this, and his stomach revolted with each touch.

She moaned, and again stale cigarettes and sugar drifted down to him. Her hips scooted closer and she rotated them, grinding against him.

His body didn't react—of course it didn't—and never would. In the back of his mind, an idea took shape. An out.

He pushed into the scene, played his part, and groaned as she continued to move against his groin. With a palm on her hip, he guided her actions and took her little mound of a breast in his hand. So fucking small. So damn young. He closed his eyes and fought against the nausea surging up his throat.

Keeping things PG-13 proved interesting when she started undoing his belt buckle. He shifted, rolled her beneath him and covered her physique with his, fighting like hell to keep to the scene. Dazed eyes stared up at him, then her gaze traveled to the ceiling above his head. He sought to run out of here, but on the same token, wanted to help these girls. She was so far gone, so drugged he doubted she was aware of even her name.

Just hold on for a bit longer, honey. We will save you.

He groaned again, tensed, and dropped his head next to hers. "Damn it to hell, baby."

"What—what's wrong, papi?"

"This has never happened. I can't—I can't get it with the program," he mumbled like he was ashamed. *That* wasn't a lie, at least.

"You can't what?" she asked, breathless.

He pivoted his hips a few times in a suggestive manner and groaned again, this time holding despair in his tone. "I can't get it up. You're a beautiful woman, damn sexy, and so damn young and hot." He was going to throw up. "But I'm sorry. Do you think if I give you some money we can keep this between us? It's so embarrassing."

He could have sworn she sighed in relief, but it had to be impossible. Her actions from before seemed to be half-drugged. "Of course, papi. It'll be our little secret."

He rose, gave her a quick grin, and kissed her on her cheek. "Thank you." Lifting off her, he made a show of buckling his pants, his back to Tom, then reached into his front pocket and tossed down a few more bills. The young girl took the money and stuffed it under her bikini top. Eyeing Tom, she stood, smiled, and left.

He pivoted and went to walk out of the room. A strong hand to his chest stopped him at the exit.

He glanced up at Tom.

"You like?" the dude asked.

Fuck no, I don't like. Learn how to form a damn sentence, dick.

"Sure. Would prefer something a bit fresher, but she was real good." He wiggled his brows, acting ten times the ass.

Giant grinned, nodded. "Then come again tomorrow night, my friend. I'll hook you up."

Dwayne smiled, clasped hands with Tom, and pushed out of the room. He worked his way through the crowd, itching for fresh air, his chest full of so much pressure it felt as if a brick sat on it. He reached the exit and burst out of the building, pulling in deep gulps of cool oxygen. The world spun faster than his body could keep up and he fought against vertigo.

"You all right, man?" a deep voice asked from behind.

He twirled, took a step backward. "Yeah, I'm tight, bro. She just rocked my world, if you catch my meaning."

"Ah…" The bouncer grinned, comprehending. "Yes, the young ones do have certain ways of composing the night better. Making a man forget who he is, no?"

He laughed with him, his much more forced, then turned and stumbled to his car, reaching it with seconds to spare before he collapsed against the panel.

It wasn't just the acts of what happened inside that bothered him. No, it was more than that. The scent of that place, the dark, hungry look in the males' eyes. It reminded him of the crap he had seen nonstop growing up. The men his birth mother brought home, the scent he used to associate with her, with family. All his history— he understood that. However, for some reason the past seemed to have reached through time and gripped him by the balls.

His phone rang and once he was inside his car, he slipped it out of his jacket, recognized the number and flipped it open.

"Luke."

"That's what they call me. I'm at the hotel. Do you want me to stop by?" his brother asked.

"Um…" He cleared his throat, tried again. "I'm not at the hotel. I decided to check out the club."

A string of curses came through the line. So loud, Dwayne had to pull the phone away from his ear. After his brother settled, he set it back and ground his teeth together.

"I'm going to forget everything you just said, and you're damn lucky Ma isn't around. You'd owe her a pretty penny if she heard what kind of mouth the Marshal Service has given you," Dwayne growled.

"Oh cut the crap," Luke snapped. "That was a bone-headed move and you know it. Going to the club by yourself. Have you lost your ever-loving mind? You don't go into a situation you are unfamiliar with, without backup. *Ma* would kick *your* ass if she knew, so don't try that threat on me."

He rubbed his eyes. Luke was right, but when it came to this, he had a hard time keeping a level head. He was exhausted, hungry, and tired of fighting Brooke. Those were the reasons why he had blown up before leaving for the club, but he recognized it was not the reason he went to the club.

"I can't stand to think of Hailey inside alone, forced to endure this shit," he said, tiredness weaving its way into his voice.

Luke sighed. "I know, man. I hate the thought of her in there, too. And I know you two were close. Hell, we recognize how you look at her mom."

"It's more than that."

"Yes, it is. Nevertheless, you gotta admit tonight you crossed that line. You can't think straight when it comes to these two. Are you sure you can do this?"

"Yes." One word said too much.

"All right, you still there?" Luke asked.

He shook his head and remembered he was on the phone. "No, I'm in the parking lot, was about to drive back and get some shut-eye. I don't remember the last time I had a full night's sleep."

"Well, how about you start tonight? You need to recharge if you're going to be any help to Hailey."

He fucking knew that. He did not need his little brother, the youngest of his siblings, pointing that out. And dammit, why in the hell was he being such a dick?

"I can hear you arguing with yourself through the phone. What's bothering you?" Luke asked.

Dwayne let out a deep breath. His brothers knew about his childhood. Hell, they all were acquainted with everything about one another, each coming from their own individual nightmares. He didn't like talking about it. Holding things back wouldn't do either of them any good, and more than likely, Luke wouldn't get off his back until it came out.

"This case has brought up memories from my childhood," he said softly.

"What in the hell does hookers, human trafficking, and kidnapping have to do with our childhood?"

He growled. "Not our childhood, dickhead. *My* childhood, before Ma and Pops. With my birth mom."

"Ah." His brother was silent for a few moments. "I can see how that could fuck with you a bit."

He scrubbed a hand over his face and shook the exhaustion from his scrambled mind. "You can say that again. Tonight made things worse. The entire place reeked of her. And the other day"—had it been only two days ago?—"I told Brooke the entire goddamn sob story."

"Awe, hell. Why?"

"I don't know!" Frustration sang through his nerves, making him ache. Fatigue fucked with him, driving his body to shut down. "It just came out. And once my mouth opened, it's like I had a case of verbal diarrhea with no Imodium AD around."

He twisted the key, held on to the wheel with one hand and leaned back, looking out the windshield but unable to focus on anything. "Then tonight I acted like a complete ass to Brooke." He wasn't even going to mention the young woman in the club. He didn't feel fit to live with the city's cockroaches right now.

"How so?" Luke asked.

"Long story, but let's just say it involves me telling her I wanted inside her body, and she expressing what she really thought of that idea, of who I am, and of my thoughts all at once. And not in a good way. Basically, she opened my eyes and made me realize who I am, and I do *not* like what I see, or how she sees me."

"Fuck, D. Come on, man. You're not married. There's nothing wrong with what you do."

"Yeah..." He glanced out the window, scanning the parking lot. "Tell that to her."

"You wanna stay in my room for the night? Get some sleep?"

Dwayne put the car in gear and held his foot on the brake. The idea held merit. Both he and Brooke could use some space. But it wasn't what he wanted. "No, I need to get back and make sure she knows I'm all right. Give her an update on things and try to apologize. What room are you in?"

"Sixth floor, number six twelve."

"All right." He eased off the brake and pulled out of his space. "We're on the tenth. Number ten-oh-one. Come by in the morning and we'll come up with a plan over breakfast."

"My morning or yours?"

He chuckled. Luke had an unhealthy appetite for being up before dawn, and that was on the days he didn't use an alarm clock. "Mine, asshole. You show your face before eight, I'm going to kick your Mr. United States Deputy Marshal ass."

"Ha! I'd like to see you try, big brother. Talk with you tomorrow."

Laughing, he hung up the phone, concentrated on the road, and fought to find the words he would need once he got back to the room.

Chapter Twenty

A thousand and one thoughts swirled like intermixed colors of black and white, shading until the gray blurred his vision. He sat a few feet away, staring at the door that separated him from *her*. Just on the other side, through a mere three inches of wood, sat Brooke, waiting on him with hope of finding her daughter. Damn if he didn't have anything, not one iota of a clue in understanding where Hailey was. On taking the suspicion away from where they thought her to be. And more so, a sighting of some kind. No, all he had was the cheap smell of women's perfume attached to his skin, and the tainted feel of dirty air surrounding him. He had no answers, and more than anything, he wasn't looking forward to the disappointment he was bound to see—*again*—on her sweet, angelic face. It was almost enough to have him renting another room just to avoid it.

Instead, he pushed out of the car, crossed the dark parking lot, and strolled up to the door. He stepped inside after unlocking it with a key card. With his attention glued to the brown carpet, he refused to lift his gaze and acknowledge her. He was disgusted with what he'd had to do. All he wanted was to wash off the hovering slime of the night. Never had he been put in such a position or fell to lowness where he preyed on others to get what he needed. And it wasn't a question of if he needed, but more so, a *craving* to find Hailey, bring her home, and lock both her and her mother up where he could keep them safe for the rest of time. A possessive urge in him demanded he do such, required submission, and refused to let its grip loosen. It wrapped around his neck like a noose, tightened by the second, and forced his compliance.

A few steps inside, unable to deny it any longer, he lifted weary eyes up and found Brooke standing across the room, staring back. Her expression scrutinized him from head to toe and propelled the already heightened emotions in his chest. Just the look of her, the raw beauty and innocence she emitted, floored him. His body swayed, wanting to cross the room. A magnetic field drew him toward her. He fought it, forced his feet to stay in place and tried like hell to hold her stare. Words caught in his throat, an unspoken reminder of how he'd left things earlier. God, she was so clean. He could smell it from here, the muted scent of soap flowing in waves. Her hair fell in a soft waterfall of red behind her back. A white camisole was all but painted on her body and held twin mounds he itched to touch and taste. The alluring display of cleavage drew his attention. A dark shadow tinted the area between her breasts. She'd paired the tempting shirt with light blue velvet track pants and he clenched his fists to fight against the urge to reach…for her.

Damn it, he wanted nothing more than to sink into her embrace, dive into her heat, and wrap himself in the clean true beauty of Brooke.

After the words earlier, the continued denial she tossed his way, and the dirty taint he held now, there was no way he could go through with it.

"Are you okay?" she asked, her words gentle.

Just the sound sent a thrill of pleasure up his spine. He closed his eyes as the tingle, like an electrical shock of minor proportions, zinged through his body. He nodded and averted his gaze, refusing to watch the dismay cross her face as he let her down.

"I couldn't get behind the scenes tonight," he said. "Well, I got back one level, but Hailey wasn't there. I'm sorry. Tomorrow my brothers should be here and we'll try again." Was that his voice shaking like a fucking newborn chick? *Get a damn grip, dude.*

Silence spread again. The resistance proved painful, and he glanced up to catch twin auburn brows raise and lower to a scowl.

"You'll find her, I'm almost as sure of that as I am that she is my daughter," she said, just as soft as earlier. But this time her words held more conviction as if she were trying to talk *him* into believing it. "I'm concerned about you. I hate how things were left and understand things may have been...tough tonight." She turned her gaze away, swallowed, took a deep breath, and spoke again, fists clenched tight by her sides. "I wanted to talk to you about earlier. About things and how they have been going."

He shook his head before she finished and took a step forward. "Stop. There's nothing to talk about. Not now. Especially not right after I've returned from a strip club and sex house. If you have ever listened to me, do it now. *Please.*"

At the word *sex*, she snapped her gaze to him, seemed to shrink back and ran a slow, thorough path down his body and up.

Before she could speak again, he continued. "Look, I have a plan. Again, tomorrow my brothers should be here and we'll figure it out, get a stronger idea of what to do once they arrive."

Her expression cut him in his gut. He hated the smell sticking to him and went to move around her, stepping in a wide arc to pass. She reached out just before he cleared. He braced for the touch he couldn't avoid, one he couldn't resist. Her hand set on his chest. He squeezed his lids shut. Decadence. That's what her one...single...touch gave.

Goddamn it, he wasn't good enough for this. Why

hadn't he seen it before? Had he been too damn cocky from the beds he'd been invited into not to recognize this? Without realizing it, he shrank from her touch, stepped away, and slammed against the wall.

Discovering her expression, jaw dropped, eyes wide with pain, he cursed the night once again. Could he do nothing right? Catching on to his mood, this time she was the one to speak and move first.

She stepped to him, set both her hands on his chest and glanced up beneath heavy lashes. His gaze was riveted to the soft curve of her cheek, the velvet sight of her skin, and the plump weight of her lips. Why? Why the hell did she have to touch him now? He didn't want this, couldn't take whatever comfort she offered. Not now.

Her palms smoothed up his chest. Inside, he cried at the loss of it all. He would not taint her. She wanted to be a friend, but he couldn't accept it. He refused to take any less than what he told her he wanted. They were made for each other, and yet at the same time, them being together was nearly impossible. He wanted her to see him as the love of her life, as something bigger than just a man. Someone worthy to take and protect her heart. But she'd never see him as anything more than a friend. The years they'd spent together told him as much.

Gripping her wrists with a gentle but firm grasp, he drew them away and sidestepped along the wall until she dropped her hands.

"I need a shower, Brooke. Please, let's talk about this tomorrow. There's nothing more we can do until my brothers get here."

A flash of impatience crossed her features and darkened her face.

"Stop it," she snapped. He blinked. "Why—why can't I touch you? Have I messed things up so much you can't accept one hug from a friend?"

He cut her a look. Exhausted, he was no match for this conversation. "No, it's not that. I need to get clean, get this night off me. Can you understand I just want to wash memories of the last few hours away? Please, we'll talk about this later. Just let me go."

Her arms locked in a tightened grip around his waist, freezing him to the spot. Her face pressed to his chest, and her body plastered to his own. He didn't return the embrace. Instead, he grabbed his upturned face and fought back the rising groan. Torture would be a better reprieve than her sweet curves pressed against the ugliness he had to endure. He wanted to shout to the heavens about the unfairness, wished he could take antibacterial spray and clean her hands. He didn't want to taint her! She didn't get it, did she? His world, the night, was one he wished to spare her.

With quick motions, he gripped her wrists from the small of his back, pivoted in her arms, and walked away without another word. He entered the bathroom and shut out the accusing and helpless gaze of Brooke. Her face crumpled just before the echo of the door bounced off the walls.

Damn it.

* * * *

Brooke stared at the closed door as if she could see through it. The easy feeling friendship she and Dwayne had held for over ten years seemed to be crumbling, and their bond hovered on a precipice. One small move and it would tumble down the mountain, forever lost. The line had blurred, and his kiss had pushed her over the edge of curiosity. Feelings she'd never considered festered inside her.

He was easy on the eyes, more than that. He held a smooth grace with an underlying lethal presence that gave his dark looks a wicked edge. A bad boy in play.

Only his appearance, always dressed without blemish, gave the illusion of civilized manners. The man she knew, and the one she had grown to know the past few days, was anything but. He held a barely restrained control in his eyes. And she'd felt the tremor of that control under her palms the last time he kissed her.

And—*didn't it figure?*—in her usual way, she had not only managed to insult him but also built a wall between them with her words. As well as, it appeared, her actions. Or lack thereof.

How could she be held responsible for any of what she did or didn't do? Right now she worried about getting her daughter back, bringing Hailey home. She was not in the position to make any sort of decisions about a relationship. But damn it, how could she not?

Spinning away from the door, she paced. Her thoughts fused together with the pained expression she'd glimpsed before Dwayne had turned from her. Was it the night he had gone through, or her, that put that look on his face?

Did he not want to touch her because of what he had done? The thought gave her pause and she sank to the mattress, stared unseeing at the ugly orange wallpaper. He mentioned going behind the scenes but not seeing Hailey. Did he take his built-up lust out on the woman he encountered? Had he slaked the desire he'd been feeling for her?

Oh dear, God.

She closed her eyes against the wave of regret as it spun through her body. Why was she doing this? If she didn't want to be with him, if she kept holding off, then why did a stabbing sensation occur in her chest to imagine him wrapped in another's arms? Why did her body call out with distress at the thought of never feeling his touch?

Her eyes snapped open and she jerked off the bed.

She had to give this a shot. Indubitably, she could lay with him and protect her heart, right? After all, she was a healthy woman. More, she craved the distraction from the reality of her world. And even she could admit she wanted him.

She wanted Dwayne, and she wanted what he had been offering her.

Was it the smell of the other woman on his skin that drew this urge? Or perhaps, was it the fact that she had discovered Hailey's dad cheating in much the same way?

Dwayne was not hers. However, nothing said she couldn't go along with what he had been trying to convince her of.

Hands at the bottom of her shirt, she whipped it over her head without another moment's hesitation. The material flung aside and landed somewhere across the room. She pushed her pants and panties down with a single swoop and turned to the bed.

All she had to do was keep her heart out of it and see where this led. This formidable draw to Dwayne and the curiosity to see what it would be like between them. Only this was a solitary thing she'd give. She had to make sure of it.

* * * *

Missing the hell out of his massaging spray showerhead back home, Dwayne stood facing the faucet, head ducked between his shoulders, and allowed the hot water to pound the tight muscles of his neck. Tension wound his body tighter than a mainspring.

The night had brought a lot of it. Nevertheless, he knew most of it had to do with the woman on the other side of the door.

Brooke.

This craving for her was so intense, he was half-afraid he would just take her one day soon. And *soon* was the key word. It wasn't a matter of if, but more, *when* it would happen. He needed to get the hell away from her if he planned to keep their friendship intact.

She had made herself more than clear, as he had with his intentions. Rebuffed at every opportunity, she gave him an unblemished answer of what she thought of that idea.

With a scowl at the reminder, and the water running cooler on his back, he yanked the faucet off and flung open the curtain. He stepped out and wrenched the white, plush towel from the rack.

Regrets, millions of them, pounded into him as he dried off. He should have told Brooke how he felt long ago instead of harboring these impulses. On the other hand, he wondered if he should have just kept his mouth shut. Why did he in the first place? Memories long gone because of his exhaustion, he shook his head and bent to retrieve his discarded clothing from the floor.

Running from Brooke had left him without a pair of boxers. As he opened the door, he expected to see her waiting for him, wanting to talk some more. Surprised, he found the room dark, a slither of yellow light sneaking through the parted curtains. A lump lay in the bed, unmoving, covered by the thick hotel comforter.

He crossed on silent feet, bent to retrieve a pair of black boxers from his bag, and pulled them up his legs, all the while keeping the towel around his hips. Dressed, he tossed the cloth aside and turned to the bed. His gaze shifted to the loveseat sitting under the corner as he debated on how smart it would be to join her. He mused the idea for a few seconds. It couldn't hurt. He shrugged and went to his side of the bed, then slid under the covers.

Settling on his back, he stared up at the ceiling in

silence, thoughts screaming through his head. Brooke's clean scent wrapped around him and, combined with the scent of the fabric softener the hotel used, it calmed his frayed nerves, cocooning him in a peaceful interlude.

The bed shifted and she slid to the side of his body, pressed her very curvy and—*fucking hell, very naked*—body against him. He hissed and went tight as a bowstring. With a punch, blood surged to his groin and his cock erected with grace at attention in a heartbeat of time.

He heaved out of her arms and rushed from the bed, standing, then rounding on her.

"What the fuck, Brooke? Christ, you're naked!"

He slammed his lids shut. It was too late. She'd sat up, and the glow from outside had caught it all. It burned in his brain, fueled the growing need rushing through him.

Thick, long hair splayed across her shoulders like a wash of silk. Desire-lidded eyes stared at him in request. Pert, round breasts on display looked almost as good as he knew they tasted. Her skin flamed brighter than the sun, which would indisputably rise in a few hours. The white sheets twisted around her waist, framed her in an absolute offering.

"Open your eyes, Dwayne."

"Put on some fucking clothes first."

"Why?"

He made a strangled noise. The noose around his neck tightened, while the control he normally tried to hold—slipped.

"Why?" he growled. "Christ, you have absolutely no idea what you do to me, do you?" With his sight gone, his other senses magnified. Cool air washed over his damp body. Her soft, rapid breath filled his ears. Her sweet smell invaded his nose. She was the one and only thing he could concentrate on, and his exhaustion vanished.

Her hand gripped his straining cock, the thin barrier of cloth doing nothing to decrease the sensation. Air rushed out of his lungs with a punch. He stilled her wrist, his precarious control waning, and opened his eyes.

Swallowing hard, he tried to extract her, but she tightened around him. Mr. Happy jerked, all too willing to join in the festivities.

"What are you doing?" he whispered with an urgent rasp.

On her knees with one arm reached out to him, she licked her lips. The sight of that pink tongue running along the seam of her mouth, moistening it, drew his attention. He stifled a groan. Her entire body was on display, smooth skin begging for his touch, each glorious curve beckoning and testing restraint.

"If I have to explain what I'm doing, I must be more out of practice than I thought." One brow lifted.

He let out a strangled laugh. "What? No, that's very clear." The high pitch of his voice had him wincing. *Christ, dude, really? She's got her hand wrapped around your cock. She's staring up at you with desire, and you're questioning it? What in the fuck is wrong with you?*

She kept that flawless, arched brow high and didn't speak. He fought to find the words. Pretty fucking hard—*literally*—with her rock solid—*yep, again, literally*—grip wrapped around his aching loin. He tilted his head back and prayed for strength. Coming into her arms after the night he had would be both a blessing and a curse. On one hand, losing himself in her softness, in the pureness she offered, would be heaven to his hell. An answer to the nightmare he experienced.

Yet, on the other, he still felt dirty. He couldn't imagine tainting her beauty, *his angel*, in any way. He shouldn't question why she had unexpectedly changed her mind—what guy would? And the fact that he was, solidified that he needed to go out and buy some tampons, get his nails done, and put on a pair of pink panties. 'Cause he had downright lost it.

Swallowing hard, pulling on every ounce of control, he lowered his head and met her eyes. "*Mi angel preciosa, me tientas.*" *My precious angel, you tempt me.* "I have to know why?" He shook his head. "That didn't come out right. Please." He gave a gentle tug on her hand. "I'm going to hate myself later, I know it, but I need to understand why now. What's going through your head? And more, does it have anything to do with where I went tonight?"

Her grip around him loosened. He nodded as her nostrils flared. Yeah, he had struck the spot. Her body's response told him as much. Hope, that bright spark of a flame, doused, but he held his facial expression in check. *Of course it had to do with the fact women had been all over him tonight.*

He sighed and pulled her hand away, then slid onto the bed beside her, taking her face between his palms. "*Si*, Brooke, you forget yourself, and you underestimate me." He smoothed her hair away. Her warm skin pierced the cold in his hands, and her eyes, even holding their frightened gaze, warmed him to the depths of his chest. This amazing woman, her strength unfaltering, showed more vulnerability to him tonight— something he never thought he would see—and it touched him more than she knew.

"*Preciosa,* this isn't you. I understand you better than you think. We've known each other for years. This…" He ran his gaze down over her and fought back a smile as her entire body tinted pink. "While it's lovely, and while I may want you so fucking bad I *ache*, it isn't something I want to take because you're feeling as if I'm slipping away." She opened her mouth, but he cut her off. "Don't ridicule me and call me an idiot by attempting to argue my point. You're failing to recall I pulled a double degree also concentrating in psychology. I know what your body, what your words, and what your actions are saying."

Her expression fell. The change as sure as a comet falling from the sky. And it scared him just as much. His heart thudded, took off like a racehorse without a rider. He could deal with her anger, handle her tears over Hailey, but knowing he put that despair there just about killed him.

Setting countless kisses across her face, he spoke through each contact. "Don't. Please." She wrapped her hands around his wrists and drew in a deep breath, then caught his mouth with hers. He froze, every muscle locking up tight as a spring coiled. The air she drew into her lungs released, capering out across his face.

She leaned up and wrapped her arms around his neck. His heart, which had been pumping on an express train up the tallest mountain, suspended. The yielding mounds of her breasts surged against his chest, twin cushions as soft as warm velvet. Her nipples pressed to his bare chest and he grumbled, felt the ground shift on his control. It stretched, so fucking tight, ready to snap.

She tilted her head, opened her mouth and sucked in another breath against his lips...then breathed, "Please."

Chapter Twenty-One

Brooke didn't understand this...this need, craving, and desire demanding she give in to Dwayne. It pulsed like a living and breathing thing. She had to have him in her arms, had to feel his body against hers, had to relent to this attraction bouncing between them. It was almost as forceful as the balls from the pinball machine a few days ago, slamming against the edges of her consciousness, punching along her skin and pulling her into a vortex of unbridled necessity to finally act.

Green eyes darkened and met her unflinching stare. She could fall into his gaze any day, wrap up in the peace of spring his eyes offered. He was normally so in control, so steadfast in his confidence and attention to what occurred around him. Tonight, though, his expression held something else, a look she wanted to comfort, something she had to wipe away. She'd caught a glimpse into his vulnerability and now that the guise was up, she had an undeniable urge to banish. A strong impulse she had no choice in fighting any longer.

"You've comforted me for so long," she said against his mouth. "Let me provide to you tonight."

She brushed her lips along his and the tendrils of need developed claws that dug into her body relentlessly.

His large palms wrapped around her upper shoulders, but he didn't push her away, nor did he pull her closer. Instead, he shook her, a small movement she believed designed to grab her attention.

"I don't need to be comforted this way," he rasped. "Do you understand what you're asking? Do you know whom you're inviting into your bed? Between your thighs? Have you realized how this will change things?" He slid one hand to her back and tangled it in her hair, then gave a forceful yank. She cried out, not in fear or pain, but more so under the sensual delight the position thrust her under. Face tilted to his, his chin rested on hers and his eyes lit with fire.

"Can you, sweet Brooke, understand how ruthless I will be in demanding you give me it all? Not just what you think you want to hand over? I will take every damn drop, ring every lick of pleasure, and push you until you no longer understand how to deny me anything. Are you sure this is what you want? Now? Do you," he said, dropping his voice until it was practically a growl, "understand you're inviting a stranger, not who you think you know, but another man entirely, between your thighs tonight?"

She met his unyielding gaze and refused to back down. He wanted to scare her; that much she was sure of. Whatever he had gone through tonight, it was something that had messed with his head. Her heart felt like breaking and as it was a fissure developed under the pain in his voice. She could no longer deny him or turn away, just as she was unable to cease breathing.

Keeping her eyes open, she leaned up, closed the last few inches between them and covered his mouth with her own. An inhuman sound rumbled from his chest as his arms tightened like bands and crushed her against his body. The hand in her hair tangled and pressed her closer, tilted her head, and forced her to submit to his ministrations. The kiss was raw, rough, and involved a demanding tangle of tongues, bites, and growls. She allowed it, refusing to back down as she gave as much as he did. It had been so damn long since she had experienced a touch from a man, even longer since she enjoyed a kiss, and never had she undergone the absolute conquest of her mouth and body. She was his for the taking.

Beneath her hands, his body was inviting. Soft, yet hard. Like stretched velvet, warmed by the summer's sun and wrapped around stone. His taste, like his scent, was intoxicating. She wanted to drink him in, take her fill of mint, the sweet taste of brandy, and something entirely just Dwayne. While fresh from the shower and smelling of soap, sandalwood filled her nostrils, a scent she'd long ago associated with him.

God, how could she have missed this? How had she been so blind to how sensual he was? He emitted a promise of sex from the way his hands forced her compliance, from the way his mouth conquered hers, and from the slow roll of his hips against her stomach. His erection pressed against her, shameless and unforgiving. He had warned her he wouldn't hold back, that she'd meet a different man tonight, and so far, his words had never been truer.

He leaned forward and she went with it until they fell back on the bed. She wrapped her thighs around his slender hips and gasped. The coolness of his boxers was such a contrast against her core. She was too hot, too sensitive, as if she would combust any moment. Threads of what hovered, some implausible release in sight, thinned, verged on snapping. He never released her mouth, though, and instead dove deeper, his tongue wrapping around hers in such a sure move, she wondered if his confidence ever shook. If she wasn't careful, this man could own her, body, soul, and heart.

The thought gave her a momentary spark of panic and she tore her mouth away. Not breaking the full speed ahead, his lips moved to her neck and suckled, nipped with love bites. The small bout of pain, combined with his body engulfing her, threaded her strings of control even more.

"God," she gasped without control, "please tell

me you plan to finish this. Dwayne, please." She tightened her legs and pressed her heels into his ass, forcing him closer. He growled and lifted his torso from hers. Thinking he was pulling away, she cried out and palmed his head, arched her back, and thrust her breasts toward his face. "No!"

"Christ, Brooke." With a helpless sound, he took the offered nipple into his hot mouth and sucked—*hard.*

"Ahhhh," she screamed as the straining peak lapped up the pleasure. Unabashed, she rolled her hips beneath him, taking the delicious thrill of indulgence each pass of her hips against his erection provided. She needed this release, refused to stand by and wait while he took his sweet time or second-guessed what they were doing. She wanted him…and nothing was going to stop her from taking what they both needed.

* * * *

Slow down…slow down…slow down.

Like a mantra, Dwayne kept chanting the words in his head. He would have said them aloud, but Brooke's tempting breasts filled his mouth. God, the sounds she made, the scent of her, and the *taste* of her drove him insane. He could barely see or think straight, much less pull his thoughts away from the finish line of falling between her sweet thighs…where no barriers existed.

While the endgame ruled his mind, a little voice nagged in the back, trying to push through. *Savor this. Keep it slow. Take your time. Who knows if you'll get it again?*

God, he wanted to. She was like a fine brandy to be sipped with patience, not some wine cooler in the hands of a teenage cheerleader. He had waited too damn long for either of them to rush through this.

With a control he didn't know he had, he lifted and took both her hands. He whipped them over her head and pinned her to the bed. She blinked up at him, then glared. A carnal look passed through her eyes, the storm at sea showing the desire and frustration. He knew what she needed, and damn if he wanted to give it to her.

"What!" she exclaimed, exasperation lining her face. If it was any other time, in any other situation, he might have laughed. Chuckling at her growing impatience was something he had no doubt wouldn't go over too well in the moment.

"Sweetheart," he murmured. The earlier edge he felt had softened at the first taste of her. A beast no longer drove his actions, and instead the man who had grown to care for this woman rose to the surface.

"Please!" Her eyes watered and damn if the sight didn't break his heart. She shook her wrists against his hold and a small sob tore from her chest. She clamped her jaw together and the muscles in her cheek bunched. *What the hell?* She tried so hard to hold it together and didn't understand what her body called for. Or, she didn't know how to ask for it.

"Shhhh," he crooned, dropping his head to brush his lips against hers. "You need something, don't you?" He trailed his mouth along her jaw, pressing reassuring caresses against the pulsing muscle until he felt her relax. Her body shook against his, and small animal sounds escaped from her chest.

"Please." This time the word came out softer, more like a plea.

He held her hands with one of his, banding her wrists together. With the other, he palmed beneath her chin and tilted up. The muscles of her neck strained and her back followed the movement, bowing under his ministrations. He placed openmouthed kisses along her neck and savored each taste of this wonderful, strong, sensual woman.

Moving lower, he took each peak into his mouth, laving and worshiping each breast until she was writhing, this time in need rather than demand. The sounds escaping her were from a woman who was with him: little gasps as he tugged on a nipple, small sighs of pleasure as he tasted the curves of her breasts.

Continuing his pursuit, he released her wrists and moved lower, stopping to dip his tongue inside her naval. She stretched like a cat while he licked his way across her body. Her palms landed on the back of his head, and he didn't fight it, simply let her guide him. She hung on for life, it seemed, but allowed him to take the lead in his sensual pursuit. He reached her hips, pushed her legs apart, and set his mouth at the top of her inner thigh, then sucked.

Brooke cried out, the sound music to his ears, and the grip she held on his head tightened. He released the skin and nuzzled at her thigh, inhaled deep. The musk of her arousal was close.

"Say my name," he commanded against her flesh. "Tell me you know who is here with you." He licked the crease and focused his attention on the muscle attached to her pelvis.

"Dwayne," she said, the sound stuttering out like a hummingbird's wings.

"Again," he urged, moving his head closer to her core. Her legs parted wider as if she understood what he was about to do. Sweet mercy in heaven, she was bare. He closed his eyes and forced his body to calm. His cock throbbed against the mattress, eager to get attention, but this moment was his, hers, a time to take things slow.

Like the parting of a flower, the petals of her sex glistened, spread for him.

"Dwayne, please…"

He glanced up and found her head tossed back.

Her hands still tangled at the back of his head. She looked like a goddess of lust, passion and carnality evident in the shape of her curves and the slow, sensual movements she made.

"Look at me, *preciosa*."

She tilted her head and focused, a slow blink telling him she was very much wrapped up in what he was doing. He held her gaze and lowered his head, darted out his tongue, and took his first taste.

She cried out and he groaned.

Never. Never had he tasted something sweeter. Control long gone, he dove in and lapped at her, addicted to her taste. He barely registered her throaty cries or the fingers tightening against his head. He licked and sucked on her outer lips, tugged with gentle pulls on the inner ones, and when he concluded in convincing himself he'd depicted her to memory, he focused his attention on her clit, covered his mouth over it, and sucked.

She shot off the bed with a shout. He held her hips down, raised his hooded gaze up along the length of her body and watched as she exploded around his mouth. Her hands released him to tangle in her hair, and her back bowed to a precarious angle. She called his name repeatedly and the sound had his cock slamming against the mattress, demanding.

He fisted his hands against her hips, curled his arms over her thighs and continued his onslaught, refusing to let up until he brought her over another glorious peak.

Rising above her, his chin and mouth were drenched with her juices. He pushed his boxers forcibly over his hips and reached for his wallet. He pulled out the condom and fought to keep his orgasm from shooting off as he wrapped the latex along his erection.

He turned back to Brooke and found her watching

him, arms open and waiting. He fell forward, felt her feet push his boxers down past his knees. He kicked them off, then dove into her mouth with a searing kiss. Her taste, both that of her mouth and from between her thighs, drove him higher. She wound her legs over his hips and as his length passed over her drenched core, he tightened his hands against the bedspread near her head.

"God, Brooke, I can't...I can't wait any longer."

In answer, she wordlessly reached between them, took him in her palm, and guided it to her entrance. Pushing forward, she lifted her hips and together they found connection. Her head slammed back with a passion-filled cry and he matched the sound. The walls of her sex gripped him so tight he thought his eyes would pop out of his head. She was heaven and hell, heat and a comforting torture in one. Silken honey gripped his cock in a fist.

He dropped his head to her neck and moved his hips. His focus was not on stamina, nor was it even centered on finesse. He couldn't help it—he had no control. His body simply took over. There was only one thought he could center on. The bright and glorious release waiting. He needed it just about as much as a starving man needed food.

He thrust in and out, helpless to the passion engulfing.

"Kiss me," she said, wrapping her hands around the sides of his face and dragging him back to her waiting lips. He fell into it, skill level forgotten, broken mouths barely connecting. He mumbled without making sense, losing himself between her thighs again and again.

"Oh God, Brooke," he pleaded. A hot ball of pleasure strung tight inside his stomach. His balls quivered with anticipation.

"Let go," she answered. "I'll catch you."

His entire body shook, and he dug his toes into the bed for purchase. He clenched and released his hands until he could no longer stand it. He palmed her ass, canted her hips, and pounded his way to the hovering orgasm. Distantly he knew this was going to be it for him, one release he'd never experienced before, one he doubted he would ever get again.

He lifted his head from her mouth, mere inches separating them, and stared into her turbulent blue gaze. She pressed a soft kiss against his lips and that was all he needed.

Time stopped, the second hands of clocks paused, the world ceased breathing, and the air around them stood still as his orgasm broke. As if he were at the top of the highest roller coaster and the car hovered there, waiting to fall into the abyss. His hips worked furiously, slammed down, and the crest broke. His eyes watered as the wave rolled over him, but Brooke was there, her gaze unwavering, her arms holding him to earth. She peaked moments after him but continued to keep their gazes connected. He fell with her, or her with him, he didn't know. All he could focus on was her arms and the sweet temptation his heart gave to fall with her.

Chapter Twenty-Two

Brooke woke with a start. Hailey's screams echoed in her ears as if her daughter was next to her. The pleading was fresh and so damn real. She itched to reach out and take Hailey into her arms. Soft light filtered through the window, a slither of the new day peeking inside.

At the hotel. On her way to get Hailey.

The brush of cotton against her naked skin, and the warm, solid feel of Dwayne's arm across her waist reminded her of the rest. Her face flamed on fire as memories blasted through her mind, each sexual act they indulged in more arousing than the last. He hadn't lied to her when he demanded she give all. She had. He'd commanded everything from her last night. If the first orgasm hadn't been mind-blowing enough, the last provided plenty of energy to power the entire building. Electricity sparked through her veins, each jolt coming from his touch, his caress, the whisper of his lips on parts of her she didn't know were so sensitive.

Last night, caught in the whirl of need, lost in the dark shadows of soft sighs and intermingled moans, it was so easy to forget about the rest of her life. Swept away to an island of sensual delight, her daughter's nightmare hadn't crossed her mind.

And didn't that just make her mother of the year.

The room grew hazy. Reality intruded and the need she had felt last night changed like a cat that discovered their hatred for bubble baths. Her focus shifted to one where she *needed* to get to her daughter. She was tired of sitting around doing nothing. It was time she put her foot inside the plan in order to get Hailey back. Something needed to be done.

Careful not to shift the bed, lest she wake the sleeping man beside her, she inched out from beneath his arm, slid off, and darted for the bathroom on silent feet.

With a quick cold shower to wake up, she wrapped the white robe hanging on the back of the door around her and stepped back into the room. She expected Dwayne to be awake now—a few dropped bottles in the shower would most likely wake the dead—and she wasn't disappointed.

He sat on the side of the bed, facing away from her, focus straight ahead on the small amount of light filtering through parted curtains. She couldn't see his face, but his rigid, broad back told her everything she needed to know. She never knew how many muscles were in the back, but after last night and memorizing every detail as he committed her body to his, she now understood how many. Dwayne was built with an athletic grace that he hid under impeccable clothing. Like an optical illusion, all steel beneath his visible charm. And as she took in his tense back, she gasped at the deep grooves left from her nails down the length of it.

"Did I do that?" Her hand flew to cover her mouth.

He glanced over his shoulder and his gaze caressed the length of her. A slight smirk lifted the edges of his lips. She loved the sight of his smiles and wished he did it more often. Handsome as he was, with his lips curved, she swore she pulled an oldie but favorite and swooned.

He shrugged. "Not complaining here, *preciosa*." His voice was rough with sleep, sexy as hell.

She dropped her hand and winced at the marks. "Do they hurt?"

He rose, turned to her, and shook his head slowly, like a panther eyeing up a fresh morsel. "Not at all. In fact, I was just thinking on how you left a few spots untouched." He took a step closer.

Her breath hitched at the raw sexuality vibrating from him. Good Lord, how could she still react to him like this after last night? After the thoughts of her daughter this morning? The last thought gave her pause and she took a hasty step back to his one forward. She lifted a hand, the temptation to go to him strong, but the urge to have her child in her arms was even stronger.

"About last night..." she started.

The tightening of his abs and shoulders, and the smooth expression washing over his face was not lost on her. She hated when he closed his face off. But what the hell did he expect? What were they doing here?

"Don't look at me like that. We can't get distracted, and you, Detective Dwayne Gonzalez, are a distraction. A very nice one, but really, we need to focus on Hailey."

Anger, quick as a whip, flashed across his features. "I haven't once stopped thinking—or *worrying*—about Hailey. Just because I spent the night between your thighs doesn't mean that I'd simply forget about my responsibility to get her home safe. For you to even come close to implying something like that makes me wonder just what kind of man you think I am?"

"That's not what I meant," she tried to backtrack. "I'm just saying that while last night was nice, I'd really like to focus on moving forward. For every day she spends wherever she is, who knows what's happening?"

"Nice." He said the word as if it was something dirty.

She frowned. What was wrong with nice? "I don't think I'm following here. Last night was nice."

He snorted, a sound she wasn't used to hearing from him. Shaking his head, he reached for a pair of jeans and a shirt, his body still bare, something she was shocked she had yet to realize. "Right. Nice." He moved to shift around her.

She sputtered. "Well, what would you call it?" Now she was getting pissed.

He stopped next to her and turned with a movement so sudden, she jerked back. Dwayne apparently wasn't having any of her moving away, and he grabbed the back of her head, slammed his mouth down and kissed her with a bruising force. His lips did not caress as they had last night. His tongue did not stroke over hers with sensual licks. No. This kiss was raw, animalistic, and *angry.*

He pulled back after landing one more kiss against her lips and stared down at her, the green jewels of his eyes blazing. "I'd say phenomenal. Out of this world. Something that touched more than my fucking body. Laying in your arms, being close to you, having your sweet cries of ecstasy filling my ears was something I couldn't use any one word to describe. Nevertheless, for it to be just *nice* might be the buffer you want set between us, then fine, Brooke. I'll allow you this word, because I know how scared you are to open yourself to anything more."

She pushed against his chest, his words a bell ringing in her head. He released her and she took a step back. "Scared? No, that's not it. Why the hell would I be scared of you?" She stared at him, trying to make sense of what he said.

He tilted his head. "No, not scared of me, of what is going on between us? Why is it so hard to accept that it can be something more?"

"I think you may be getting a little ahead of yourself, no?" She crossed her arms. He caught the movement and tossed his hands up, then shook his head.

She refused to let him intimidate her. So what if he thought she was closing herself off? She could not deal with this now.

"Is that what you really think? Tell me something," he said, mimicking her actions, folding his arms across his wide chest. He set his feet shoulder length apart, the clothes balled in his hand not covering any of his nudity. He acted as if he couldn't care less. Of course, jumping beds as he did, modesty was probably the least of his worries. "How do you think I'm getting ahead of myself? What would you call what's going on between us?"

He tilted his head, his body language a taunt.

"Stop that," she snapped.

He scowled. "Stop what?"

"That." She pointed to his stance and uncrossed her arms. "You will not intimidate me into having this conversation with you. Last night was a great fuck, Dwayne. The best I've ever had. Is that what you want to hear?"

He blinked at her crude words.

She tossed her arms around to emphasize her point. "But I know you, and I know how you are. I cannot be one of those bunnies who allow you to hop in and out of her bed. As it was, that one time is going to hurt enough."

His eyes snapped and narrowed. "Bunnies? A fuck? What kind of man do you think I am?" he thundered. His face etched with livid, lovely lines of hurt and anger.

"Why so many women?" she asked, her voice softer this time but no less angry. It really did hurt that he did what he did with *all those women.*

"Why not?" he snapped.

Again, she tossed her hands. She was beginning to

feel like a damn bird. But the pain was so much, and it caused so much energy to boil inside that she needed to just let it out. She knew last night would come back to haunt her. But right now, this morning, *this* moment, she only wanted to find her daughter, dammit!

"Do you even love any of them?" she asked, although she really didn't know why.

The anger on his face cooled. Night and day came over his features. He clenched his jaw, set it as stubborn as a mule.

"You can't answer that question, can you?" she pushed.

He glanced down and away from her.

"This is what I'm talking about," she continued.

His phone started to ring. They both ignored it.

"I may speak Spanish, but I'm fluent in English, *preciosa*. And I know you are, too, so how about you put together an actual statement and clear it up? What are you saying?"

"I'm not saying anything. I was asking. But apparently, you're going to pick and choose what you want to answer. Fine. I'll answer this, and then, can we please move on? I may be a stereotypical female when it comes to sex, but I'm attached to my emotions, my feelings. You refuse to comprehend any of it. I see you. I know you. I've been around you so damn long." Her voice started to shake. Oh, no, she would not break down. Not now. "You use physical attentions as a substitute for emotions. Tell me I'm wrong."

His lips thinned. "Maybe now isn't the best time to have this conversation." He glanced at his phone as it continued to ring.

"Of course," she snapped.

His gaze whipped back to hers. "Now, what's *that* supposed to mean?"

"Nothing." She sighed, feeling defeated. "Just proving a point."

He let out a heavy breath and scrubbed at his face. His phone cut off, and the room fell silent again. "If both parties are willing to...indulge, then what's the problem with it? I'm safe, I use protection, get tested. What's the damn deal with sex?"

His phone started ringing again. She squeezed her eyes shut, calling for patience. "Get your phone, Dwayne."

"Fuck the phone. Talk to me."

A lump, thick in her throat, lodged in her windpipe. "Sex isn't a substitute for love," she choked. Interesting that she should say that after all Hailey's father put her through. Visions of her ex-husband between his secretary's thighs made her flinch.

"Don't you dare put me in the same circle as him."

She opened her mouth to deny it, but he cut her off.

"Don't you dare lie to me. I see it on your face. You think just because I've been with a few females that it makes me like him. Let me make this clear." He took a step forward. "I am nothing like your ex-husband. I never cheat. Every woman I'm with knows that I don't commit and that there are others."

She knew it, but his words still stabbed her chest. Of course he didn't commit. He never had. This was her point entirely.

"That's exactly what I meant," she whispered, then said louder, "and it's exactly why last night can't happen again. I need more. Unless you can sit here and tell me that it would eventually come, that maybe, just maybe you could grow to love me, I would rather us just break this off now. Clean cut for everyone. More of a chance that we can be friends down the road."

His expression softened, but his next words were still hard to hear. "I don't believe in love, Brooke."

His face was so resolute she bit her lip. "Then this is for the best. You really should get that." She gestured to the phone.

"But, wait—" he started.

"No, please! I can't handle this right now. If you have ever listened to me, then please understand and respect this request. Just get your phone." Despite already having taken a shower, despite coming from the bathroom, she turned and went back to it. She needed the escape and yeah, call her a coward, but the pain in her chest was too damn much. She refused to break down in front of this man and let him see how deep his words cut.

She was lying to them both when she said they needed the clean break. He had wrapped around her heart, something she'd known would happen, something that terrified her. Their friendship was important to her, and a normal part of Hailey's life. And one night of sex had pretty much shattered it all.

* * * *

Dwayne stomped over to his phone, yanked it out of his pants, and snapped it open. "What!"

"Well." Luke's deep voice vibrated through the line. "Someone seems to have pissed in your Wheaties this morning."

Dwayne sighed and walked over to the bathroom door. The vision of Brooke's red face, eyes filled with tears, haunted his mind. His brother didn't deserve the treatment his frustration drew, but neither did she. He still didn't speak but listened to the soft sobs coming through the wood. *Damn it.* He wanted to go inside and comfort her, take her in his arms and talk to her.

Now wasn't the time, though. Luke reminded him

they needed to move today and do so soon. With his brothers coming in town, they were more than prepared to act. It humbled him that they were putting their lives on hold in order to help him. Then again, that was what brothers were for. That, and the ability to have a never-ending supply of embarrassing stories.

"Dude, seriously." Luke's voice interrupted his thoughts. "Did someone piss or shit in your cereal?"

Dwayne moved from the door. "No. Nothing like that. Although I really hate myself this morning."

He heard the frown through the phone as his younger brother sighed. "All right, when mister high and mighty starts cutting himself down, something's wrong. At the risk of sounding like a chick, what the hell happened?"

Dwayne shook his head. "Nothing. Just female drama."

And as if that summed it up. "Ah, gotcha."

"Right," he answered. And in brotherly communication, the topic closed. "What's the plan today?"

Luke changed gears and downshifted, relaying the information. Apparently, last night his brothers had pulled into town, Charlie and Trent arriving an hour ago. The plan was to head over to the club this afternoon, which, from the clock was two hours away, and start to scout the place out. Once they all had a solid feel, they would head inside after dusk and try to blend in. Luke and Matt, being the more "colorful" of the group, read: able to blend in more to the "bad" side of the crowd with their longer hair and tattoos, would try to work their way into the back. Mike, the ever politically correct Secret Service agent of the group, had already coordinated with local LEO and everyone was in on the plan. If they found— *no*—once they found Hailey, they would wait for her to exchange business. Then she, along with the rest of the transacting club, would be taken down and arrested. It was for Hailey's safety they were doing it this way. She needed to be arrested at the same time as everyone else so as to protect her future. This would make retribution less likely.

The guys that ran this type of operation were more likely to hold grudges. They didn't need her life to be threatened for years to come. They needed to shut this down and get her home.

"When you explain it like that, it sounds easy," Dwayne said.

Luke clucked. "Don't jinx us, bro. You know as well as I do, nothing ever goes off smooth. Not even a traffic stop."

"Marshals conduct traffic stops now?"

"Bite me," Luke snapped. "Not at all, but maybe you should ask Matt about his latest seizure. Seems the DEA agent is getting into more than drugs nowadays."

Cursing and laughter filled the line and Dwayne smiled, picturing the two youngest going at it on the other end.

"All right, girls," he teased. "Settle down. I'll get dressed, get Brooke ready, and then meet you at the Tick-Tock Diner down the street in about an hour. Have everyone ready to go then and we'll head over."

"Sounds good, *princess.*"

"I'll give you princess, fucker."

Laughter cut off as the line went dead. Assholes. But he smiled.

* * * *

Less than an hour later, Brooke leaned against the red vinyl covering of the chair and took in her surroundings. Booths lined the outer wall of the fifties-style diner, colored intermediately with red-and-white leather. Scattered inside the outline were freestanding tables, like the one she sat at, where they held the ability to push them closer to fit additional parties. Inside that was a classic car she couldn't recognize.

Dwayne slid into a seat next to her and drew the attention of almost every female in the room. Goddammit, how in the hell could he be so cool and calm? Her nerves felt frayed as if anything that touched her would send her crumpling to the floor with shock.

Dwayne sprawled back in the red pleather chair like he didn't have a care in the world. His eyes lit with laughter, twin beacons of emeralds cresting over the horizon, as his attention turned behind her.

Brooke peeked over her shoulder, prepping herself for this reunion. She froze, dumbfounded. As with the few times she'd interacted with the brothers, each time in their presence was a whole new visual treat.

Four huge men walked their way, each moving with a deadly grace, the type of walk that didn't waste any energy. A loose swagger that spoke and defined confidence. The scrape of a chair told her Dwayne stood and yet still, she couldn't take her gaze away from these men.

Dwayne was adopted, but if the physical appearances hadn't said they weren't related by blood, one wouldn't know. Their bond was almost unbreakable, something both the brothers and their adoptive parents had worked to develop. Although they weren't related by blood, these men were definitely brothers.

Brooke turned back to Dwayne and stood as if on autopilot. He greeted each of his brothers with that whole man hug, slap-on-the-back kind of way she never understood. God forbid two men who loved each other show some sort of physical affection. Just like, God forbid, the New Jersey governor should learn to stop talking as soon as his point was across.

But both hopes were pointless.

Only after each embraced, while she stood there making her best impression of a goldfish looking out of a bowl—*damn the universe!*—did Dwayne turn to her.

"Brooke, let me reintroduce you to these hoodlums I *sometimes* choose to claim."

For a moment, the goldfish impression stuck, and now she outright gaped. Dwayne's smile lit up his entire face as if that was all it took to make the world spin on its axis. Ridiculously handsome even when his face was stoic, the wide curve of his full, plump lips and the crinkles of lines around his eyes turned him from panty-dropping good looking to clothes-disappearing-just-take-me-here-and-now.

In addition, the audacity that he could be smiling at her, affecting her body *this* way, really burrowed under her skin like a chigger. But in a way she was grateful for the distraction from the reason they had to meet with his brothers. Anything to get her mind off all the ways Hailey could be suffering right at that minute.

With a teeny-tiny portion of her brain, she turned and greeted a man about a foot taller than her. She craned her neck—*way back*—in order to meet deep brown eyes sprinkled with gold dust. Like his brother, creased lines formed around his wide-set eyes, and full lips curved with reception. Short brown hair, slightly longer on the top, fell across his forehead with an easygoing grace, sort of like the vibe pulsing off him.

"You should remember Mike. He's an agent with the United States Secret Service, and, despite his mammoth size, still my little brother."

"Pfft," Mike replied. "By six months, bro. But we'll discuss that and the last whooping I gave you later." He turned that amber gaze her way and as if his stare was not captivating enough, his voice rolled over her, a deep bass like a sensual caress.

"Brooke, it's a pleasure to see you again." Mike took her hand between both of his baseball glove sized ones and gave a small squeeze.

"Back 'atcha, Mike. Thank you for coming." Her voice did not shake—*thank God*. Inside, though, her stomach did its version of J-E-LL-O on a roller coaster. And although Mike had always reminded her of Josh Holloway from Lost, her reactions had nothing to do with the bedroom/surf-boy man. She wanted to lean on the strength of someone, anyone, who would hold her up and tell her everything would be okay.

Dwayne's gaze, his knowing scrutiny to every movement she did, wasn't lost on her. It was like a brand, and Lord help her if she didn't acknowledge it with a quick shift of her eyes.

Green emerald stones sparked with humor. While he smiled, his body relaxed and the words flowing from his mouth carefree, there was some sort of censure in his eyes. He moved closer and placed a warm palm on her back. The contact had her chest constricting.

"Easy, *preciosa*." His voice brushed close to her temple, low enough it didn't carry. "Breathe. They are here to help."

Brooke drew in a deep breath, determined to push down the rising panic threatening to burst free. While she felt the urgency to get to Hailey, one that had her wanting to spring to the club ASAP, this other building emotion bullying its way up her throat was foreign and confusing. She wanted to lean on Dwayne for that comfort and him alone. Like her mind and body gravitated to him and knew without a doubt he'd never let her fall.

Her cheeks burned as, once again, she realized she gaped. The low clearing of a throat brought her attention back around. Mark Wahlberg's doppelganger stood before her wearing a loose navy blue shirt with a gray sports coat. Jake. Jeans covered legs seemed able to crush her neck with one flinch.

"Brooke, you remember my other baby brother."

"Hey!" Jake laughed.

Dwayne matched the chuckle and with it being right next to her, her entire body focused on the sound and craved more. Her mind sluggishly struggled to place who he was.

"Yeah, yeah. Now he goes by NYPD Detective Jake Gonzalez."

Jake gently shook her hand and smiled with the warmth of an immediate friend. "It's been a long time, Brooke. We're going to get her back. Have no worries."

Now that she could breathe, she gulped in air like someone who had almost drowned. Yes, this was exactly what she needed to hear. But…

Damn it, Dwayne, your touch! Stop touching me, please!

She wanted to shout at him, but each time she shifted away, he followed her movement as if they were two pieces of a magnet fitting together. She tried her best to focus on greeting each of his brothers, but it seemed with every movement, each breath, she became more and more aware of Dwayne. The side of her face itched. He still watched her. Taking a chance, she glanced over.

You stupid, stupid girl.

Did she wear her feelings so open on her face? Could he see the turbulent wash of emotions? Because, make no doubt about it, the sweet desire and affection he must have been experiencing was like the front page of the NY Times, reading in fifty font print across his face.

What is this? Her heart seized in her chest.

"You're going to have to pardon my language,

Brooke," a low voice said, pulling her attention from Dwayne's face, "but you two are going to have to stop looking at each other like that. My boy parts are starting to twitch."

All the men at the table started laughing and Dwayne's voice rose over the warm-sounding humor, and again Brooke was grateful for the distraction. Her mind kept conjuring images of what Hailey was forced to endure, and none of it, from those thoughts to her realization of her dependence on Dwayne, could she control.

"Luke," Dwayne barked out in a rush of laughter. "You asshole."

A hand tightened on her hip and she turned around to greet Luke, the baby of the bunch.

"Brooke say hello to US Deputy Marshal Luke Gonzalez."

She coughed and eyed the tall, dark, and handsome man. "It's good to see you again, Luke." Of all the brothers, Luke had been the most reclusive of the bunch. His hair was short and as dark as the center of a black hole, which was saying something. But then her attention shifted to his eyes.

A hematite stone was the first thing to come to mind. He had a steady gaze, but the metallic gray seemed to swirl as if the irises were in constant motion. And no, not moving around with an intense, protective scan like the rest of them. More like the color was a liquid, hot and molten. She peered closer, taking note of the baby blue and soft purple dancing within. Since she hadn't had a whole lot of interaction with him, this was the first time she noticed.

"Amazing," she breathed.

Dwayne let out a strangled cough next to her and she jerked back, pulling away from Luke's captivating gaze. Her cheeks burned hot as the desert, but an overwhelming sense of relief sagged her shoulders at his pink cheeks, too.

Oh my, God. He is too adorable.

She must have said it aloud because Dwayne made an animalistic sound next to her and Luke pulled his gaze away fast, like lightning struck. His lips curved and he rubbed the back of his neck. Colors danced along his arm, tattoos on display. Now that she noticed, dotted along his neck were tiny blackbirds curving up as if flying around his nape. Beneath those were a bunch of black lines. She couldn't make out what completed the design, as his black shirt concealed it, but boy was she curious.

Still feeling the pull, with a sigh, she resigned to a key point and refused to deny it any longer. Able to catalog all of these details using about 0.1 percent of her brain, her attention was still glued to Dwayne. She was ridiculously clued into his presence and his handsome smile, his addicting gaze. The other 99.9 percent of her brain was occupied with two thoughts...

Dwayne, Hailey, Dwayne, Hailey.

"Hey," one of the objects of her thoughts grumbled. "How come the kid gets a compliment five minutes after seeing you again after years? Yet, we've known each other, been around each other for years and I get a scowl at best?"

Brooke took a deep breath, turned, and braced for the sight of him. The preparation was useless as his dark—yet petulant angst—looks hit her like a fist.

Surrounded as she was by beautiful men and yet all she had eyes for was this one.

No, no, no!

"Luke gets a compliment," she began, her voice cracking, "because his eyes truly are one of a kind. The blush was pretty cute, too." She cocked her head. "It's amazing what happens when women aren't falling over someone, huh, Dwayne?" She was such a bitch, but she couldn't accept this connection between them. The focus had to stay on her daughter.

Instead of coming back with a snappy, off-the-wall rebuttal, his jaw hardened and a ticking pulse in his cheek drew her attention. "Some things aren't what they seem. You, of all people, should realize that."

She did. What she did *not* get was why now, why right at this moment, she wanted to do nothing more than toss her arms around his neck and tell him she loved him.

No! her mind shouted. She gulped, the sound audible not only to her ears but from the widening of Dwayne's eyes, his too.

She blinked to soothe the prickle and he narrowed his gaze.

"Holy shit, bro," another deep voice boomed. Brooke snapped her head to the source and found a smiling man, built as all the rest, with long brown hair tied at his nape. Matt Gonzalez.

"Matt," Dwayne said next to her, "Remember Brooke? Brooke, this is now the famous DEA Agent Matt Gonzalez."

Matt flashed a grin and tipped some imaginary hat on his head. "Nice to see you again."

Before she could respond, he turned to Dwayne. "Dude, you all are not only messing with Luke's boy parts, but you're sure as shit making me nervous with this entire intense gaze BS. How about you two kiss and make up, put whatever is going on behind you for now?"

Brooke squared her shoulders and shook out of the slump she seemed to be stuck in. In the proverbial sense, she literally had lain in her bed, and now she had to deal with it. She loved him, and it was a fine time to realize it, but more so, she had to remind herself like a mantra that he would never love her back. He'd even said he couldn't.

She had to be strong for tonight and pretend as if her whole world was not crushing in around her like some central Florida sinkhole.

With a careful breath, she pasted on a bright smile and took a step away from Dwayne. She faced all the brothers, each different down to their blood types, no doubt. Yet, the family bond pulsed around them like an aura, almost visible.

"All right, guys," she said. "As soon as Charlie and Trent get here, let's talk about the plan for tonight."

Five pairs of brows went up and Dwayne cleared his throat. She shifted her attention and forced her face to remain impassive. All she wanted to do, all her body screamed for, was to stomp her feet like some tantrum-throwing five-year-old screaming, *I can't love you! I refuse to, you big, dumb, dillhole!*

"You're not coming, Brooke. It's too dangerous," Dwayne rumbled softly, but his voice held command.

His tone brooked no argument, but he had another think coming if he thought she'd just lay down and get run over by some lawnmower.

"Yes," she responded, the word clear and concise. "I am. You know I'll go even if you leave me behind. My daughter is going to need me. You have already run down just what I should expect, and from that, there's no doubt in my mind that in this situation she'll respond better to her mother than she will anyone else. I will not argue this. What's it going to be?"

His green eyes turned hard as stone and the pulse in his cheek pumped double-time. Seconds ticked like the countdown to a nuclear explosion. She waited him out. Had to. This was her daughter and her responsibility. *If...*

She shook her head. *When* they found her, she would want her mother. Refusing to back down, she lifted her chin and put resolve in her expression.

Dwayne must have seen something for in the next moment he cursed.

"Dammit, you will stay by my side. Like my shadow, sweetheart. You hear me?"

The endearment rushed through, a pain in her chest. It unfurled and stuck its tendrils straight through her heart. She drew in a deep breath and held out her hand. Sandalwood and wooden spices filled her lungs.

Dwayne.

Needing the promise, pushing him to give his word, she gave a pointed glance at her hand and met his questioning gaze.

"Promise me," she said.

He sighed and wrapped his large palm around hers. Her gut clenched.

"I promise. But you will be my shadow. Don't forget it."

"All right, then," Matt drawled with a clap of his hands. "Let's kick some ass like the big 'ole happy family we are."

Chapter Twenty-Three

Just after dusk, bass buzzed through the brick building, vibrated through the air, and with each beat, tightened the knot of nerves in Dwayne's stomach.

He squeezed Brooke's hand around their interlaced fingers, the only thing holding him from picking her up, tossing her lithe body over his shoulder, and hiding her away where none of this ugliness could touch or harm her. He was used to this scene. The preparation and mind-set just before successfully infiltrating the bad-guy's domain. This life was a part of his job. He had to face it. Having her innocence in this dank place and her life in danger gave him nothing but apprehension. On one hand, they had to get Hailey. This operation had to work. There were too many young lives affected. Without someone to stand up for these children, they'd be adrift in a vortex of lost memories.

On the other, having Brooke so close to where one wrong move and he'd lose more than her heart, had some protective instinct screaming in alarm. It went against everything he was, the opposite of what he had been trained to do. Protect and serve had no spot in his life tonight. Civic duty was forgotten as a child's dream.

Bouncers, big stocky men wearing tight red shirts and blue jeans, controlled entry. Two staffed the doors while a third stood off to the side, eyeing waiting patrons in line. Despite the darkness descending, the third wore black sunglasses blocking his eyes. All you could do was guess at what he was seeing, but Dwayne could feel his attention like twin laser beams, a target on his head.

Brooke shifted against his side. Whether out of nerves or sensing his unease, he didn't know. Clad in denim practically painted along her legs, and a loose low-cut black tank top, she stood out amongst the young crowd. Her long, curling red hair looked softer than down feathers, shinier than the brightest star above. Charlie had given Brooke a gorro cap to try to disguise her a bit, but nothing could really hide her gorgeous hair.

His partner had also gone a bit batty with Brooke's makeup. Heavy, smoky color brought out the blue of her eyes and her lips were a pale shade of glimmering pink that highlighted what he was sure every other man saw: sexiness, long erotic nights full of pleasure, and a woman who could unwind a man and send blood south with just a glance. Her gaze darted up to his, then away. At the same time, she sent a shaky smile. She couldn't seem to stand still, and her concentration never centered on any one thing.

He dropped his head to her ear, his attention on the woman in his arms, their safety covered by the circle of his brothers surrounding them.

"Easy, *preciosa*. You looking like you're actually searching for someone will raise red flags." He shifted her in front of him, tucked her back tight into his front, and pretended to nibble on her neck.

"These guys are looking for anything that stands out," he murmured at her ear. "And as it is, I can feel their gazes on me. When we get up to the door, stay close to my side, don't speak, and keep your eyes on the ground. Once we're inside, make sure you become my shadow. I don't care if you see Hailey, or if you have every instinct to run, sweetheart. You will be so close to me, you'll think I'm still inside you."

She gasped.

Lifting his head, he took in her pink cheeks and smiled. Wrapped around Brooke as he was, he doubted he'd get behind the scenes tonight, but his brothers had his back, all understanding the game, each eager to get their hands on the assholes running this operation. With a few local police undercover officers already inside, and about an army of them outside, he should feel more at ease. But he didn't. He couldn't, wouldn't, leave Brooke's side. He had to have been kidding himself to think that allowing her to come along wouldn't cloud his judgment.

They shifted and moved up a few feet in line. Dwayne dropped his head to hers and inhaled. Her scent wrapped its tendrils inside of his lungs and dug thorns into his soul. This woman, one he'd cared about for so long, was a very real and unmistakable part of his heart. He'd put his life down for hers. Hell, he'd do the same for Hailey. And he'd do it without a second's hesitation.

Shifting forward again, he resisted the urge to lash out at the bouncer watching him. The constant attention wasn't easing his tension. Staying cool and in control of the situation slowly fell away. At the front door, each of their IDs were handed over and given a brief cursory glance before they were granted access. Inside, the black walls led down a long hall. Numbers and letters flashed in purple, the only source of light leading the way.

Dwayne followed closely behind Brooke, the curve of her rear pressed against him, his arm wrapped around her waist. Getting separated wasn't an option he felt comfortable with in this dark club. It wasn't just the circumstances of having her so close to danger that bothered him. It was the thought of losing her because he was doing his job, because he was trying to bring her daughter home. His brothers had always given him shit for giving too much to others, putting his feelings on a back burner to help out those in need.

And if tonight wasn't a night of revelations, wasn't this just the time to realize they had been right?

Jake and Matt caught Dwayne's gaze and nodded

toward the bar. He returned the gesture and caught Mike's retreating back pushing through the crowd, most likely heading off to some dark corner. Having them all together gave him a sense of rightness, a bond only captured through family. Yet even with the six of them standing next to one another, you'd never be able to tell they were brothers. The fact that they'd all been adopted kept their looks from being too familiar, but it was something deeper, that something being that each of them were entirely different. Had separate reactions to situations and ways of dealing with their own problems.

Being able to count on one another was the commonality they could always bet on.

He pulled Brooke tighter against his hips and turned to catch Luke's gaze. His younger brother stared back with a look Dwayne hadn't seen before, one that had a hint of unease skittering up his spine. His almond-shaped eyes pulled down in a silent apology, and he drew his bottom lip into his mouth before uttering a harsh, "I need you to ignore anything you see tonight," and walking off.

What the fuck was that?

Dwayne almost went after him but drew up short, remembering Brooke in his care, his responsibility, his to keep safe. Whatever was going on with Luke, whatever kind of warning he'd been given, was something he'd have to deal with another day.

Trent brushed by, caught Dwayne's gaze and nodded toward the dance floor. Turning in that direction, he scanned the crowd, taking in sweaty, gyrating bodies pressed too close to one another, replicating acts that stated clearly it'd be considered an X-rated event had their clothes suddenly disappeared. A Latin beat with some guy singing along pulsed through the room. The singer's raspy voice spoke of hips moving, parts of the body touching, tasting, smelling, licking…all of it adding to the very sexual atmosphere, something no doubt the owners were trying to achieve.

He slipped his arm from Brooke's waist and stepped around her, grabbed her wrist as he passed, and tugged forward. She resisted the pull, and he looked back, inquiring. Her gaze jumped from the floor to him, both lips turned inside her mouth, pursed with a frown. He had to laugh. The sight just did him in. Clearly, as he well remembered, Brooke wasn't the most enthusiastic—*or greatest*—dancer, and the fear was written all over her face. He tugged her forward with a quick yank, and she tumbled into his arms.

Pressing his mouth to her temple, he spoke loud enough that he hoped she could hear. "We need to blend in, *preciosa*. Standing here won't do it."

She lifted on her toes and the length of her body pressed to his. It was innocent enough, but he had to fight a groan at the feel of her curves. "Won't we be better hiding in the shadows or something? Keeping a look out?"

He shook his head. "Trust me when I say if you hide in the shadows someone is going to notice. Brooke, sweetheart, you draw attention just being in the room." He pulled his chest from hers but kept their hips pressed together and rubbed his lower body back and forth, letting her feel his desire.

Pink bloomed on her cheeks, and he smiled.

"Come on." He pulled her onto the floor as the song morphed into a new one. Trent and Charlie were already on the dance floor, grinding against one another, lost in their own little world, yet aware. And from the looks of both of their eyes, very much in tune with their surroundings.

He shifted his hips, flowed to the rhythm, and let

his body do what he'd been doing for as long as he could remember—dance.

Brooke stood like a statue, her hands just above her shoulders and, after his encouragement, gave a little shimmy.

His lips twitched, but he fought against the grin.

He pushed her to move more into his body and urged her to follow along to his rhythm. She did—or at least *tried to*. He adored her, he really did, and even understanding he could actually love her wasn't something that surprised him. She was gorgeous, caring, funny, and loyal to almost a fault. But dance, that she couldn't do.

Brooke, now opening to dancing more, jerked and convulsed as if she were having a seizure. There was no rhyme or reason in her steps, and nothing about the way she moved said she had any beat in her head. It was so unlike her, so completely *unsexy*, that he burst out laughing.

She stopped and scowled. Chuckling, he drew her closer. She still tried to pull away.

"I'm not a good dancer," she hissed.

"I'm getting that," he said through hilarity. "Relax." He turned her until her back was to his front. With her hips settled to his groin, he set one hand on the curve of her waist and the other to her belly.

Then he began to move. Slightly, at first, but still keeping the beat.

"Brooke," he murmured with a brush of his lips at her temple. "Relax. Feel the beat. Let it move you, don't try to move it."

She growled and let out a little sound of frustration. "This isn't going to work."

He pressed her closer to him.

"Follow me," he said. "Let my body move for

you. Feel it…"

He rocked their hips stronger, putting pressure on her stomach until the crowd around didn't exist. It was all a blur, she, his entire focus. That's what she did to him every time. She took the thoughts from his mind and caused his brain to stop working until all that continued, all that he smelled, tasted, or knew was Brooke.

She swayed against him and pressed her bottom to his groin. Their bodies were in sync, two beings becoming one. A few seconds passed and she brought one hand up to curve behind his neck. Her body arched and just like that, the exuberance she gave to him, the way she let him lead her, the way she gave him her all, caused a jolt of desire to tighten his groin.

Lost in his world of her, he blinked as another female stepped up to Brooke. She stiffened against him but relaxed once Charlie came into view. The desire, the calm, and his elation at having Brooke in his arms disappeared with a snap. Both Charlie and Trent's faces were hard, worried, and sent alarms pinging through his head.

Charlie pressed against Brooke, but she lifted her head so she could speak to Dwayne. Trent continued to look over the crowd, his front to Charlie's back.

"Luke," Charlie hissed and pulled her head back. Her focus shifted over to the corner, and Dwayne followed her gaze.

Standing off to the side of the room under a blue light was Luke with two women. The females kissed each other and Luke's gaze was hard, hot, and more than a little dark. It wasn't something such as two women kissing that drew his attention. Dwayne tightened his jaw. It was more. Those women looked young, too young, actually. And they were stiff in each other's arms like they didn't want to be there. Dwayne watched as his youngest brother dipped his head toward the two girls and said something that caused them to look at him in fear. Luke leaned back, took a sip of beer and lifted a hand as if to say, "Go on."

One girl turned and leaned against Luke, her back to his front, and pulled the other into her arms. Even at this distance, Dwayne saw her hands shake. She played with the silver strap on the brunette's tank top. Her head dipped and she touched her mouth to revealed skin.

"What is he doing?" Brooke hissed.

Dwayne looked down to find Brooke watching the action, too.

"I don't know," he answered and remembered Luke's warning earlier. *Shit!* Shit, they didn't need this. Whatever his brother was doing was bound to fuck the entire operation to hell. He didn't think…no, he knew Luke realized how important Hailey was to him. He couldn't believe that his brother would toss it out there and fuck around with little girls, women who didn't look older than seventeen, all for a piece, or two pieces, of ass.

Just then, a shadow stepped under the blue light and the four of them stiffened as Jaxon's face came into view. With a mischievous look on his face, he stepped right up to Luke.

Luke didn't move away from the girls but turned his head toward the newcomer.

"Jaxon," Brooke said with a low warning and went to move away.

Dwayne tightened his grip around her waist and used his other arm to wrap a band around Charlie's neck until the three of them were sandwiched together. Trent went with the action, falling close behind, clearly realizing how the situation could seriously deteriorate if Brooke got free.

"You will stay right here," Dwayne growled.

"But it's Jaxon," she snapped.

"Exactly, Luke's got it."

"No, Luke doesn't have it," she mocked. "I don't know what the heck he's doing, but he definitely does not have my daughter's best interest at heart. Look at him."

"Yes," Charlie said, wrapping her arms around Dwayne's neck. She pressed closer to Brooke, but her eyes were intent on the scene in the corner. "Look at him. I know Luke. I grew up with him, and I understand he has secrets. But look at him, and look closely."

Dwayne did what Charlie ordered. Jaxon and Luke were exchanging words and when Jaxon tossed his head back and laughed at something Luke said, then reached out to shake his hand, Dwayne knew.

They were in.

Chapter Twenty-Four

Luke didn't like this.

Not.

One.

Fucking.

Bit.

He'd been trained to work on his own in some of the most dangerous situations possible. The duties of a US Marshal demanded it. Hell, working undercover as much as they did, you never knew what types of crimes you'd come upon.

But this.

Pretending to be into this underage shit. Like a mere child could handle a man, even one like him. He couldn't imagine a child, some seventeen-year-old girl, trying to take on his six-foot-one, two hundred and twenty pound frame. Just the thought of it tore his stomach to shreds.

Of course looking the way he looked, there was no doubt why he'd be chosen to come to a back room separate from the club. And wasn't it just his luck that he was here? Yeah. Right. At least that's what he kept telling himself.

Really, he needed to be there for his family, the only he'd ever known. Losing his own mother so young, for reasons out of both of their control, he'd been shoved into a life where everyone he knew was a stranger. No family for him to fall back on, no friends to take him in. He'd been a scared four-year-old little boy thrust into the state's care.

He would never have enough gratitude toward the Gonzalezes for taking a chance on him and giving him a possibility to survive. If this small act was one way he could repay his family, so be it. He'd fake his way as far as he needed to. Do *anything* it took to help repay his debt.

The stocky guy he'd been following pushed open a door and motioned him inside. He stepped through the frame and shoved his hands inside his pockets. A king-size bed sat in the middle of the floor, a deep red silk spread covering the mattress, inviting carnal thoughts unneeded. For whoever came back to one of these rooms sure as shit wasn't looking to talk.

Sheer burgundy-and-black curtains fell around the bed and the walls were painted black. The low-lamped lighting gave enough to see, yet kept it dark enough to keep one from looking too closely. The room felt dirty, and the thoughts of those who'd be invited back here were guaranteed to be even dirtier.

"She'll be here in a few minutes. Get comfortable," the dude who introduced himself as Jax, said.

Luke glanced over his shoulder and fought to keep the sneer inside. "Remember what I asked for."

Jax nodded, waving a hand. "No worries, my friend. We'll take good care of you. This little treat I've tested personally. You'll like her, no doubt."

The door shut.

God, he wanted to puke. He stepped forward, kept his face neutral in the instance that the room had surveillance. No doubt it did. What was a little privacy invasion on top of human sex trafficking?

Fuck.

He crossed the room and sat on the bed, clasped his hands between his knees and dropped his head. All he needed was a few minutes. He had to get into the character for this. They were depending on him. And he wouldn't, couldn't, allow a child to continue in this place knowing what he did now.

The shit he had to push on those two teenagers out front was bad enough. But he had to do it, had to do this for his family. For Hailey's safety, and for his older brother and his woman.

A whisper of movement behind him.

His head jerked up and his upper body spun around. Now he knew why the lighting was set as it was, why the walls were black, why the damnable sheer curtains were up.

Hailey—yeah, he recognized her—stood looking back at him on the other side of the linen. Her long hair sat in big tumbled curls around her shoulders, the color somewhere between the sand of the desert and the mountains of Arizona. Her body was clad in ivory, adorned in only a lacy bra and panties. Garters attached the cloth in the same color and disappeared beneath the ledge of the mattress. Her breasts almost tumbled out of material a size too small and entirely too provocative for a girl her age.

None of that held his attention, though. With air stuck in his lungs, he watched her doe-brown eyes try to keep focus on him. She held his gaze as if a challenge, but it was glossy, hazy, not all there. She bit her bottom lip, trailed her fingers over the material separating them, and kept the hold on his gaze as she walked around the mattress.

He couldn't speak. He'd lost the ability to focus. She was Pandora, a wicked siren of temptation. In that moment, she wasn't a teenager verging on being eighteen. She was downright one of the most beautiful women he'd seen.

He shook his head. She was underage. She was here against her will.

"Do you like what you see, mister?"

Her voice rolled over his skin, little rose petals, all velvet and smooth and utterly too sensual.

Keep it together, dude. She needs to offer her services. It won't have to go too far. He hoped.

He cleared his throat, then darted his gaze around the room, looking for those damn hidden cameras. "Um, yeah. What's not to like?"

She swayed as if some unspoken music played. Muted notes of something whispered through the air. Teasing, like the minx that stood before him. She'd moved around, and now that he took note, he found himself cocooned inside the sheer curtain, which wrapped around the entire circumference of the bed. The panels of burgundy and black had been sewn together to give the entire thing a majestic feel. No doubt enhancing the power of lust.

Hailey stayed on the other side of the curtain, though, and continued to watch him. Her body grew bolder, swayed to the music and flourished in confidence as if a wave teased, cresting over its peak. Her breasts caught against the material and flowed with her. She never broke eye contact, their connection palpable. Just danced. For him.

He was caught up in the arch of her back as she moved, the length of her neck when she stretched, the sway of her hips. Each movement was smooth, transitioned from one to the other as if designed together.

A cold sweat broke out along his neck. How could he shiver when the room was so hot?

"Show me," she whispered.

"Show you what, sweetheart?"

"Show me," she started and licked her lips. The pink gloss glistened under the muted light. "Show me what my body does to you. Tell me what my movements do for you."

Christ! His throat went dry and he tried to swallow several times to no avail. *Come on, honey. Enough of the small talk. Get to it.*

"You're uh…very sexy." He winced. *Way to be smooth, Luke.*

"Will you…?"

He started at her unfinished question. "Will I what?" Something ugly festered in his stomach. *Please, don't. Please no, no, no.*

"Will you save me, mister?" She continued to hold his gaze and stepped closer. The sheer curtain plastered and caught on her curves, spread across her breasts, pulled taut between her legs. He didn't know if that was the effect she looked for, but it damn well did its job. Blood rushed south and he fought against the reaction. *Think of something, anything. Fat dudes eating hotdogs. New York City subway rats. Barney singing that annoying damn song.*

Her earlier question pierced through his attempt to control his reaction to her. He tore his gaze from her body and studied her eyes, imploring a silent question. Did she recognize him? Know who he was? "S-save you?" he croaked.

She moved forward and nodded, stepped between his legs and he looked up, forced to hold her gaze by tipping his head back. "I want you to stay with me. Here. Just us." She dipped and came closer. Her mouth brushed along his, the sheer curtain the only thing separating them. Her small palms cradled his head and pressed their mouths tighter, deepening the kiss. Having the netting between the absolute touch of their tongues annoyed, yet provided a coquettish sensation.

Sweet Lord in heaven. I'm sorry.

How could he not react to this? The situation broke his heart and sent a crack a mile wide through his chest. Here was this sweet girl, forced into a ring without a choice, drugged up beyond understanding anything going on around her.

He fisted his hands on his thighs, forcing himself to remain still while she kissed the daylights out of him. Conscious of the cameras perhaps trained on them, on the soft music playing through the room, and of the feel of her silken lips teasing his through the soft material, he silently called himself every type of bastard.

She moved closer. On instinct, he reached out for her legs. Bare skin brushed under his palms and she jumped at the same time he tensed. He broke his mouth away and glanced down. The sheet had risen to her waist and she was stepping through.

No, no, no.

No one heard him, though, and she pushed through the material—stood glorious, gaze expectant on his.

"I'm not really sure how I feel about this."

She cocked her head to the side, studied him and trailed her fingers along his cheek. "Do you dream?" she asked.

The question took him by surprise, nothing new in the few moments he'd been here.

"What?"

"What do you dream about, mister?"

He shook his head and held her gaze. "I don't." She didn't say anything and he really needed her to talk, needed her to offer her services. To get things going, he tried, but stupidly asked the wrong damn question. "What do *you* dream about?"

"You." No hesitation in her answer.

He groaned and moved his head, rested it against her bare stomach, and squeezed his eyes shut. She cradled him to her body as if he was the one that needed to be comforted, as if at twenty-five years old he needed to be protected. *If only, sweetheart.*

"Dance with me, please," she whispered.

Her soft request sounded like a plea and he was unable to deny her anything. She had set a spell on him and he was bewitched. He rose from the bed and took her small waist in his hands, intending to keep space between them. She plastered her body to his before he could think, then pressed her mouth against his and kissed him.

He crushed his hand in her hair and wrapped his free arm around her, pulling her closer. She tasted of sugar, plums, and sweet temptation.

He had to get control of this situation before things got out of hand.

"Do you dare to come closer, mister?" Her sweet breath whispered over his mouth.

Through the fog, her words registered. "Call me Luke. What if I said I do?"

"This isn't something you can take, Luke. It's something I'm going to give."

Morbid images floated through his head. He had to stop this, had to get through to her. And he had to do it without alerting anyone else.

"I'm so enchanted. Sugar, you have no clue."

She kissed him again before he could continue. The cold, dark despair that had accompanied him since being a child began to melt a little. He palmed her face, as she had done his earlier, and pulled her back. Pressing chaste kisses over her face, he prayed for strength, for courage...for the chance to get them out of here.

"It's funny," he began between kisses, "it seems like you're saving me, instead of me rescuing you."

"What?" she squeaked, just a little semblance of control peeking through. Hell, she was going to blow this.

"How much?" He buried his head in her neck.

Speaking louder, he asked again, "How much?"

Wrapped around him, and he around her, their two bodies were lost in the middle of some ugly operation. Yet, he wouldn't want to be anywhere else but inside her arms. *Fucking hell!*

"How much?" he snapped, this time whipping his head up and glaring at her.

She blinked, drew her head back a bit, and glanced up to a dark corner. Yep, cameras were in the room. "Um, five hundred dollars."

He swallowed, forcing the bile down his throat. "What do I get for five hundred? That's quite the check, honey."

Her delicate nose wrinkled. "Anything—anything you want."

Bingo.

He pulled out his phone, sent one waiting text, and removed himself from her arms. "Ms. Mason, you're under arrest. You have the right to remain silent."

"What?" Panicked features swelled past the drug-induced haze. "What are you talking about?"

He didn't bother with the handcuffs. "Anything you say will be used against you in a court of law."

She sputtered. "What are you doing? They'll hear you! I need it now. Please, keep your voice down."

Her eyes filled with tears, but he pressed on. "You have the right to an attorney during interrogation. If you cannot afford—"

The door to the room burst open and two beefy guys entered.

Hell...any moment, guys. He waited for the sound of his brothers crashing through the walls. For the sounds of shouting from the local police. Anything. All he got were the heart-wrenching sobs from Hailey. She stepped between him and the two new arrivals, fleetingly taking him by surprise. Cursing, he grabbed her hand and tried to pull her behind him.

"No! Don't. He was just role-playing. Please!" she screamed, panicked.

"Christ, get behind me."

He grabbed her around the waist, tried like hell— *and failed*—to ignore her curves pressing against him as he shoved her to his back.

One of the guys reached for his waistband and Luke reacted, grabbing the Glock from his groin, then drew it on the first guy. He had one gun. They had two between them. He didn't like the damn odds left and all the while, Hailey continued to clutch at his shirt.

"Who are you?" the shorter guy thundered. He wore black pants and a black shirt, baldhead, and a murderous expression.

"Name's Luke. Would shake your hand and all, but unless you plan on lowering your weapon, I don't think me drawing mine down is such a good idea."

The taller of the two sneered. He wore the same outfit—*must be their uniform*—and cursed in a language Luke didn't understand. The only reason he knew it was a curse was the ugly sound it made coming from the guy's mouth. He didn't think it was a compliment.

"Well, Luke," Baldy spat his name. "Couldn't help but to overhear something that's alarming."

Luke smiled, his lips feeling rigid. "Invasion of privacy?" He tsked.

The guy snarled. "I'm going to ask you again, who the fuck are you? Are you a cop?"

Luke drew back, affronted. "A cop? Fuck no."

Baldy and Jolly Green both looked like they took a deep breath, but he wasn't finished.

"I'm a Deputy US Marshal. Do you realize how annoying it is when you fuckers use that term, or slang as it may be, on just about every law enforcement officer?"

Their guns, which had lowered a few inches, took aim again. Luke tensed. *One of these days, your mouth. Dude!* He sighed.

"Well, Deputy, what the hell do you think you're doing? You realize that you're outnumbered, no?"

Luke shrugged, when he felt anything but at ease. Baldy narrowed his eyes.

"You might as well give up," Luke said. "Your club is going down."

Jolly Green scoffed. "In case you missed it, you're a little alone. Are you stupid? Who's going to follow through with this said 'taking of the club?'"

Luke grinned a slow smile, and both chumps' eyes narrowed. "Just me." He paused and continued, "And the FBI, SWAT, State PD, ATF, DEA. None of you are making it out of here. Alive, that is."

Jolly Green took a menacing step forward. Luke leveled the sights of his gun on him.

"Please fuck with me. I'm really hoping you'll take me up on the offer because I'm fucking itching to kick some ass. I'm giving you a fair warning, though, asshole, the second you get within two feet of me, so help me God, I'm going to snap your neck."

"And I'll shoot you," Baldy responded.

"But then," Luke seethed, "his neck will be snapped. So either way, I'll win."

"But you'll be dead."

"So will he. So it really doesn't matter." Crap, what would happen to Hailey, though?

"You shouldn't be a smart ass with a gun in your face," Jolly Green inserted. "It could get you shot. Not a good idea."

"Yeah." Luke shrugged. "I'm a smart ass, or so I've been told. It's probably not a good idea, but you know what, I'll take your stereotype and raise a big, fat, fuck you."

The sounds of shouting broke out down the hall and both Men in Black glanced over their shoulders. His brothers. Luke grinned wider. "Now, if you'd direct your attention, I'll give you two hooker helpers some choices."

Chapter Twenty-Five

The next day, Brooke sat in the hospital, staring at her daughter. Hailey looked too small in the big white bed. Her normally shiny red hair laid around her face like wiry strands begging for a dose of moisture, just another sign of the effects drugs had on a system. The life usually sitting in her cheeks also reflected a dull, drab complexion. It had been less than two weeks since she'd disappeared, yet she didn't look like the rambunctious teenager Brooke knew her to be.

This was someone else entirely.

A stranger holding the real Hailey captive.

Brooke dropped her head, tightened her grip on Hailey's hand, and willed her to pull through. She'd gone to sleep late last night after arriving in the ER and now, fourteen hours later, she still hadn't woken. The doctors checked in every hour, double-checked her stats, and gave her more fluid and medicine to help wean her off the drugs.

All Brooke could do was sit back and let others help her daughter. She felt worthless and a complete failure as a mother.

The door clicked behind her. The on-duty nurse, a middle-aged round woman who wore tight pink-and-white scrubs, stepped through, humming beneath her breath and smiling as if she didn't have a care in the world. Like her entire estate wasn't crumbling down around her feet.

She stepped beside Hailey's bed and started the routine process of taking her vitals.

"How she doing so far, hun?" the nurse asked.

Brooke glanced back at her daughter's face and her heart squeezed.

"Still sleeping. Shouldn't she be awake by now?"

She shook her head. "Not necessarily. I'll double check with Doctor Johnson, but right now, her body is doing what it needs to. Rest." Shrewd blue eyes turned her way, measuring. "It looks like you may need to take a bit of a break as well. Have you caught any sleep yet?"

Brooke shrugged. "A little here and there. No more than you can imagine any mother would want to, seeing as my daughter has been missing for almost two weeks."

The nurse nodded and jotted something down on Hailey's chart. "Well, yes. But honey, you have guards right outside the door, big menacing men, who, no offense, but can raise anyone's temperature with just their presence alone. Do you really think they'd move away and let anything happen in the few hours you need to get some sleep?"

Brooke frowned. "Who?"

"And they have hospital security running tight shifts. I tell you, in my fifteen here, I've never seen Doug jump so quick at someone's beck and call. Those boys belong to you?"

Pulling away from the bed, Brooke crossed the room, curious. She hadn't seen anyone since they'd been brought in and honestly thought they had been left alone to deal with this. Just like they always had done, on their own. She hadn't heard from Dwayne. His expression through the back of an ambulance's glass as they sped away from the scene haunted her. His eyes had spoken a million things at once, his gaze steady and sure, but at the time, she'd been too focused on what they were doing with Hailey to really think or plan anything.

She tugged on the door and held it open with her hip, then peeked her head around the jamb. Luke straightened from his perch on the wall, eyes shaded beneath the brim of his ball cap. He wore a black t-shirt, this one with a dark gray skull etched on the front, which pulled taut across his chest before giving way to a trim waist. Blue jeans that had seen better days encased his legs, and finishing off the full package were black boots, scruff with use.

She pulled her gaze back up and caught a small hint of a smile before he said, "You done?"

Frowning, she crossed her arms over her chest. "What are you doing?"

He lifted one brow. "Contemplating life. What does it look like I'm doing?"

She narrowed her eyes at his tone, his words. Luke hadn't seemed talkative last night either, but this was a little much. Or not much at all. He kept shifting his gaze toward the door at her back, almost as if he expected someone else to come out.

"Have I offended you or something, Luke?"

His shoulders stiffened. "No."

She waited. When he didn't offer any more, she tried again. "Then what's your problem?"

He stared straight ahead and mirrored her pose. "I don't have a problem. At least, not with you, Brooke. Is there something you need?"

She frowned, disturbed even more by his words. "Why are you standing outside my daughter's room? Are we still in danger? Is someone still out there?"

He shook his head and let out a breath. "No, no, God, no, it's not that. We just want to make sure you don't have anything else to worry about while Hailey recovers." He swallowed hard and glanced again at the door. His face looked vulnerable, which had her confusion ramping up more. "Has she said anything?"

How odd of a question. It wasn't as if he was in the room, knew Hailey was still asleep, but she figured one would ask how a patient was doing rather than what they were or were not saying.

"No, she's asleep," she answered, measuring each of her words.

His shoulders relaxed and she could have sworn the lines around his mouth smoothed away. How very strange, indeed. Before she could ask additional questions, Luke nodded to someone approaching behind her. She turned her head, but she should have prepared for it.

Dwayne stepped up to them. He stopped two feet away, but she could feel his presence as if he had touched her. His gaze roamed over her body and lingered on her face. She must look like crap, could only imagine what last night's makeup, the outfit, her appearance, revealed after all they had been through. She fought with the instinct to check her hair and kept her hands planted at her sides.

He stepped closer and lifted a hand, slowly, as if gauging her response. Intrigued and craving a little of his touch, she stood still. He cupped her cheek and wiped his thumb beneath her eye. "You catch any sleep last night?"

She shook her head, unnerved with the zing his touch created. The heat from his palm spread like lava through her system, warming her completely. After being so cold, battling with the storm of concern for her daughter, she wanted to wrap the cloak of warmth around her body and give in to the comfort.

His mouth went grim and he sighed. "What about Hails? How is she doing?" His gaze shifted to Luke behind her and he frowned at whatever he saw before turning back to her.

"She's going to have to go through detox. They keep talking about different options but are keeping her comfortable for now while her body recovers from what she's been through. Her mind needs to rest as well, so they are trying not to disturb her too much."

"Good," he said, then dropped his palm to her hand, entwining their fingers. A possessive hold, one screaming of his intentions, and one she liked way too much. She sucked in a breath and fought to control her growing nerves. There was no way she could manage this man, his appetite, and the care of her daughter, as well as protect her heart. He didn't give long term. He'd told her that, right? Or, at least, he'd shown her that with actions over the years. She knew this man, knew what he did, and that he'd always have another offer with just a flick of his wrist.

Dread formed a knot in her stomach. There wasn't another option to give here other than break things off now, before she fell any more in love with this man, before she gave him all of her. She feared she had already given him too much.

He pressed his lips to the back of her hand, their joined hands between them, a stark contrast in their coloring capturing her attention for a quick, distracting moment. He nipped her knuckle as if he knew.

"She needs her rest. As do you. Why don't you go back to the hotel, get some sleep while Luke and I hang here? If she wakes, I'll call you immediately," Dwayne said.

She shook her head before he finished. "No. I won't leave her." She tried to tug her hand, but he wasn't having any of it and tightened his grip.

"You're practically asleep standing up."

"No," she snapped, yanking her hand away. God, she knew she was being unreasonable. He was doing what he always did—making sure others were taken care of. But she couldn't allow this to happen, couldn't have him hanging around and settling deeper in her heart than he already was. She and Hailey would be fine. They always had been. They would be now, too. She needed to break this off before things twisted any more.

With an apologetic glance over her shoulder, she faced Dwayne head-on. "I think you should go home."

He blinked slowly. "Come again?"

She shifted, seeing the change in his body, the tension radiating off him. "I think you should go home. I can handle things from here with Hailey. We'll be fine."

His eyes narrowed. "So you can handle a seventeen-year-old drug addict who has to detox, in a place three states away from home, without support? Am I hearing you right?"

Shoot, when he put it that way, it sounded pretty rough, but that was exactly what she was going to do, what she had to do in order to protect not just herself but Hailey as well. "I want you to go."

He crossed his arms. His face was hard and unreadable. "You want *me* to go? Not Luke? Just me?"

Her throat grew tight and needles pricked at the back of her eyes. She fought to maintain control. This was the only way. "Yes. I'm sorry, Dwayne. I think it'll be for the best. I have Hailey to concentrate on and that's all I can handle right now."

"I want what's best for Hailey, too. You do know that, right?"

She nodded. His words were lovely, but this wasn't about his feelings. Unfortunately. And that may make her a bitch, but she had to put her daughter first, and in order to do so, she couldn't care about anything else. "I do. But I also know I can't be who you need me to, what you expect. I just think it'll be better for all of us if you go home and we settle back into our old friendship. You can't handle anything outside of that," she said and rushed on to add, "and that's okay, but it's time for us to stop this. It's time I need to spend with Hails."

His shoulders snapped and his back went stiff. "You really think we can just go back to being friends?" he asked incredulously.

She blinked and whipped her head up, shocked to realize she had never considered that he wouldn't want that friendship anymore.

Riiiiip.

So many years, so much lost. It was almost too much to bear. The pain in her throat spread to her chest. "You don't want that?" she gritted out, fighting to keep the pressure inside. It built in her chest, an explosion of epic proportions. With everything happening the past few weeks, the emotional release threatened to erupt as sure as a geyser.

His gaze roamed over her face before his expression softened. "I think you know what I want, Brooke."

Sex. Didn't he say that? That's it. That's all it was? She drew in a deep breath and squared her shoulders. "I'm sorry, I can't be that to you."

He stared at her for long minutes. She kept her gaze on his strong jaw, knowing if she met his eyes, she'd break down and let it all out. Her love for him, the craving she always felt. Her desires needed to be set away, placed on a back burner until her daughter was healthy. Maybe then, maybe they could discuss being friends again.

Unbidden, hundreds of memories flew through her mind.

Dwayne laughing, his smile shining brighter than the sun.

Her three-year-old daughter wrapping her arms and legs around one of his, holding on for dear life as he played Giant and ran across their backyard.

The muscles of his back flexing as he bent below the sink to fix a leak.

Teaching Hailey how to throw a curve ball.

Mowing her lawn when she hadn't asked him.

Corralling them over to his parents' house for Thanksgiving the year after her mother died.

Taking care of them. Always.

She turned, needing the escape, and pushed open the door. His voice behind her was rough with emotion, pain, and something she couldn't identify. She wouldn't look back, couldn't, for surely he'd see her tears, and he'd know she lied.

"Luke will stay and watch over you. He'll take care of you from here." A heavy pause floated between them. "Goodbye, Brooke."

Goodbye...

Crack.

The ominous sound ripped through her chest, the heart she'd been trying to protect shattering.

Chapter Twenty-Six

A week later, Dwayne pushed through the front door of his parents' house, the home where he had started his new life. A life that belatedly began at six years old. The foyer had coats and shoes scattered haphazardly, tossed aside like a forgotten item. It was the way of things, a simple reminder of how his life with his brothers had been when they'd done the same—still did the same—as they were each brought into this new bright, loving world.

He toed off his Italian loafers, kicked them gently under a wooden bench by the door, slipped off his jacket and hung it on a hook. Voices sounded from down the hall, just on the other side of the stairs, and he recognized Charlie, Trent, his mother, and father laughing and carrying on. He gave a small smile at the sound of family, and that Trent would be accepted into the mix as easily as Charlie had been. His parents were like that, loving and kind, always freely giving something they never expected in return. Patience. Understanding. Love.

God. He squeezed his eyes shut and rubbed at the phantom pain in his chest. The whole saying about your heart breaking had always been something he thought silly, because really, how could feelings cause that much grief when they weren't physical. But after the way Brooke had kicked him out of the hospital, and effectively out of her life, the pain in his chest hadn't lessened at all.

He was standing in the foyer, staring at pictures from his childhood, ones where he'd been laughing, smiling and covered in mud with his five brothers, when his mom walked into the room.

"Baby, when did you get here?"

One side of his mouth lifted in a grin and he glanced over his shoulder. Karen wasn't as young as she used to be, but she was still very mobile and spent tons of time outdoors doing gardening, hiking with his father, and pulling them both on outings to explore the world. It showed in her sun-kissed skin dusted with wrinkles, and her toned shoulder where a white cardigan had slipped slightly. Her gray hair had hints of brown beneath. Her eyes, a clear hazel, held years of knowledge and a lifetime of love.

"I just got here. Was remembering how you had to hose us down after this." He nodded toward the picture he'd been looking at.

She stepped next to him and glanced at the picture. "Oh, yes, hose you down good, I did. I warned you boys. Your father kept harping on me to leave you alone, said it was only a little dirt."

Dwayne scoffed. "A little? You were installing the pool, it had been raining for two days, *two* days," he emphasized, "and to us it was way more than a little dirt." It had been a big 'ole mud pie, and they had a blast pretending to be pirates attempting to dig their way from the trenches.

She chuckled, and the sound soothed him. This was why he'd come home, to experience a little piece of comfort. To remember what it was like to be accepted unconditionally. No matter what. His adopted mother turned to him and he looked over at her. She studied him, frowning.

"What is it?" he asked.

"Why don't you tell me? You boys work out whatever it was you needed to do up north?"

Surprised she knew, he asked, "Who told you?"

She offered a smile, one that looked like she was only tolerating him being so silly. "I'm your mother, I know all."

He let out a short, disbelieving laugh. "Yeah, and I distinctly remember you telling me the same thing after I came home from an all-nighter with Cindy Squalls."

"You were sixteen, and it was three o'clock in the morning."

"I was sixteen and a half," he corrected. "And Jake had a big mouth then, too."

She shrugged and asked again, "So tell me, what's got you so upset?"

He sighed, then hung his head. "There's no easy way to tell it."

"Then just say it, baby." Her small hand reached out for his. He accepted her connection and linked their fingers together. With a tug, she motioned over her head and he followed. The short hall opened into a huge kitchen with wraparound counters, a kitchen island, and a bar to separate the cooking area from the eat-in dining. Charlie and Trent glanced up and smiled.

They sat at the bar that extended out from the kitchen counter. Trent had his arm wrapped around Charlie, smiles on both of their faces. His dad turned laughing eyes toward him. Charlie was wiping beneath her eyes, and Trent's lips were turned up in a smile. He'd obviously walked into something, but really, it was no surprise to have Charlie here when he wasn't. She'd been accepted long ago, and if she was bringing over Trent to meet his parents, ones that had looked over her as she grew, too, then it meant things were getting serious between them.

Not that they weren't serious already.

A blissful scene, and he was more than happy for them all. His problems seemed so pathetic when compared to the lighthearted feeling in the room. He shifted his feet and his mom squeezed his hand.

"How's Brooke?" Charlie asked.

Dwayne pursed his lips, fighting to find the right words to explain the situation she was dealing with. He didn't know if he could, though, and fought to stop thinking of himself and his own damn feelings. It was ridiculous. Here this woman was dealing with her seventeen-year-old daughter who'd been kidnapped and was now trying to detox, and all he could think about was how he wanted to be at her side, comforting her, helping her, just being with her.

His mother reached out and soothed the area between his brows with her finger. "Tell me, what's causing my son to develop wrinkles. Is she hurt? I thought you two were getting along nicely."

He tilted his head away from her touch. "Ahhh, hell, Mom," he whined.

She grinned. "I told you, mothers know everything."

Blowing out a breath, he looked around the room, not seeing anything but the woman he left behind. *Was forced to leave.* "She's fine. They've got the best care in the area and as soon as it's safe, she'll be bringing Hailey back down to Nyack."

"She'll get through it. That girl is stronger than she thinks. And her daughter takes after her, so I'm not worried about it," Karen chirped.

"Yeah, there's that."

"Okay, so go on," she prodded, nudging him lightly.

"On?" he asked.

She looked at him with the same expression she used to get him to confess to stealing a beer from his dad's fridge.

"Son, give it up," his father stated. "Something is wrong and it's written all over your face. Out with it."

Hadn't he come home for this? To be accepted, to not be afraid to put it all out there? His mom covered his hand lying on the tile countertop. She gave it a squeeze and he closed his eyes. "I've wanted Brooke for longer than I could remember."

"Nothing new there," his mother stated.

"Things between us have always been tenacious at best. She was married."

"Got divorced," his dad, Daniel, added.

He opened his eyes and nodded. "Got divorced, and still, I kept a distance. I wanted to let things come along on their own terms. I didn't think I could give her something she didn't want, nor did I want to ruin our friendship. I look at Hailey now as if she is my own, care for that little girl like she's the world."

Charlie leaned against Trent. Dwayne didn't think either of them realized the silent support they offered one another, even when their attention focused elsewhere.

"Well, things changed in the past week. Between Brooke and I. But unfortunately, they really didn't change for the better." He winced.

"What do you mean, not for the better," his mom asked.

"Not going to get into it. Not with you. No way, no how. Sorry, Mom, not happening."

She huffed. "Oh please, you clean your sons' rooms through their teenage years and you learn everything you ever wanted to know, including things you didn't."

He grimaced. "Mom! Please!" Shaking his head, he laughed. "Christ, woman!" He laughed again when she smacked his arm. "Let's just say Brooke thinks I'm not one to settle down. Doesn't seem to understand how I care for her."

"Ah." One word. Understanding dawned in his

mother's expression. "I see exactly what's happened."

A feeling akin to a needle prickled at the back of his neck. "You see? You see what?"

"Oh, baby," she said, eyes sad. "I wish I could have been there for you sooner."

"Mom—" he tried to interrupt, but she cut him off.

"No. Don't you *mom* me." She took his hand and squeezed it to her chest, staring at him with so much conviction he reared his head.

"I wish I could have. Your birth mom wasn't a bad person, baby. She had her vices, though, and those issues of hers have passed on to who you have become as a man. I tried to show you that it's okay to express your love, to voice it, but I have a feeling I may have failed.

"I have very few regrets in my life, but this one is on the list. I allowed you boys to do as you needed. I wanted you all to test the limits, to fly, to learn. I wanted you to feel as if you could figure out the world on your own, make your mistakes, and solve your way out of them yourselves.

"With you, though, it was a bit harder because of what you went through. I wanted to protect you from all that ugliness, wanted you to have the innocence you were denied as a child. She brought those men into your home, screwed them in front of her baby, and left you alone again for hours to fend for yourself."

His throat grew thick. Memories swamped him as he remembered.

"You came for me, though," he rasped, his words rough.

"Not soon enough. I wish I could have been there sooner." His dad stepped up behind her and set his hands on her shoulders. A show of support. She glanced at him, then at Dwayne. Tears filled her eyes but didn't spill over.

"You were eating flour out of a bag that had been left in the closet. You'd been alone for only God knows how long. That's what they told us. You were so young, yet your eyes so old. I wanted to shelter you for a bit longer, babied you into not being pressured to talk about it. Because no one really wanted you to remember."

"But I do," he said.

"You do," she confirmed. "I didn't want this, though. I didn't want you scared to touch life, touch someone for fear of the unknown. Life isn't written in braille, baby. Neither is love, friendship, experience, or knowledge. Life is just that, to live, to learn, to experience, and to love."

Her tears spilled over and damn him if he didn't feel one slide down his own cheek. He understood what she tried to say. Many nights he had talked to her about his birth mother, about the way she used to toss the words of love around as if they were air, nothing special. It was her actions that affected him most. She didn't do things that showed love, and in some way, he was almost reliving her life through his own.

"Don't you do that," his mother snapped, her voice angry.

He startled. "Do what?"

"You are not her," she said, gripping his hands with a strength that surprised him.

"Ma, I didn't say…"

"You didn't, but you were thinking it."

He pursed his lips and bowed his head. Fuck, when had life gotten so out of control? When had he lost it all?

"Say it," she whispered.

"Say what?"

"That you're not her," she replied and her voice broke. The damn sound tore at his heart and his chest caved in. He never wanted to hurt her, never wanted to mess things up between him and Brooke, and he never wanted to feel this lost again.

"I'm not her," he whispered.

"Louder, baby, I don't think your dad heard you."

He lifted his head and looked at both of his parents. "I'm not her."

They smiled.

"Now, go talk to her, you ass," Charlie quipped from behind.

* * * *

Luke sat back in the chair, legs stretched out before him, crossed at the ankles, his arms folded across his chest. He'd been sitting like that, outside of Hailey's room, for hours now, so many he'd lost count. He hadn't gone back to the hotel room, hadn't really moved from this spot other than to piss or get some coffee and a bite to eat.

So maybe he was being a little over the top with keeping watch here. Sure, the bad guys had been taken down, the threat against Hailey gone, just as sure as the meatloaf he'd had for dinner last night in the cafeteria wasn't made with real hamburger.

He didn't know why he stayed, well, other than the fact that his brother would have his ass. But he wanted to stay even outside all that.

Why?

He didn't know.

"Fucking hell," he muttered and sat up, scrubbing his hands over his face.

He did know, and the reason sat in the room behind him, resting fitfully, trying to recover from an ordeal of hell. He'd peeked in earlier, and the sight of Hailey lying so small and sick beneath the white covers… His damnable heart tore apart.

"Shit, damn, shit, damn, damn," he said and stood. He paced two steps to the left, pivoted and paced another four, then turned again. He needed to get back to work. The problem was he wasn't due for another seven days. He'd expected things to take a bit of time, and who knew how long they'd have Hailey here, but he didn't think he'd be able to handle another seven days standing around, watching her, thinking about her, wanting...her.

"She's seventeen, dude," he told himself.

Technically, she turns eighteen next week.

And wasn't that just another kick in the balls? That Hailey would have to celebrate her eighteenth birthday with an injection from the good 'ole drug of methadone. *Welcome to the world of feeling faint and like you're going to throw up. Have another!*

"It's not your problem, Luke," he muttered.

No, no it wasn't, but damn if it really was. He still remembered her as a skinny little girl following his big brother around, coming over to the house for holidays, and he'd watched her grow into a teenager up until a few years ago when he left to become a US Marshal.

But the girl he remembered from three years ago was *not* the same as the one who'd seduced the shit out of him in that room back at the club.

She was high!

"I know!"

She's underage, asshole!

"I know!" he snapped.

"Luke?" a soft voice asked from behind.

He whipped around and damn if he didn't feel his cheeks heat like a schoolboy caught peeking in the girls' locker room. *Brooke.*

"Yeah?" he asked hesitantly. How long had she been standing there? She must think he was a complete moron.

You are.

"Who are you talking to?" She looked up and down the hall with a question in her eyes.

Hell.

"Uh, no one," he answered and pushed on. "Is everything okay? Has Hailey said anything?"

Her faced twisted and he mentally kicked himself in the nads. Like full-out, David Beckham in his best shot to get to the goal, kick.

"Why do you keep asking that?"

"Asking what?"

"If she's said anything."

He jammed his hands into his pockets and rocked back on his feet, his mind scrambling for an answer, because telling her what happened back in the club wasn't an option, and telling her he wanted to see if Hailey remembered him just made him a dick.

You are.

Shut. Up.

"I mean," Brooke went on, "normally one would ask how someone is doing in the hospital, how they were feeling. Not if they've said anything."

"I'm curious to see what she's going to remember, if there's anything we've missed during the takedown is all."

Brooke stared at him, and he fought not to fidget. He didn't think she'd buy the story, hell, he didn't even buy it, but after a few moments, she nodded.

"Okay, no, she hasn't said much. She's awake, though, and I think they are going to want to transfer her home today."

Luke frowned and glanced down at his watch as if it held all the answers. "Already? She's only been here a few days."

Brooke offered a sad smile and shrugged. "That's

what I thought, too, but apparently the worst part is over and she'll continue her recovery at home with an aide. The hospital will be sending a nurse down to explain and work on getting someone local in Rockland County."

He rubbed at the back of his neck and shook his head slowly. "I'm not familiar with all that, but if they say it, then surely it must be what's best. When are they thinking of discharging?"

Brooke stared at him and he really wanted her to stop. *Dude, seriously, you're squirming again.*

Stop that!

"In a few hours. Do you have a car, or should I arrange to rent one?"

He shook his head fast. Surely, she didn't expect him to leave her to take care of everything. His brother would have his ass if he abandoned them now. "Don't worry about that. I still have the rental and will drive you all back down. Just let me know what she—what you both need," he amended, "and I'll make sure to get it ready."

She nodded, then glanced over her shoulder. "Okay, thank you, Luke."

"Anytime," he said, but she'd already walked back in the room, leaving him standing there wondering about what the hell he'd gotten himself into and how the hell he'd ever get it out of his head.

* * * *

The next day...

Brooke shut the door to Hailey's room with a soft click and waited, listening for any sign her daughter would need her. The hall was dark, surrounding her with its comforting silence, but inside she wanted to scream and shout at the unfairness of it all.

The drive had gone by smooth enough, with

Hailey resting fitfully in the backseat. There had only been one instance in which she woke with a piercing shrill, but Luke's calm voice had soothed Hailey in a way Brooke hadn't seen in the days since she'd been rescued.

Brooke had seen him watch her daughter from the reflection in the rear view mirror more than once. But each time he saw she caught him, Luke turned his attention back to the road with a tightening of his lips. She didn't know what happened in the back room, didn't want to let her mind wander, and as grateful as she was that he'd helped, she didn't think she could handle the attention he gave Hailey for too much longer.

She wasn't ready for her daughter to grow up. She wasn't anywhere near close to accepting that men looked at her. And they were, just as Luke did.

When Hailey's soft snores remained constant, Brooke turned from the door and tiptoed down the hall to the living room. Luke sat on the couch, his ankles crossed and resting on the ottoman's footrest. He typed furiously on his cell phone, his relaxed pose deceiving.

"Idiot," he muttered and tossed the device down. He glanced up at her and winced. "Sorry, not you. Dwayne."

She couldn't help it, she smiled. Related by the bond of adoption or not, the six brothers acted as if they'd been born of the same blood. Her smile wilted at the reminder of the dark, good-looking older brother and she crossed the room to sit on the couch opposite of Luke.

"If he heard you say that," she started, "I'm sure heads would roll."

Luke smiled and it was a thing of beauty, completely transforming his face. She tried to remember the last time she'd seen him smile but came up short. "He keeps asking about Hailey. I told him to stop by, that it'd be good for her, but he's so damn stubborn and won't do it."

She snickered when inside she felt anything but humor. In fact, at the thought of Dwayne stopping by, her stomach flipped and her heart clenched. She clasped her hands on her lap to try to hide their shaking. "I'm sure he'll come around in his own time. He's probably got things to do, people to see."

Luke stared at her, studying. His gaze dropped to her hands and lifted again to her eyes. "You and I know that's not true. His mind isn't anywhere but on exactly what's going on in this house." His words sounded measured, spoken slow as if he gauged her reaction.

Behind her breastbone, her heart thudded painfully fast. If she was being honest with herself, she missed Dwayne more than she could let anyone know.

"How many times have you seen his cruiser pass the house today?" Luke asked.

She bit her lip and looked at the window. More than she could count, or rather, she stopped counting hours ago. "A few."

Luke snorted softly. "And I'm the gingerbread man. A few…" He shook his head and stood, unfolding to all his six-foot-high glory. "Look, I'm not going to get in the middle of whatever is going on, but I will tell you this. You have been around us a whole lot longer than a few weeks. You know all of us as well as you know yourself. We love you like you're a sister to us, and so when I say this, I'm saying it with the absolute conviction that because we've known each other so long, and I wanna think that love is mutual, it's in the best interest of everyone involved."

She sat up straight and held his gaze, not wanting to hear it, not wanting to have to focus on what she was sure he'd say, but unwilling to look away. The impending advice was coming and she couldn't stop it.

"My brother isn't the only idiot. You're acting like one, too."

She frowned and stood. "Luke—"

"No," he interrupted. "Don't. I don't want to hear it. I've never seen two people dance around each other so much for so long. I'm surprised that a grown man who is highly successful in what he does, studies people for a living, and figures out why they do what they do could be so damn blind when it comes to how to voice what he feels. And you," he continued. "You should have more faith in him—and yourself, for that matter."

She sighed and opened her mouth, but he cut her off once more.

"Like I said, I really don't want to get in the middle of what's going on." He rounded the coffee table that had been between them and grasped her arms. "I have to go."

Yes, yes he did. But she didn't want him to. She didn't know if she was ready to face this alone. "Are you sure?"

Luke glanced over her shoulder and she saw what he did. A dark hall leading to where Hailey lay sleeping, recovering.

"I do. I need to get back to work. It's for the best. But know this, Brooke, you're safe. You'll always be in good hands, and if you need anything, call any one of us. We're here for you. Do you understand what I'm saying?"

Tears stung her eyes, but she ruthlessly forced them back. She nodded. "I do. And I will."

He offered her a smile, then swept her into his arms and gave a surprisingly strong hug. "Take care of yourself...and her," he added almost as an afterthought.

She hugged him back. "I will. And Luke," she called as he pulled away and headed for the door. He looked over his shoulder.

"Yeah?"

"Thank you."

His smile was less so, and he glanced at the dark hall again. "Anytime."

He walked out into the cold, dark night and she stood there watching the door long after he was gone. She'd never felt so damn alone.

Chapter Twenty-Seven

One week later…

"Mom, I'm fine. Seriously, though, you need to get out of the house," Hailey said with no hidden amount of exasperation.

Brooke hovered over Hailey, who sat on the couch, scrolling through the latest social media craze—she could never keep up with it—and fought the crazy impulse to check her again.

"I don't know, honey."

It'd been a week since they'd been home, a week of hell and nightmares, of sleeping next to her daughter only to wake up to the sounds of her screams, or to simply listen to the reassuring sound of Hailey breathing and living next to her.

She hovered, she got it. She had put the needs of her daughter ahead of everything else, as it should be. The aide the hospital assigned reassured her on a daily basis that Hailey was strong, that she would recover, that the time she'd been away hadn't done too much damage on her young body.

Not too much damage…

But there had been some, and that ripped at Brooke. A mother was supposed to protect her child from it all, and every day was a reminder that she had failed.

Hailey huffed and looked up, lines straining around her mouth.

"Mom…seriously, Hilda is here." She waved a hand toward the kitchen where the aide was fixing Hailey something to eat. The two of them had been on her all day, wanting her to get some fresh air, both claiming it would do *her* some good. Like she needed to be taken care of, too.

Brooke slowly sat on the couch, bent to retrieve her running shoes, and slipped them on, taking her time in tying the knot. She still wasn't sure this was a good idea and almost wanted to give it another day.

The sound of a plate meeting the coffee table drew her attention to Hilda, who had entered the room and gave her a smile, one meant to reassure, she knew, but damn if she felt anything of the sort.

"We'll be fine, Brooke. Go get some air. If there's a problem, I'll call you on your cell," Hilda said.

Brooke stood and nodded, her lips thinned.

"Okay, one run, really quick. If anything seems out of sorts or if you need me in any way…"

"Mom, we'll be fine. I'll be okay. I feel great today."

Brooke glanced at her daughter and saw the strain of the last week on her young face, and in the slow way she moved to grab the sandwich Hilda had made. Tears stung at her eyes, but she forced them back and turned away before she changed her mind.

"Okay. I'll be back."

She stepped outside, did a few stretches to warm her muscles, then kicked off. Heading down toward the river, she lost herself in the rhythm of her feet slapping against the pavement, soothed her body and mind in the constant in and out of her breath, matched her breathing to the example her body set with the jog.

Trees passed in a blur. Houses lined the street and grew sporadic closer to the Hudson. The fall air blew around her, kicking up leaves long fallen, the promise of snow a full reality as Old Man Winter made himself known.

She turned onto a path that ran along the edge of the river and stopped immediately in her tracks. Dwayne ran toward her in the opposite direction and the sight of him was like a physical kick in the gut. Breath stuttered out of her. It shouldn't be like this. He shouldn't have this kind of hold on her after only a few days together.

But he did…

He drew to a stop a few feet away and she found it hard not to stare at how the long-sleeved thermal clung to his body. It reminded her of how she'd wrapped herself around him, how she'd gripped his arms and ass as he pounded into her, long, hard, and without falter until they'd both exploded in pleasure.

His jogging pants rode low on his hips and, further down, his battered running shoes reminded her of how often he used them. In a world where this man perfected his appearance, his shoes were so out of place.

She stared at those shoes for long minutes, knowing damn well she couldn't look at his face for fear of what she'd see.

Lust or hatred?

Disgust or sympathy?

She didn't want any of it.

"Hey," he said.

She looked up, focusing her attention on the hard line of his jaw. Sweat ran in rivulets along his cheeks, another thing that was out of place in this man. Who knew he could sweat?

She did. God, she remembered all too well.

"Um, hi," she answered, sounding like an idiot.

His jaw tightened. "How's Hails?"

Brooke glanced away, looking over the water. It glistened under the lowering sun, sending sparkles of diamonds glittering across the river.

"She's doing…okay. Getting along. We've…we have an aide who comes in and spends the day with her. Nighttime is rough, especially on the nights she has nightmares, but we're getting through it."

He shifted closer and she closed her eyes, fought to stay still. Her shoulders stiffened.

He sighed, a long, drawn breath that sounded as frustrated as she was tired. "And her father? Has he come around?"

She shook her head, remembering that hateful conversation she had days earlier. Leo had been too busy in Europe, on some honeymoon with his secretary. "No, he's away on business."

Dwayne cursed. "Asshole."

She let out a brief laugh and opened her eyes. "That's true, but nothing new."

Silence spun between them, the web getting thicker as the slow minutes ticked by. This strain they'd developed was her fault. She knew that. She should have never let things get so convoluted, should have never crossed that line into a sexual relationship. She missed her friend. Missed his company.

Would she regret her decision to sleep with him? To get below the skin of this man?

No.

But she couldn't stand this wall erected between them.

"Look," she started, shifting back to him. Meeting his eyes was next to impossible but she did it and regretted it immediately. He stared at her with a cool expression, but beneath the façade, frustration was clear as the sky was above.

"Oh, Dwayne, I'm so sorry," she breathed.

He frowned, then reared his head back. "You're sorry?"

She sighed, hating this all. "Yes, I'm sorry. I shouldn't have led you on. I shouldn't have let things get so off path between us. We shouldn't have slept together.

I shouldn't have let you think I could be like the rest of your—"

"Stop it right there," he said, his voice low but all the more menacing.

"Stop?" she asked, exasperated. What the hell did he want her to say? Her world spun around her and her heart kicked against her ribs. "But…"

"No, stop," he repeated and the cool face he'd been holding fell, revealing the man beneath. She took a step back and let herself see it all. The pain, the exhaustion clouding his features. The man who wanted her. *Her.*

He closed the distance she had set with another step in her direction. "Brooke," he began, "you are not like anyone else in my life. You are you. You're who I want."

She shook her head. God, couldn't he see she wasn't built for that? She couldn't just toss her body out there without ramifications. "What we had was great," she said. "We had fun, but I can't continue to be that kind of friend to you. It's not something I can just hand out."

He growled and clenched his hands before him. "Sometimes I wanna strangle you," he shouted.

Her eyes widened.

"Do you really see me as some guy who just fucks whatever walks around?"

She couldn't answer. Even if she wanted to, she couldn't, because he plowed right ahead as if she were a twig in the middle of a snowstorm.

"I know I'm not the most communicative type of guy. I know you've had your issues with men in the past, and goddamn I'm sorry you've had to go through that. But I want you! I don't want someone else. I don't want to be with anyone else…but you. Do you understand what I'm trying to say?"

"I-I," she stammered. "I can't lose your friendship. I don't think I can do that."

"You won't. God, open your eyes," he growled.

"They are open," she snapped, getting pissed.

"No, they—" he started but she'd had enough. That pressure in her chest, the unfairness of it, boiled up and exploded before she thought twice.

"Do you love me, Dwayne? Can you tell me you love me? Can you really settle for someone as used up as me, someone who will always put her daughter first? Can you stand there and tell me you love me? If you want to be with me, can you give me that kind of connection, one such as *love*." She spat the last word, the taste of saying it foul.

He stumbled back a step and stared at her, wide-eyed.

Of course.

"Yup, you see? This is what I'm talking about," she said. "This is why I can't do this with you. It will change everything between us, and I have to be with someone dedicated to me." Her vision wavered as tears filled. "I can't be with you, because I'm trying to figure out how to open myself up like that again. I'm trying to understand *how* I can love again."

She turned her face away and cursed herself for showing too much, for letting him see how he affected her.

More silence passed. Minutes ticking slower than she thought possible.

"You want to hear me say the words?" he asked.

Her face heated again, except this time it was from embarrassment and anger. God, this was humiliating. He'd meant so much to her for so long, and while she'd wanted something from him, some sort of clue that she meant as much to him as he did her, the fact that she was making him say anything really stung. "No, Dwayne, you don't get it. I don't just want to hear them. I want to know you understand them."

He ran his hands through his hair, grabbed what short strands he could and let out an animalistic sound. "Christ! You—you don't, you can't mean to sit here and tell me you don't see it? You can't stand there and tell me you don't already understand?"

She stared at him, uncomprehending.

"Of course not," he continued and paced toward the water, then whirled and faced her again. "I'm—I'm not good with those damn words, and I thought I was showing you, but fuck, I guess I was wrong all along, wasn't I? I did it just like my mother said."

"What?" she asked.

He shook his head. "Those words, the ones you really want to hear? Brooke, they mean shit."

Her mouth fell open in shock. She gaped at him like some fish sitting in a tiny tank in a dentist office somewhere.

His expression softened. He took a step toward her. "Brooke, I don't know how else to say it, because damn if I'm going to waste oxygen telling you three words that could mean absolute shit. In case you've missed it, I'm an action kinda guy. I thought I've shown you that, how I care for you, about how much you and Hailey mean to me, but I guess I was wrong."

Had he really shown that? She fought to keep her head in the present but memories slammed into her, the years he'd remained at her side. The laughs they'd shared. The tears he'd helped mop up. The lovemaking from a few short weeks ago.

She opened her mouth, but he cut her off again.

"Love," he spat the word as she had earlier, "isn't something that can adequately be described. It's not meant to be that way, because no word can capture what the emotion really is. Love is an action. Love is showing that no matter what, someone will remain at your side and stay there. Love is something that when it gets rough, you don't have to worry about shouldering the burden alone, or in the darkness by yourself. Love is showing the one you care about that you're there. I don't have to hear the simple word from you, Brooke, to know you love me. I see it. Tell me I'm lying."

He waited her out, studying her face intently.

Air rushed up her throat and choked her. His words had stolen her power of speech. She couldn't answer. She had nothing to say. She wanted to, but she couldn't think. A sob escaped her chest and she pushed down on her heart for fear it would break out of her body.

He took three long strides and captured the side of her face, then tilted her head back with his fist full of her hair.

"Dwayne," she sobbed. The musk of man and evergreens rushed into her lungs on an inhale.

"You love me. You've shown me that. I was too damn blind to see it when you kicked me out of the hospital last week, but I've had time to think." His eyes bore into hers. "I've had time to really step back and see. You love me. Nod your head if I'm telling the truth."

She nodded. Wind blew against them, brushing her cheeks with cool air. She shivered, but it wasn't due to the cold. It was the feel of this man holding her in his arms.

"That feeling," he continued, "is exactly what I feel. I can't say the words you want to hear, and God, it pains me to tell you that, to know that those three simple words could fix everything between us. But I can't. They don't mean the same thing to me that they mean to you. And I refuse to utter something when me saying it would be a lie. I don't believe in those three words. But if you believe that love can be what I've just explained, then you should consider yourself loved...by me."

He kissed her then, hard and fast. The world around her dimmed until they existed in a realm of nothing. The hard muscles of his chest pressed against hers. His height towered above her, and his body cocooned her from the cold. It was only Dwayne and Brooke.

She tightened her fists on his shirt and whimpered into his mouth when he sought her to open. She complied and let him take his taste while she drank him in.

All too soon, he pulled away, brushed his thumbs over her cheeks and stepped back.

"You know where to find me, Brooke. If you need me, if you want me as I want you, you know where and how to find me." He dropped his forehead to hers and squeezed his eyes tight. She wanted to say something, tried to force her mouth open, but nothing came out.

Before she could respond, he turned and resumed his run in the opposite direction. She stared after him for long moments, even after he'd disappeared.

Chapter Twenty-Eight

A few days later...

Dwayne pulled to a stop on the curb outside Brooke's house and looked up at the red door. After their last conversation, he wasn't sure if she'd welcome him stopping by, but he couldn't put off seeing Hailey any longer.

He cared for that girl like she was of his own blood, and after helping raise her, after rescuing her, he was in his right to make sure she was getting along okay.

Right?

With a nod at his own question, he pushed open his door and jogged across the lawn to the front steps. He gave a quick knock, something he usually didn't do, and it felt weird to be doing it now. Normally he'd just walk in the house as if he belonged—because dammit, he *did* belong—but again, something had changed in his relationship with Brooke, and that right seemed to have been taken away.

The door opened and Hailey stood there in a pair of pink sweatpants and a white tank top. Her hair was piled on the top of her head in a messy ponytail and on the perch of her nose sat rectangle glasses.

"Hey," he said and peeked over her shoulder. The house looked empty and as much as he wanted to see Brooke, he hoped she wasn't there.

He was lying to himself. He so hoped she was.

"Hey," Hailey answered with a smile. "Why are you knocking?" She stepped back in invitation, and he moved inside and closed the door.

"I wasn't sure if I should just walk in."

She scoffed and rolled her brown eyes, ones that

looked tired behind the rim of her glasses. "Oh please, you know better. You're always welcomed to come right in."

She turned and tucked herself on the couch, folding long legs beneath her and tossing a throw across her lap. Two fingers lifted and rubbed at her temple.

"Are you okay?" He followed her over but didn't sit.

She nodded. "I'm fine. But I'm getting real sick of that question. I had to kick Mom out earlier because she was driving me insane."

His hopes fell, but the girl on the couch was his biggest reason for coming. He sat next to her and rested his elbows on his thighs, clasped his hands between his legs. "We're all worried about you. That's all. It should feel nice to know that people care, your mom especially. Do me a favor and don't give her too hard of a time."

Hailey sighed and looked over. "I know, and I try. I just, I really want to get better, you know? But when she's constantly hovering, it's hard to think straight."

He had to remind himself that this girl was only eighteen, her birthday passing a few days earlier, and she was dealing with a lot. That she and her mother were trying to work through things wasn't any of his business, but it still bothered him to know it. "She's worried. We all are. So tell me, how are you feeling, really? What's up with the glasses?"

She sat back, drew her knees up, and hugged them to her chest. "I'm getting through things. It's hard, but I'm talking to someone. I just can't tell Mom some stuff. It's not that I don't think she wants to hear it, but I don't think she's ready. I don't think I'm ready to face all of it with her. It's like you said, it's hard on her, too."

He thinned his lips and looked down, lest he show too much about how her abduction had affected them all, him included. A few moments passed. He drew in a breath and reached into his coat pocket. "I've got something for you, birthday girl."

Her low chuckle brought his gaze to her face. She smiled and the light in her eyes told him she'd be okay, and that stopping by was the right thing to do. Holding out his hand, he presented her with a pink box wound with a white ribbon. The trip to the city had been no problem, and the visit with the jeweler was a favor owed to his brother Jake.

She took the box and unwound the bow slowly, set it down on her outstretched hands. "You know you didn't have to. Coming to get me was a present I don't think I'll ever be able to repay."

She hadn't opened the box yet, and her hands paused on the top. She looked into his eyes. Hers filled with tears and bubbled over. "Thank you," she said with a catch in her voice.

He couldn't stand it any longer. He reached for her at the same time she tossed herself into his arms. Her face pressed into his neck and he held tight. This little girl had grown into a young woman overnight, one who'd seen too much in her short life. He palmed the back of her head and let her cry against his chest. With her safe now, being held by him, he finally gave in to the emotions that had been bubbling up since she'd been taken. Tears flowed down his cheeks and fell into her hair unchecked. Harsh sobs from the both of them filled the air for long, sorrowed minutes. Losing her for almost two weeks had been one of the hardest things he'd ever went through, and the thought of never getting her back was something he hadn't realized would have buried him.

Her crying jag waned after a bit and he wiped at his cheeks with the back of his hand. She pulled back and sat at his side, tucked under his arm. She gave him a watery smile and he chucked her nose.

"All better?" she asked.

He laughed, a short bark that relieved more pressure he didn't know was left. "All better, brat."

She grinned and grabbed the box that had been tossed aside, put it back on her lap, and lifted the lid. Inside, against blue velvet, sat a gold necklace with two interlocking pendants at the end.

"Oh," she breathed. "Dwayne, you shouldn't have."

"I wanted to. This is something a young woman needs to have. Something from *Tiffany's*."

He unwound his arms and reached for the pendant, took it gently out of the box and clasped it behind her neck. She leaned back and fingered the charms, a small smile hovering on her face.

"Thank you."

He knew what she thanked him for, understood it needed to be said. "Anytime, Hails. I want you to think about the bond we share every time you look at that and know if you ever need anything, someone to talk to, a shoulder to cry on, or even food in your belly, you can come to me."

She leaned her head on his shoulder and let out a sigh. "I know all that, but thank you for the reminder."

He wrapped his arm around her and played with the ends of her hair. A question hovered on his lips and he needed to ask it.

"Where's your mom?"

"Shopping for food. Hilda, the aide, left just a short while ago. It's nice to finally have some alone time."

"Until I came breaking the bubble," he said through laughter.

She matched the laugh but settled her head on his

shoulder. "I'm glad you did. I've missed you and wondered where you were."

"I've been around, watching, but I'm always around."

"Did you and Mom have a fight or something?"

What a loaded question. He leaned his head back on the couch and closed his eyes. Hailey snuggled to his side. "We'll be fine. Just working out a few things."

Hailey yawned. "Sorry, whew, I'm more tired than I thought."

He popped his eyes open. "Want me to leave?"

"No," she said and fisted the side of his jacket. It reminded him of the time she had the chickenpox and had held him tight saying if she did that then she wouldn't scratch at her skin. He laid his hand gently over where she held him.

"Please stay. I'm not sleeping well but feel like I may be able to sleep better if you're here," she said softly.

The admission broke his heart and he closed his eyes against another onslaught of stinging tears. He squeezed her shoulders and settled back in silence.

A few minutes ticked by and Hailey asked, "Can I ask what you and Mom are working out?"

He let out a heavy breath. "I don't think that's such a good idea. But I don't want you to worry. We're going to be all right."

"I hope so," she murmured sleepily. "You two were made for one another."

His eyes shot open, and he stared ahead at the wall. It held pictures of family, ones where he was included as well. He couldn't talk, didn't know if the statement required a response. Hailey's soft snores filled the air and he let out a breath he didn't realize he'd been holding.

They sat like that, Hailey sleeping, tucked against him. Him, staring at the wall and seeing how well the three of them fit. It held years of memories, ones he wouldn't take back for anything in the world. He'd made a home here, physically living there or not, and he hoped Brooke saw it the same way. She hadn't reached out to him after their conversation on the jogging path and, remembering his parting words, it chipped a bit of his heart away each time he thought back on it.

He didn't know how much time passed, but the door opened and Brooke stepped inside carrying two plastic bags. He tensed, not sure if he should get up and leave, get up and help her, or stay right where he was seeing as Hailey was sleeping soundly.

Brooke paused and looked at them, her gaze jumping between him and her daughter before coming to rest on his face. "She's asleep," she said with surprise in her voice.

"Yeah," he said softly. "Been out for a while now."

Brooke closed the door, set the bags down, and stripped out of her coat. She turned toward him. "I was wondering when you'd come by."

He didn't say anything, just continued to stare back.

"You could have come sooner," she said, her voice still soft.

"Could I?"

Her shoulders sagged and she nodded, then looked away. "Of course, Dwayne. She cares about you, too, you know." Picking up the bags, she turned and walked into the kitchen.

He struggled with the need to remain at Hailey's side, or to go to Brooke. While she didn't say anything about what was going on between them, and he really didn't expect her to with Hailey sitting so close, it still stung. A simple statement such as she missed him, too, would have gone a long way toward his bruised ego.

Right now, in this moment, though, his ego was the least of anyone's worries.

Gently extracting from Hailey's clutch, he stood and tucked the throw around her shoulders, watching her snuggle into a pillow on the couch for a moment.

He turned and checked his pockets, making sure he had his keys and phone before heading toward the door. He should leave. Staying around and taking in additional reminders that Brooke was ignoring what needed to be addressed between them wasn't something he thought he'd stay cool with.

He didn't have it in him tonight to deal with it.

Just as his hand slid around the knob, he heard her come back into the room. "You're leaving?" she asked.

He dropped his head to the door. Tired. Weary of it all. Missing the hell out of her. "Yeah, I need to get going." He didn't move, though.

She shifted behind him. "Dwayne…" His name, one word. It held nothing but pity and he hated it. This must be what people felt like when their hearts bled, because inside his chest his had torn in two. He'd been the asshole on the other side of the room far too many times and despised that he'd ever put anyone through anything that even resembled something like this.

He turned the knob.

"Stop. Don't go," she whispered harshly.

"God," he said against the door. "I need to. I can't keep doing this. I can't dance around what I feel any longer, and I can't stand knowing that things with us have gotten so mixed up."

"I know."

"No," he answered, "I don't think you do. I

understand what I've done, hate that I've done it, and get now what I must look like to others. It's not right, I know that. But I just can't pretend that I don't want you. I can't dance around the subject any longer, and I can't say something that I know you want to hear.

"I want you to trust me, Brooke, I do. And I can't stand that you don't. I want you. Only you. And no one else."

Silence met his bold statement and he hated himself more. The soft brush of a hand against his back felt like heaven, and he lost it. Disgusted with himself, he whipped open the door and stepped outside. He was a masochist when it came to her and could only hope distance and time would heal things.

"Dwayne, stop," she called from the door. He halted in his tracks and closed his eyes. Could he deny her anything?

Her footsteps sounded, drawing closer until he knew, even with his eyes closed, that she had stepped up before him. "I'm not good at this," she said.

He let out a laugh that was anything but humorous. "You're plenty good at it. Trust me."

She palmed his face. "No, that's not what I'm saying."

His breath hitched and he opened his eyes.

"It's not?"

She shook her head, a small smile on her lips. "No, it's not at all."

He laid his palm over hers on his face and stepped closer. "What are you saying?"

She inched her fingers around the back of his neck. "I'm saying I want you, too. I want to give us a shot. I want to show you that I do trust you. I trust you with my daughter, with my life, and with my heart, my body."

He blinked, hearing words too good to be true. It took a moment, but they finally hit him and he surged against her and planted his fingers in the soft strands at her nape. "Say it. Say it again. I don't think I heard you."

She laughed then and the sound released every bit of tension. It flowed and made him soar like an eagle high above the Hudson. "Even if you don't believe in the words, I do, Dwayne, and when I say them they may not be as pretty as yours."

He winced. "Pretty?"

She grinned wider. "Yes, as pretty, but I love you, and I want to make things work with us. I want you in my home, in my life, and in my bed. You're my best friend, my lover, and my rock."

Unable to wait any longer, he kissed her. Hot and deep, the contact heated him down to his Italian loafers and did things to his body he never thought he'd feel again. *Only with Brooke*... With her mouth fused against his, he knew things would be okay, that *they'd* be okay, and that they'd face whatever approached, head-on, together.

"Come inside," Brooke whispered, tugging on his hand.

He watched her and followed, one foot in front of the other until he stood inside again. The door shut with a soft *swoosh* of air and it was as if that small sound, the one minor act, solidified it all: the worries, the doubt, the questions on if she'd ever accept him. She'd told him as much but looking at her, smiling up at him, holding gathering warmth in her eyes, said so much. The one tiny act spoke more than her words outside. She was inviting him not only into her home but also her life.

Hailey roused on the couch and glanced over. Her gaze landed on their linked fingers and instead of a question, she smiled, slow and sure. He couldn't help but answer her with one of his own.

The words that came next shocked him down to his toes.

"It's 'bout time, you two." Hailey sat up. She hunched her shoulders slightly as if she still carried a burden there, and he figured she did. She'd been through a lot in the past few weeks and he hoped that this transition, this big change in her life—because it was huge—wouldn't be too much for her to handle.

"Are you okay with this, Hails?" he asked.

Her sleepy smile turned goofy and it reminded him of a few weeks prior, when she'd been an innocent jokester with her whole life ahead.

"I'm more than okay with it. You two have been dancing around one another for years, and you've been in our lives for so long, it's exactly as it should be."

Such simple words stated so much.

He cleared his thick throat.

"Ah hell, Hails, come here," he said gruffly.

She rose and crossed the room. He held his arms outstretched and she walked right into them. The scent of baby powder wafted through the air as he hugged her tightly, knowing without a doubt he'd do anything to protect her, to protect her mother, and to provide for them both for as long as he lived. In a world where people had surrounded him, his true home was here with these two remarkable women.

Brooke's hand brushed the back of Hailey's hair, and she lifted her head, then stepped back from them both.

"So, I'm just gonna, you know…" She tilted her head toward her room.

He laughed.

"And I'm probably going to put my earphones on really loud, so you two can just enjoy, you know…"

He laughed harder and Brooke gasped next to him.

"Hailey!" she said.

Hailey's goofy grin returned and she walked backward down the hall. "You know, don't mind me, and don't do anything I wouldn't do!" she sang before darting into her room.

A moment later voices came from behind the closed door. "I'm watching TV, too!" she yelled.

Dwayne couldn't help it, he doubled over laughing and looked up at Brooke. Her face was two shades of red, her mouth gaping at her daughter's room.

"I cannot believe…" she started.

He rose to his full height and took her hand.

"Where are you going?" she asked.

He grinned. "My mother taught me to always listen to the advice of a good woman."

She balked and mockingly tried to resist his tug down the hall. "You are not thinking of…"

He nodded. "Oh I'm thinking it all right. You don't argue with my momma."

Her eyes widened as he pulled her into her room and shut the door. "You're not thinking of your mother right now…"

He pushed her against the closed door and breathed out a groan as his body met hers, every glorious inch of her curvy, beautiful existence. "Oh, you've got that right. I'm definitely not thinking of my momma anymore."

Her breath fluttered from parted lips and washed over his face. He gripped her hips and brushed a kiss to the side of her mouth.

"What-what are you thinking about?" she asked on a breathy gasp.

Trailing his mouth to her ear, he gloried in the

scent of her, all ripe with the feminine smell of vanilla. He whispered naughty things designed to make her blush, words of promise, and told her how high he wanted to take her, how much he wanted her, how he craved her more than his last breath.

"Oh," she breathed.

He leaned back and grinned briefly at her dazed look but didn't get another word or thought through his head. She wrapped her arms around his neck and jumped him.

Yes, she *jumped* him.

He staggered back and met her kiss for kiss. Their tongues clashed and tangled in pleasure. He nipped and sucked on her mouth, groaning as she repeated his ministrations on him.

Falling to the bed, he couldn't get her clothes off fast enough. She must have had the same idea as she growled under her breath, tugging and pulling on his belt. He laughed.

"You are not laughing!" she huffed and glanced up. Her hair fell over her face, her beautiful blue eyes blazing with heat. The white camisole she had worn beneath her sweater pulled down on one side, showing him tantalizing glimpses of the lace beneath. He groaned.

"No, no, I'm not laughing. God, I want you."

She sat back on his thighs and pushed her hair from her face, bit her lip. With agonizing slowness designed to drive a man wild, she slid her camisole up, inch by beautiful inch. Rich, tanned, and smooth skin revealed with each slow shimmy and shake she gave. Then, in one fell swoop, it was pulled from the top of her head and tossed aside, forgotten.

Gripping her hips, he rolled her over and rose above her, kissed the exposed cleavage of her breast, then the other. He worked at his pants, whipped his belt off, and undid the zipper. He struggled with getting his pants over his hips as she pushed his shirt off his shoulders, lifted, and put her mouth on his chest.

His eyes rolled back in his head. "God."

"Hurry," she pleaded.

With as much finesse as he could muster, he kicked off his shoes, tore away his shirt, and discarded his pants. She wiggled beneath him and finally—*finally!*—they both lay as naked as they'd been born.

Her warm hand wrapped around his erection and he saw stars. She slid her hand down the length and back up, giving him a squeeze that threatened with an impending release.

"Stop, Brooke," he said roughly.

She spread her legs and guided him between, to where he belonged, his home, nestled in the body of this woman. Once she posed him at her entrance, he reached down to make sure she was ready and, feeling she wanted this as much as he did, he filled her with one stroke.

Embedded inside her, he sat to the hilt and stilled, taking it all in. Her scent wrapped around him as her arms and legs did. Her love and acceptance took his heart and locked it safe. His head swam with pleasure, but she anchored him to this world, kept him afloat in a sea of desperation to be closer…to her.

"Please, Dwayne," she whispered, her hips moving anxiously beneath him.

He couldn't hold back and surged forward. Their movements were in sync, the rise and fall of hips meeting one another, their bodies both chasing the release coming, the ecstasy that would take them both over the ledge.

He dropped his head, captured a dark nipple in his mouth, and sucked. She greedily arched her back, gave him more, and took it all.

She whimpered and he glanced up, feeling the

rising tension in her body. Her legs tightened around his waist. Her hand was over her mouth, teeth biting into the tender flesh, pleasure awash over her face. She tilted her head down and reached for him.

He met her halfway, their mouths a clash of passion as the crest lifted and broke. Her nails dug into his ass, pushing him deeper into her, harder into her sweet heaven. She cried out and he sucked it all greedily down, his orgasm bringing a groan from his chest.

For long moments, the world held suspended, turned into nothing but a buzz of orgasmic bliss as they tumbled and fell together. He slowed his thrusts, gentled his touch, and deepened his kiss, letting her know with his actions how much he cared for her, how this thing called love could take him to such heights and all because of her.

She kissed him, brushed her fingers through his hair, and let them trail down his spine.

Pulling back, he brushed one, two kisses across her lips and rested above, making a point to hold his own weight so he didn't crush her. Her expression was sated and happy, her mouth relaxed. Her long hair spread beneath her like a waterfall of the Arizona desert. Beautiful.

"I want you to know how much you mean to me," he said softly.

She smiled, and brushed the back of her fingers over his cheek. "I do. I see it clearly, Dwayne. And I love you."

He swallowed, the words sitting thick on his tongue. He wanted to say them, yearned to give that to her, but he didn't see them as she did. But God, he wanted to try.

"I know the words don't mean the same thing to you," she said as if reading his mind. "But I know you love me, too. In time I'm sure I'll hear them, and I don't want you to say them just to make me happy. I want to hear them come from your mouth because you believe in them, and not a moment sooner. Okay?"

She lifted and brushed her mouth over his while he stared at this amazing woman. "Okay—"

His cell rang from his pocket, cutting off anything he'd been about to say.

"I need to get that," he said and she smiled.

"I'll be right here."

He lifted off her, grabbed his pants, and hit the answer on his phone.

"Yeah?"

"Dwayne," a low voice rumbled, one he hadn't heard in months.

"Chris?" He pulled his cell back, looked at the blocked display and put it back to his ear. "Where are you? I thought you were out of touch for a few weeks." Assigned to a Special Forces team, both Chris and his military working dog Delta Alpha two niner, affectionately called Dumb Ass amongst the team, had been conducting some super-secret black ops mission in Afghanistan for the past few weeks.

"I'm—" A racking cough sounded down the line, weak and wet, and Dwayne stood straighter, suddenly alert. He didn't sound right. Something was off.

"Chris," he demanded, this time with a bit of force due to fear.

A wheeze came down the line and his stomach turned to a knot. "Chris!" he shouted.

"I'm here." Another cough. "Fuck, damn, shit! Argghhhh!"

"What the hell, Chris?" He looked around, searching for the answer to why his brother sounded like he was on his deathbed.

A slow and ragged breath rang down the line. "Give me a second, douche bag."

Dwayne breathed out a sigh. The tension in his shoulders eased slightly. He sounded hurt, sounded like hell. But if he was using his term of endearment, as he so liked to call it, surely it couldn't be too serious.

Another big breath pushed through the phone. "My team was attacked," Chris said.

Dwayne's heart stuck in his throat. "Shit, are you okay?"

He coughed. "Peachy."

"Ass. Seriously? Where are you?" Dwayne asked.

"Ramstein."

"That's Germany."

"No shit, Sherlock."

Dwayne sighed. *Jesus.* His heart was beating out of his chest and all he could get out of his brother were a few simple words. As if the sun was shining in la-la land and all was hunky-dory. Brooke moved off the bed and grabbed a robe. He jammed his legs inside his pants.

"I don't know how long it'll take me to get there, but I'm sure I'll know in a few hours."

"What?" Chris asked.

"I'm coming to you. Ramstein, right? That's what you said?"

"Just like that, you're going to drop everything and come to Germany?" He asked the question as if he was asking someone if they needed a glass of water.

"You're my brother, you asshole," Dwayne snapped.

"Fuck." Chris sighed. "Look, I'm sorry. They've just given me some really good drugs and I'm a bit loopy at the moment."

He sat on the bed and dropped his head. "Tell me what you need."

"For you not to get on a plane. I'm coming home," Chris answered, his statement so simple, but everything so, so wrong.

"You're coming home?" Dwayne asked again, not knowing why he was repeating things, but needing to understand what was going on.

"Didn't I just say that? DA is coming with me. He's hurt." His brother's voice cracked and Dwayne sucked in a breath. Never, ever had he seen Chris break down. No tears when he broke his arm, none when Jessica Sorstein broke up with him in high school, not even when he left for basic training. Never.

"Hell, Chris," he breathed. "How bad?"

"Bad. Look, I called you first because I need you to tell Mom and I know you'll be able to keep her calm. I also need a favor."

"What's that?"

"Get my place open. I've got someone from the unit coming by to make sure DA will have what he needs, and I wouldn't normally bother you with this…"

"Consider it done," Dwayne answered. "Anything you need, man. What else?"

"He jumped in front of me, the dumb ass." Chris sobbed on the other end and Dwayne's heart cracked open.

"Who did? Who jumped in front of you? And what were they doing? Why?"

"I can't talk," he answered, his voice rough and broken. "When I get home, you'll hear all about it. We'll be there in a week."

Dwayne went to respond, to ask more questions, but the line had cut out, his brother's way of saying goodbye. He looked down at his phone, stared at it, willing it to ring again, but silence spread through the room.

Beside him, Brooke touched his shoulder, her eyes sad, her face concerned. "What happened?"

"I don't know," he answered. "But we're about to find out."

Epilogue

A week after everything in his life changed, after *he* changed, Dwayne walked up behind Brooke, who sat in a chair and typed furiously over the keys. He grinned, loving that she'd thrown herself back into finishing her articles. Sure, she'd hemmed and hawed for the first few days and complained that she needed to dedicate her attention to Hailey and the struggles she was going through. But, after both he and Hailey sat her down, she'd finally given in and agreed. This was her time, a chance for her to pursue her dreams and follow what she'd always wanted. Plus, while her editor had been giving her some time to recoup, there were still deadlines to meet and a promise left unanswered.

The thing he'd been surprised about was her revelation that she was through fighting against her original idea of writing. With a few tweaks, her "creative juices" had flowed to allow her articles to practically jump off the screen. Her shock on how well the words came out was almost as strong as his, but that was his Brooke. Her ability to adapt to change and overcome struggles was something he loved most about her.

And there was that word, or rather, that feeling again.

Love.

How about that?

He brushed his lips against her neck. She shivered and her hands paused on the keyboard. A smile spread across his mouth.

"Come on, *preciosa*, it's time. They're waiting for us."

Her gaze darted to the clock on the wall and widened. "I totally didn't notice the time. Is Hailey ready?"

He nodded.

"Okay, give me five minutes to freshen up and we'll go," she said.

She jumped out of the chair and he left her to do what she needed while he went to the front door and grabbed his jacket. His parents, ever loving and completely accepting, had announced they were throwing Hailey a birthday celebration. They'd wanted this girl they'd known for so long to have a party with family, nothing too big, but rather smaller and intimate, just the family together showing they loved her and that everyone would support her through her struggles.

Hailey, sitting on the couch and typing on her phone, stood and made her way over to grab her jacket.

"She coming?" she asked.

He took in the dark shadows, lighter than last week but still present, under her eyes. She wore black leggings with a silvery-purple tunic that fell over her hips. Hanging from her neck were three thin silver chains and some sort of green jewel at the end. She looked like a tired teenager, and no one the wiser would have guessed all she'd been through in the past month. Her strength, the strength of her mother, and his support would get them through this. He'd make sure of it.

They were establishing a routine, and while Brooke was worried about Hailey and what she'd think if she caught him in their house in the same clothes the next morning, he still stayed the night, only to sneak out before the sun rose.

It was just two days earlier when Hailey had been waiting at the front door with a comical expression on her face, that they'd been busted and set straight.

She'd welcomed him into her home, just as she'd always accepted him as a part of her life. It spoke of their relationship, one he felt growing stronger each day.

"Yeah, she'll be out soon. Are you gonna be okay with this gathering?" he asked, cupping her cheek. His thumb brushed the dark bruises under her eyes.

She tilted her face until it rested fully in his palm. "I'll be fine. It's going to be nice to get out for a bit."

Dwayne gave a gentle tug, and she went willingly into his arms. He held her, still feeling the overwhelming relief that she was back home safe. "Let me know if it gets to be too much. We'll come home and make s'mores."

She giggled and pulled back to grab her scarf. "Deal."

Brooke rushed down the hall, tossed them both a smile, and grabbed her jacket. Within minutes, they were on the road and pulling up to his parents' house. An old style colonial, the twin beams framing the front door rose with a colorful display of Christmas lights. The curtains to the bay windows were open and showing several of his brothers walking around with their dates, laughing and having a good time. Inside his chest, warmth grew, a statement of how much he considered this home, a place to be loved and safe. He wanted to build this same environment for the three of them.

He took Brooke's hand and led them inside and out of the cold. The scent of baked potatoes, warm turkey, and spices filled the air.

"Oh my God, if that tastes as good as it smells, I may just pass on those s'mores, D."

He winked at Hailey and nodded. "You've had her cooking before. Is there any doubt?"

She shook her head and hung up her jacket, then immediately walked toward the kitchen. Cheers of Hailey's name filled the foyer seconds later and Brooke chuckled next to him.

"She's got your parents wrapped around her finger, you know."

He shrugged. "I think it might go both ways, if you ask me. But even if it doesn't, they love her and are here to support her, too."

Brooke's eyes turned sad as a shadow passed through them. "I know. And God, I'm so grateful." She bit her lip.

He finished hanging his jacket and turned to tug her into his arms. "Hey, none of that. She's going to be fine. She's going to get past this, and we'll all see to it."

Brooke tugged at the top of his sweater and studied something there as if it held the world's secrets. "I know," she said. "I'm just worried about how this is all going to proceed. She's doing so well. Her nightmares don't seem as bad anymore, and she's even talking about going back to school after winter break."

"Yes, but why do I hear something else in there that you're not telling me?"

She sighed. "Her case."

Ah. Yes. They'd gotten a call yesterday from the prosecutor's office handling the case. While the attorney understood what Hailey had been through, while he promised to use extreme care, they still wanted her to testify in a few months. Brooke had vehemently said no way, no how, but Hailey had surprisingly been the one to break that argument up. She'd said she wanted to do whatever she could in order to make sure other girls didn't go through what she went through.

"What if it messes with her recovery?" Brooke asked, bringing his attention back to the present.

He echoed her sigh and squeezed her tighter. "Look, she wants to do this, and if she thinks she's strong enough to handle it, then we have to give her as much support as we can to get through it. If she has a moment of weakness, we'll handle that as it comes. We can't keep sheltering her from everything. We need to let her live her life and make her own decisions."

Brooke frowned and glanced up from beneath long, brown lashes. "Since when did you become the all-knowing? Do you have kids somewhere I don't know about?"

He choked on a laugh.

"What?" he asked.

The side of her mouth tipped up wryly. "That seemed like some advice found in one of those parenting books. And it's good advice, Dwayne."

His cheeks heated and he shifted. "It's not from anywhere but from what I've been taught, what I've learned in my own life, sweetheart."

She smiled and lifted on her toes to brush a kiss over his lips. "It works. Thank you."

She went to pull away but he had none of that. He fisted her hair and pressed his mouth back to hers, kissed her deep and hard, right there in his parents' foyer, where at any moment anyone could walk in. He didn't care, though. All he cared about was drowning in this woman. In the taste of mint in her mouth, on the velvety stroke of her tongue against his, in the warmth she gave him even on the coldest night.

A throat cleared. Brooke pressed her hands against his chest and jumped back. A quick glance at her face showed it turning two different shades of pink. Cute.

"Duuuuude," Mike drawled, leaning against the frame of the doorway. He lifted one brow high and smiled. "Feeling your girl up with Mom in the other room? Ballsy, man. Big time."

Dwayne snorted and opened his mouth, but Brooke jumped in before him.

"He wasn't feeling me up."

Mike turned his amber gaze toward Brooke, and Dwayne faced her, mouth agape. He had no clue why she'd straight up lied, because yes, he had been feeling her up. And he'd been two seconds away from closing them both away in the hallway bathroom for a more in-depth discovery.

"Brooke," Mike said with a deep laugh.

She blew air into her pink cheeks and waved her hands in front of her face. "Whatever." She looked anywhere but at him and Mike. Dwayne grinned. Not only was she embarrassed they'd gotten caught—which had happened more often than not in this house, with six boys and a happily married couple—but she was a horrible liar and fidgeting under their gazes.

Again, cute.

He grabbed her hand, tossed a look to Mike and led her down the hall. Once the room opened up, before them spread the family and dining rooms. His dad, Luke, Jake, and Trent were watching some game on the big screen in the family room. The deep baritone of the announcer hardly reached his ears, as above their heads were the speakers, which were connected to the house's stereo system. A raspy female voice cut through the chatter, football, and just overall business of the house.

In the kitchen to his left, Charlie sat with his mom, Hailey, and Matt, who was giving puppy dog eyes and trying to steal a deviled egg from the container in her hands. She laughed and held the dish out for Matt and he made a show of worshiping her feet, professing his love and undying affection.

Dwayne shook his head, laughing at the scene. His family, both legally and—with a quick glance at Charlie—from a meaningful friendship. He took in a breath, finally feeling as if he could take a deep breath, the first in forever. A weight on his shoulders lifted. It didn't leave completely, and with just a look at Hailey, he knew why, but it still lifted from his shoulders and a sense of peace moved into him. He could get used to this, life in a warm home with a warm woman in his bed, one he not only loved as his friend but also admired for her strength. His family opened their arms yet again and accepted more into the clan.

It was how life should be lived.

"All right, let's eat," Karen called. Everyone turned from what they were doing and grabbed a dish to set on the long, ten-seater, oak table that sat between the two rooms.

Dwayne released Brooke's hand to help his mom with the turkey and frowned after he set it down. He wasn't a math genius, but even he could count. There were eleven in the room, yet only ten chairs sat around the table. Chris hadn't made it home yet, just another troubling thought in the back of his mind, but with his mom and dad, Charlie and Trent, Luke, Matt, Jake, Mike, Brooke and Hailey, then himself, it made eleven.

He glanced across the table. "Luke, grab the computer chair from the office, will you?"

Luke shook his head and reached for a piece of turkey, which surprisingly his mom allowed. "Why? I'm not staying."

Dwayne's eyes widened just as Hailey asked, "What?"

Luke shifted his gaze from Hailey and back to Dwayne. "I thought I told you, bro, I gotta jet. I'm back on assignment and have a mission that requires me to be on a plane in three hours. I don't have time to eat."

"Oh, nonsense," Karen chirped. "I'll make you some sandwiches to go. You still need to pack, right?"

Luke glanced at his mom. "Yeah, I'm heading up now. And thanks, Ma."

"Of course, my son."

Dwayne stared after Luke in concern. He knew his baby brother was a grown man now, understood they all had dangerous jobs, but with everything else happening, he didn't feel as if he'd gotten the chance to catch up. He missed his brother, hated that their time had been cut short, but vowed to make sure they met up soon.

At last, he sat down for a feast and celebration.

* * * *

Twenty minutes later, Luke stepped out of the shower and grabbed a towel. His body hummed with the pulse of excitement. Half that excitement was because of his mission coming up, something so secret they decided to brief him only in person.

That should have been enough.

It wasn't.

The other half of this zing, one that sparked along every inch of his skin as if he were suddenly sensitive to any touch, was because of the female sitting downstairs.

Hailey.

"Fuck," he grumbled and rubbed his face viciously with the towel.

Getting away was going to be good. Sure, he would miss the hell out of his family, but he wouldn't last another day in Hailey's presence. He felt like a damn pervert. And being the man he was, liking the shit he did and seeing the stuff he had, the fact he felt like that spoke volumes.

Each time he looked at her, he flashed back to that dark room in the club. His vision tunneled until it was only the two of them. And her scent invaded his space, even from twenty feet across the room. It wasn't just her visual presence that drew him, but more, he knew without looking when she'd enter the room. He could *feel* her.

After he dried off, he snapped the towel around

his waist and ground his teeth together, sat his knuckles on the counter and looked hard at his reflection in the mirror. He didn't look like a pedophile. Cocking his head, he changed the angle, searching for some clue, something that explained this unrealistic attraction he had to a damn eighteen-year-old. His hair was cut close to his head. Darker now that it was wet, it looked the color of the sky on a moonless night. He stared hard at his reflection, the swirling silver of his eyes something his mother loved, hell, something that had most women tossing themselves at his feet to get a close look at.

He had a strong jaw, high cheekbones, and was the only Gonzalez brother who hadn't had his nose broken, so it was straight and narrow, looking to be on the opposite path than he was treading with his control. He felt as if he were in a maze, dodging temptation and lust, bucking out of the way of any contact with one Hailey Mason.

He stepped back and pinched his nose, blew out a breath and turned for the connecting door to his room. Each of them had shared a bathroom as a kid, something their mom had demanded they have. A space to call their own, one that held the responsibility of cleaning it, and being the baby of the bunch, he'd gotten out of that chore until he'd been the last to be stuck with it long after Jake had left for the city.

Stepping into his room, he'd just crossed the threshold when he froze. His head snapped over to his bed. Sitting on the end, hands in her lap, gaze directly on him, was Hailey.

"Fuck," he breathed and she winced.

He couldn't move, his body stuck in the moment like some super speed drying cement. His legs refused to backtrack in the bathroom and hide like the pansy ass scaredy cat he really was.

Hailey stood and her gaze ran over his chest, down lower, and he'd never felt more on display. He watched with dismay as her eyes warmed, heated, and her full lips parted on a sigh. *Goddammit.*

That look, the one that said more than her actual words and communicated what was going on in her mind, spurred him into action. His legs came unstuck and he crossed the room, whipped a pair of jeans from the floor and shoved his legs inside with more force than necessary. He made sure to keep the towel around his waist, but fuck if it wasn't going to be interesting to see how he'd be able to snap his jeans closed with the massive hard-on he now sported.

"What are you doing in here?" he asked, his voice gruff.

She crossed her arms over her chest, more of a protective measure rather than a body communicating it wanted to close itself off. She seemed to hunch her shoulders as to hold herself together and yeah, after all she'd been through, he got it.

And didn't that make him feel like an ass?

Well, yeah, but better she stay far away from him. They couldn't, wouldn't, go anywhere near what her eyes said as they roamed in a heated caress over his body.

"You're leaving?" Her voice was soft, so soft he strained to hear her speak. This quiet girl wasn't the same he remembered running around with, playing in deep mud pits and driving his older brother insane. She'd been traumatized. That's what he kept telling himself. She needed to heal. She needed time. But he couldn't help but feel a pang of loss at the rambunctious woman—*no, girl*—she used to be.

He sighed and turned to her. Giving up on the impossible action of shift, press, and grunt his way into buttoning up his jeans, he kept the towel around his waist.

"I have to go," he said. "I have a job that needs to get done." That's it, that's all he could give her. Hell, even he didn't know more than that. Her scent, the sweet, crisp smell of apples, surrounded and threatened to suffocate him.

She shifted, her gaze still glued to him. "Where are you going?"

He tried not to let the impatience, the need clawing through him just to reach out and touch her, show. Instead he clenched his fists and crossed his arms, widened his stance, and gave her a hard stare.

"Like I said, to work."

She took a step toward him. He ground his teeth together. "Stop," he gritted out.

Her gaze searched his. She looked so small, so vulnerable, yet so heartbreakingly beautiful it hurt to look at her.

"I remember you," she said and he sucked in a breath. *Bad move, dude!* She was all he could see, all he could smell, all he wanted to reach out to touch and see if she was as soft as she looked.

He shook his head, not wanting to go down this path, *any path,* with her. Not now, not ever.

"No," she said, her voice stronger but no less vulnerable. "I remember you, Luke. In my mind where it's dark and scary, I remember the feeling of you. Even not understanding who you were, I knew I was safe, finally safe, because you were there."

"Look—"

"You're my knight," she said and took a step toward him. He took one back, needing to get away, wanting her in his arms anyway. Fuck, he was royally screwed. Like tendrils of velvet, her voice, presence, and scent ran over his sensitive skin. Instead of reaching out and giving in to the need to touch, he lashed out.

"That's a child's fantasy, little girl. I'm no knight. I was just doing what needed to be done."

She froze, her eyes wide and brimming with unshed tears. "What's wrong with you?" she snapped.

Good. Anger. He could deal with anger any day. Anything to get her out of his room and away from him. Anything other than giving in to the sweet temptation.

"Nothing's wrong," he said. "Yet everything is. Don't you get where you are? Again, you need to think before you do something. You're standing here in a man's room, with a man who is half-dressed. What if I would have come out of the bathroom naked? Would you have wanted to be put into a situation that got you in trouble a few weeks ago?"

He hadn't meant for it to come tumbling out the way it did, but damn if he could control himself around her. Her tears spilled over the lids and tracked down her face. She sniffed, her mouth agape, and swung away from him. He felt like all kinds of an ass for hurting her. But she had him on edge, and she had no clue what he wanted. Hell, he didn't even want it.

But he so did.

When she reached the door, he heard her choke on a cry. He closed his eyes, regret brimming over anything else he felt. "Wait," he called, keeping his eyes closed. He pinched his nose again and heaved out a heavy breath. The door didn't open and he didn't need to look to know she was still in the room. He could *feel* her still present.

"I'm sorry," he started, "I shouldn't have said those things. I'm just worried about you and the situations you've been put in. What you've seen, what you've had to do…no one should have to experience that. I wish we could have gotten there sooner. I wish there was something else I could do or say to make things easier for you. I don't have anything, though. I can only tell you to watch where you go, don't go somewhere alone, and please, just stay safe. For your mom, for Dwayne, for all of us."

Something brushed his chest and he snapped his eyes open and jumped back, slammed against the wall. "Christ!"

Hailey stood there, silvery tracks from her tears still wet on her cheeks, looking up at him with so much affection and hope he damn near fell to his knees. "Hailey," he said and she closed her eyes as a soft smile curved her lips.

"Say it again," she demanded softly.

He frowned, then shook his head, uncomprehending. "What?"

"My name?"

"Hailey."

"You've never said it before."

Surely he had. His brows drew together as he thought back. Taking his attention away from where he was trapped, and how Hailey had advanced on him, was the wrong move. Her hand reached out and he braced with a lock down of every muscle in his body. "What are you doing?" he asked.

"These," she said with almost an awe in her voice, touching his neck, right where he knew his tats were. The contact zinged across his skin, drove into his bones, and pulsed with the steady beat of lust. *Fuck.* "The blackbirds. I've seen them on your neck but didn't know how far they went down. What do they stand for?"

The blackbirds she talked about started on his left pectoral, rose into flight up over his shoulder and across his neck, with the last one tucked behind his ear. He had his reasons for getting it—ones he wasn't ready to tell her about.

"It's just a bird," he said instead.

"They're beautiful, like the man."

"Hailey—"

"No, don't. I know you think I'm a child. But I can tell you I've grown up fast in the past few weeks. I know exactly what I was doing when I came in here. I'm not looking to jump on you if that's what you're thinking. I only wanted to say thank you…and I want to ask for you to keep in touch, wherever you may go."

She was killing him. God, he wanted to give her that little request, but he didn't know where he'd be next week, much less if he'd have access to e-mail. He didn't want to get her hopes up, either. "I'll try, but I really don't know how long I'll be out of touch. If you need me, though, D knows how to get ahold of me."

She nodded, her attention still on the birds at his neck. "Can I have a goodbye hug, then?"

He dropped his head to the wall behind him and looked to the ceiling. Denying her would be smart, but if he was honest, he couldn't hold out any longer. He blew out a breath, lowered his face, and nodded. "Sure."

She smiled and like a light, it lit up the entire room. Carefully, he allowed her to step inside his arms as he wrapped them around her and tucked her head to his chest. She made a noise in the back of her throat and the sound pinged right down to his groin. Her sweater brushed against his bare nipples, causing them to tighten. Her hands crept behind his neck with surprising familiarity. He held her for a few moments and went to move away. Immediately he knew he'd made mistake number three thousand, two hundred and eighty-six since she'd walked into his room. He'd let his guard down.

She pulled back slightly and tugged on his neck, rose on her tiptoes and pressed her mouth to his for a kiss. There were no tongues involved, just a meeting of lips, but it was one of the most spectacular kisses he'd ever had. Her lips were moist and full under his. She parted her mouth, and her breath shook, betraying her shy confidence. He gripped his thighs, fighting not to react and dive into the deep recess of her mouth, not to plunge his tongue inside and conquer her.

She cupped his face, tenderly, surely, and rubbed her lips back and forth over his. Each caress had his gut curling in pleasure. He was one second from the snap of his control.

Reaching up, he gripped her wrists gently but firmly and pulled his head back with a murmured, "Hailey."

She smiled at him, not looking at all disappointed. In fact, her face flushed with the first hint of color. Her skin was dewy and radiant. She glowed with a sensual promise.

He needed to get the hell away.

"Thank you," she said.

He nodded and held her gaze. "That can't happen again, Hailey."

She didn't say anything, just kept smiling before extracting herself from his grip and heading to the door. He watched her go and tried to ignore the pang in his gut at seeing her walk away. At the door, she turned to him and met his gaze from across the room. Their connection, as always, was instant.

"One more question?"

As if he could deny her anything. "Sure, what's up?"

"How do you know if your life is the one you're supposed to live? Or if it's just…this is it?"

His brows drew together, her words causing a mix of emotions in his chest—fear, concern, empathy. He shrugged, unprepared for and a little surprised by the depth of that question. "I'm not really sure I can answer that."

Her lips curved slightly, not a full smile, just a hint of one. She yanked on the door and stopped as Dwayne stood there, his facial expression first shocked and, with a glance at Luke, pissed.

Fuck.

* * * *

"Get downstairs," Dwayne snapped at Hailey.

She bit her lip and looked back at Luke. Fucking hell, he'd gone looking for Luke, to say goodbye to his baby brother, only to find him half-naked with Hailey. His vision turned red and his blood pressure shot through the roof.

"Hailey," he warned.

She sighed softly and slid around him. He didn't watch her go but listened for her steps down the stairs. His gaze stayed on Luke's, and his brother glared right back, shaking his head slightly.

Only after he was sure Hailey was out of hearing range did he explode. He stomped into the room, slammed the door behind him, and snapped a finger toward Luke. "What the fuck, dude? She's eighteen!"

"I know," Luke said, his mouth a thin, tight line.

"What the hell was she doing in your room?"

Luke laughed, a harsh short bark of a sound. "Are you kidding me right now?"

Dwayne stared at him.

Luke stared right back.

The tension in the room diminished the early regret for not spending enough time with his brother. Now, after seeing Hailey walk out, he just wanted him gone. But first, he'd tell him exactly what would happen.

"She's a child," he said.

"I know she's a child, goddammit!" Luke snapped. "I know she's eighteen damn years old."

"She's been through hell," Dwayne said, refusing to back down.

"Fuck!" Luke exploded, his hands coming up to grab his head. "I know, dude, I fucking know. I was there. I saw exactly what she was stuck in. I *know*."

Dwayne winced at the helplessness that crossed over Luke's face. Dammit, when had this happened?

He sighed, fought to rein in his temper. "She's a child," Dwayne repeated.

"For Christ's sake, D, why don't you put on your running shoes and get to the fucking point?"

"What I walked in on here, whatever happened, it can't go any further. It can't happen. Do you understand? Hailey's off limits."

Luke clenched his fists in the air and tossed back his head with a growl. If Dwayne wasn't so angry, if he wasn't so concerned about what *had* been going on between Luke and Hailey, he would have laughed. As it was, Luke reached under his towel and the action brought the cloth up so he could see that his brother's pants were not only unbuttoned, but he was commando.

"For fuck's sake, Luke!" he thundered, gesturing toward his pants.

"For Christ's sake, for fuck's sake, what a vocabulary we have," Luke said with no small amount of sarcasm. He finished buttoning up his pants, reached for a light blue Henley, and tugged it over his head. "Nothing happened, D, not that you're going to believe it. She just wanted to say thank you."

"And you just so happened to be half-naked?" he asked with matching sarcasm.

Luke shook his head and reached over to zip his luggage. Dwayne's heart pounded against his ribs at the reminder that this was it. Luke was leaving, to return only God knew when. He didn't know what was going on with him and Hailey, but with him leaving, obviously nothing would happen. Not only that, but with Chris coming home with an injury, with everything they'd all been through, his temper went from boiling to a slow simmer.

"Look," Dwayne started, "I lose my head when it comes to those two women. I'm just worried."

Luke finished zippering his luggage, set it next to the bed, and grabbed his big, black monstrosity of biker boots. "Nothing happened. Nothing is going to happen, D." He sat on the bed, bent over and laced up his shoes. Only when he stood again did he continue. "But really, do you think I'd be such a bad choice."

Dwayne sucked in a sharp breath and held in the initial thing he'd wanted to say, which was, "Hell yes." His brother had darker cravings, and while he didn't know much about it, he knew Hailey couldn't be a part of that world. Not after everything she'd been through.

Apparently taking his silence as an answer, Luke shook his head and let out a short, disbelieving laugh. "Yeah, whatever, stupid question. I gotta go."

Dwayne watched as Luke set a heavy duffel bag on his shoulder and picked up his luggage. They couldn't part like this. Not knowing what was coming. There was no way. Just as he went to pass, Dwayne set a hand on his shoulder. Luke turned his head and stared at him.

"No matter what, Lucas, I'm here for you. We're family, yeah?"

Luke closed his eyes, dropped his head to Dwayne's shoulder and nodded. "I love you, too, bro."

A few silent moments passed. Then his little brother walked out the door.

Dwayne stood there for a moment, taking everything in, which if he really stopped to think about it, was a hell of a lot.

He puffed his cheeks and blew the air out, then

headed out of the room. Halfway down the stairs, his cell rang. Pulling it out of his pocket, he sucked in another breath. Just when he thought things would be settling. Well, he was about to make it settle even more. He was done with his old life.

"Yeah," he answered.

"Detective Gonzalez," the dark voice purred as he hit the bottom of the steps. He stared at the front door and tried to feel an ounce of anything other than finality. Nothing came. Not the exciting prospect of a sexy night, not lust at what a sultry voice could do, nothing other than wanting to go back to Brooke's side and spend time with her and Hailey.

He sighed and shuffled his feet, wondering where to start.

"I'm thinking," she said, still with the same erotic promise in her voice, "we should get together tonight."

"I'm sorry," he answered. "I don't think so."

"Oh," she said, sounding disappointed yet still hopeful. He crossed his eyes. "Maybe tomorrow night, then?"

"Listen," he started, "Renea, tomorrow won't work either. The night after that, too. I've met someone and I'm happy, settled, with just her."

A few beats of silence passed before, "You're settled?" He winced at the complexity of the question, the confusion in her voice.

"I am. And I'm going to marry her. I'm sorry. If you need anything, anything involving detective related duties," he rushed on to clarify, "you know how to reach me."

"Uhhh, okaaaay."

He chuckled. "Goodnight."

Pushing the disconnect button, he turned to find Brooke with a grin on her face and laughter dancing in her expression. He groaned. "How much?"

"All of it," she said and giggled, practically dancing on her feet.

He groaned again and had to brace himself as she crossed the remaining feet between them and flung her arms around his neck. "So, you're going to marry this girl?"

He smiled down at her and held her gaze unwaveringly.

"I am. What do you say to that?"

"Yes," she said with a kiss.

The End

www.authordcstone.com

D.C. STONE

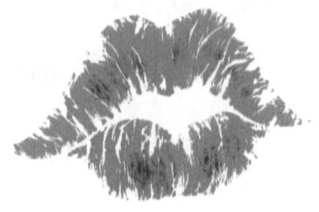

EVERNIGHT PUBLISHING ®

www.evernightpublishing.com